THE HOT BODY CLUB

A Jack S. Hunter Mystery

Also by Tom Arnold

Checkpoint Charlie

Chambers of the Human Heart

Tom Arnold was born and graduated form high school
in California, but has lived and traveled around the world.
He has been a factory worker in Denmark; a drug counselor
in a Methadone program in New York; a VISTA volunteer,
the owner/manager of an auto repair garage, a race car driver,
and a ski instructor in Oregon; an English teacher in
Cambodia; and – always – a writer. He currently
lives and writes in Eugene, Oregon.

Tom is the proprietor of Bleugene Press.

THE HOT BODY CLUB

A Jack S. Hunter Mystery

By Tom Arnold

Bleugene Press
Eugene, Oregon

Published by
Bleugene Press
Eugene, Oregon, U S A
www.bleugenepress.com

This is a work of fiction. Names, characters, places, and incidents either are the product of the author's imagination or are used fictitiously.

ISBN 978-0-9849954-2-4

Printed in the United States of America

I dedicate this book to my sister, Mary,
who appreciates a good mystery.

I hope you enjoy this one.

Acknowledgements

I would like to thank the following people for their invaluable
help with this project:

Jennifer Andrews of Helios Creative for designing the cover.

Dan Armstrong of Mud City Press for technical help formatting.

Breanne Henke for final proofreading.

And, of course, the many loyal readers who read
<u>The Hot Body Club</u> as a manuscript and
were not shy with their comments and opinions.

THE HOT BODY CLUB

PROLOGUE

"Ladies and gentlemen, up next on the main stage of the Hot Body Club for your viewing pleasure and total enjoyment is the one and only, Winter!" The disc jockey's tone of voice lacks the conviviality with which he introduced earlier dancers. He halts his line of chatter and scans nervously around the tavern, pausing briefly when he comes to the big bouncer checking IDs and collecting money at the door. The DJ adjusts the lighting and the music. Disco D's Booty Bar Anthem *Keys to the Whip* throbs in synch with the footlights. The warm tones saturating the bar give way to cooler hues. A mirrored disco ball, suspended over the stage, reflects the footlights as it revolves.

"Yes, friends, summer in Eugene is almost dead and soon the weather's gonna change for the worse. But the Winter we have in the Club tonight is hot, hot, hot! So please welcome her, our very own Winter, to the main stage!"

As the house lights dim, a cold, blue spotlight illuminates a young girl standing at the foot of the steps leading up to the raised dance floor. Her round face is framed by glossy, black shoulder-length hair, scissor-cut in bangs across her forehead. She wears white fishnet stockings with snowflakes woven into the pattern and a white thong that is little more than a misplaced cocktail doily. Her bulging breasts look ready to burst out of her faux-fur white bustier. A column of shiny silver rings, counterpoints of light to the disco ball, glints along the edge of one ear. In the smooth, pale moonscape of her face, her eyes are pools of deep blue outlined in black mascara. The only splash of color is the oasis of her mouth; the girl's garish lips curl in a perpetual, tempting kiss like the petals of a crimson rose in full bloom.

1

"Remember," the DJ continues, "tonight is amateur night at the Hot Body Club. That means the lovely ladies dancing for you this evening are unpaid amateurs. Each and every gorgeous girl is performing not only for the sheer thrill of sharing her charms with you, but also for tips and the chance to win the grand prize of $500 in cash and a job offer right here at the Hot Body Club." His voice has taken on the rote tone of a message machine. "So dig deep and be generous." The DJ slides a lever on the sound board, ramping up the volume of Donna Summer's *Last Dance*.

In a curtained alcove sandwiched between the DJ's elevated booth and the end of the bar, hides a fat man with an unlit Romeo Y Julieta clenched in the corner of his mouth. He stands, motionless, with his pudgy hands clasped behind his back. Although the man is mostly shrouded by the dark drapes, his field of vision takes in most of his bar. His attention is focused on the girl, her netted legs and thonged buttocks, and his fleshy face forms into a salacious smile. He fumbles in his shirt for his lighter and ignites his cigar, never taking his eyes off the girl.

"Ladies and gentlemen, let's give it up for Winter!" The song's slow introduction gives way to a harder beat: Donna Summer at the top of her game.

Whistles and cheers fill the room. Someone bangs the side of a pint beer glass with a spoon. Feet stomp. Hands clap. This is the moment the crowd has been waiting for.

As the girl slowly climbs the first and then the second stair up to the stage, a muscled, tattooed young man in frayed Levi's and a sleeveless tee-shirt jumps from the shadows. He bear-hugs the girl from behind, pinning her arms, and lifts her away from the stairs.

"Jimmy, you fucker, let me go!" The girl thrashes helplessly against the kid's overpowering embrace. Her breasts escape the flimsy confine of her bustier and flop against his forearm. "Get your fucking hands off me!" She screams, kicking her legs uselessly in space.

The gargantuan bouncer dashes the distance from the padded entrance door to the stage with swiftness that belies his bulk.

2

"Get off her, Jimmy! You know the rules. You aren't allowed to touch the dancers." With lightening speed, the bouncer clenches the kid in a headlock and then just as quickly relaxes his grip when the kid jabs a perfectly-aimed elbow deep into his solar plexus. The bouncer doubles over, gasping for air. The kid releases the girl, spins around and crouches in a martial arts stance to face the bouncer.

That's when all hell breaks loose.

CHAPTER ONE

I could hear the damned thing even before I could see it. The fire-engine red Hummer, festooned with grill and light guards, fog and driving lights, a full-length roof rack, busty chrome license plate frames and every other bit of macho bling imaginable, rumbled down my dead-end, unpaved, potholed alley, agitating clouds of tan dust that took a while to settle in the hot afternoon sun. It was early October and Oregon was having an Indian summer. In another month or so, that dust would become squishy brown mud. My old cat, El Gato, an orange, semi-retired mouser with a cauliflower ear and an astute judge of character, vanished with a noisy clatter through the kitty flap door I'd cut for him through the kitchen wall. He's no fool.

Behind the wheel of this red monster was none other than my landlord, Charles Thurgood Winetrout. Shortly he would be making yet another attempt to squeeze me for the rent. I was about an hour into *The Big Sleep*, one of my favorites, but it would have to wait. I clicked the pause button on the remote and start composing a strategy for keeping the old fart at bay. I didn't have the rent, back or current, and didn't have any immediate prospects of coming up with it. On the other hand, it wasn't likely Winetrout had another fool waiting in the wings eager to inhabit the ageing singlewide I've called both my home and my office for more years than I care to remember. The trailer balances precariously on concrete blocks in the middle of a skinny lot in Glenwood like a fat lady squatting on a folding chair at a picnic. If you put a marble on the floor of the kitchen nook by the refrigerator, it will roll lazily downhill to the dented vent below the sink like a slow eight ball scratching its way toward a side pocket. Picture the 'before' dwelling in an episode of Home Makeover Extreme Edition and you've got a rough idea.

What we stubborn residents euphemistically call 'our town', Glenwood is sandwiched between the cities of Eugene and Springfield, in the west central part of Oregon. This is the green part of the state, west of the Cascades. In a wet year, we'll catch about five feet of rain in the valley and maybe that much snow in the mountains.

Our puny burg is an unincorporated collection of struggling mom and pop businesses, taverns, pawn shops, discount auto parts stores, and last-stop used car lots of rolling wrecks headed for the scrap yard. We host the county dump and the local transit bus garage, but we don't have a ZIP code to call our own. Our big sisters to the east and west, (known with derisive affection as Bleugene and Springtucky), prefer to squabble over the division of the meager property taxes we generate rather than upgrade the bare minimum of city services we survive on. Glenwood isn't much, but it's ours. Somehow, amid the weeds and blackberries that thrive here, a slender shoot of civic pride struggles to survive. For better or worse, I'm a part of this bedraggled community. My name is Jack S. Hunter. I'm a private investigator.

The dirty red SUV skidded to a stop, spraying unraked maple leaves and three-quarter-minus gravel against the trailer's galvanized skirting, making a sound like a quick riff on a snare drum. The car door slammed shut before the dust and debris settled. Out stepped Charles Winetrout, an oversized guy who does nothing with a light touch.

"You really ought to put in some landscaping around here, Hunter. Plant a few flowers or something. No wonder your business is in the shitter. This dump looks like the last stop on Tobacco Road." Winetrout's plump face was flushed and he wore a garland of grimy sweat like a hippie headband across his forehead. They say people end up looking like their dogs; you know, the sad-eyed guy with the basset hound, the tattooed skinhead with his pit bull, the old, blue-haired biddy with some species of yippy froufrou hand warmer in her lap. People choose and personalize their cars in much the same way and I couldn't help thinking Winetrout matched his Hummer, fat, red, and full of gas.

"If there was an outside water spigot, my front yard could be a Garden of Eden. If you're here—"

"Don't worry, Hunter, I'm not gonna hump you for the rent. I know damn well you don't have it. So chill out." Winetrout barreled past me into the trailer, slamming the ripped screen door against the siding. "I assume you're open for business." At six-five and pushing three-twenty easy, he displaced a considerable amount of the air in the narrow space. I squeezed in after him in.

"What, then, to what do I owe—?"

"And you're not in the middle of scouting out some extra-marital hanky panky?" Winetrout arched his eyebrows in his approximation of a leer. "Not out spying on any cheaters? No juicy—"

"What do you want, Mr. Winetrout?" I was beginning to feel uncomfortable. I knew more about my landlord from scuttlebutt than I did from personal contact, but there he was in my office, a bombastic force, confirming the rumors. Since I didn't have any work scheduled for the day, or for the foreseeable future, if you want to know the truth, I was dressed in worn Levi cut-offs, a faded Rogue River Adventures tee-shirt and a heavy bristle of unshaved beard. I'm one of those skinny, hairy, pale little guys who make one day away from the razor look like a bum's three-day stubble. Not likely I'll ever go bald, either; my hair was a messy thatch.

"My daughter, Summer Rain, has gone missing. Again. I want you to find her."

"Missing? What do you mean, missing?" *Again?* I'd heard through the grapevine that Winetrout's daughter was often MIA, but the old man had never asked for my help finding her before so I felt it prudent to act surprised. Keeping my eyes and ears open was an integral part of my job; that part was easy, but keeping track of what I knew, what I was supposed to know, where I'd learned it, and so on was more challenging.

"Damn it, Hunter, don't you speak English?"

"Sorry, I just wanted—"

Winetrout flicked his hand like he was whisking away a pesky horse fly. "She's been gone about a week. I can't tell you exactly how long, because sometimes she spends nights with friends. What I can tell you is that neither Jimmy or the housekeeper has seen the little…" he paused for a beat or two, his face scrunched into a scowl "…seen her since last Friday." Winetrout settled his bulk onto one of the two straight back chairs on the client side of my well-worn desk. My heart went out to the chair as it creaked under the overload.

"Jimmy?" I wasn't sure whether I should interject questions along the way or just wait for the old blowhard to finish. I sat down opposite him but I didn't lean back.

"Yeah, Jimmy!" Winetrout's tone of voice implied that everyone within earshot should know who Jimmy was. "The kid who takes care of the pool, mows the lawn, washes the cars. All the usual outdoor stuff. Mind if I smoke?"

Charles Winetrout wasn't the type to wait for permission. He fumbled in the pocket of his garish fuchsia-and-green orchid-flowered Hawaiian shirt and came up with a cigar case, a cutter, and a gold lighter. In short order, pungent blue smog was rolling across my desk like incoming gloom. I'm an ex-smoker, so this was more than annoying.

"I want you to find her, Hunter, and I'll pay you damn well when you do."

I sat with my mouth shut trying to not to inhale and waited for Winetrout to get on with his story.

"Are you listening to me, Hunter? I want Summer found and brought home. That's what you do when you're not spying on cheaters, isn't it? Find people who go missing?"

As a matter of fact, finding missing people is outside my normal range. My niche is infidelity.

"Have you filed a missing person's report with the police? That's the best place—"

"I don't want to involve the goddam cops!" Winetrout was bombastic. "Summer was, is…" The old man paused, wagging his head imperceptivity like he was considering and discarding possible categories for his wayward daughter. The folds of his fat neck spilled over the collar of his damp, unbuttoned shirt. "Let's just say that girl is a teenager in name only. The cops wouldn't be much help anyway. All they wanna do anymore is write up tickets on I-5 to gouge you for more money." Winetrout picked a piece of tobacco from his lower lip, scowled at it for a moment, as if considering the audacity of an expensive Cuban cigar disintegrating in his mouth, before flicking it onto the worn rug. "I'm keeping this goddam county afloat with fines."

I glanced involuntarily at my own pink moving violation citation thumb-tacked to the cork board beside my desk and concluded that there was some truth in Winetrout's assessment of the state troopers. I wished I could take a deep breath.

"You said 'again'. What makes you so certain her disappearance this time is different from all the other times?" My eyes were beginning to water and I wondered how long it would take for the stink to blow out of my trailer.

"I got a gut feeling."

A gut feeling. The worst kind of motivation. Nothing solid you could lay your hands on or get your head around. As a private investigator, my job is to gather solid evidence. I barely trust my own hunches and I don't trust other people's at all. I like proof I can see or touch. Or, better yet, photograph. If I had a Lincoln for every suspicious husband or weeping wife who washed into my office with a 'gut feeling' about their possibly wayward spouse...

"If I decide to look into this for you, Mr. Winetrout, I'll need to ask you some very personal questions and you have to promise me you'll give me honest answers."

"*If* my sweet ass, Hunter. You're two months behind on the rent. I don't exactly see a line of cuckolds beating a path to your door." Winetrout took another couple of puffs on his stogie and inspected the glowing end. By the time he got around to asking, "What do you want to know?" his face was hidden behind thick, bluish-gray fog.

"For starters, I'll need to talk to Mrs. Winetrout, as well as—"

"Ha! Good luck with that one. I haven't seen that whore in months. I threw her ass out a long time ago. As far as I know, she lives on another planet."

I digested this ugly outbreak for a moment before I continued. "What about Summer Rain's friends? I assume you've checked with them."

Charles Winetrout's florid face emerged from the cigar smoke like a whale breaching. He hammered a hammy, hairy fist down on my desk, knocking an inch-long cone of ash onto the glass, which he swept onto the rug. "Damn it, Hunter, do I look like the kind of dimwit who'd hire a private dick if I hadn't already tried everything else?"

"No, of course not. I just—"

But the old man was already on his feet and lurching toward the door. "You come out to the house and we'll talk some more and you can question Jimmy and Consuelo, if you want. You know where I live, right?" I did, but he didn't wait for an answer. "You can look at some photos of Summer, too."

"Consuelo being?" I asked, feeling on safe ground.

Winetrout ignored my question. "I'm headed home now. I'll be there most of the afternoon. Get your butt in gear. Oh, the code for the gate is sixty-nine-twenty-four-seven."

"I still haven't agreed to go searching for your daughter, Mr. Winetrout."

"Five thousand bucks when you find her, plus any normal business expenses you run up along the way, whatever 'normal' is in your line of work. See you this afternoon."

"What about the back rent? If I take this case—"

Winetrout didn't bother turning around as he passed through the door. "Fuck the rent. You just get my girl back home again."

El Gato made it half way through his kitty door before the cloud of smoke made him change his mind and back out. I propped the front door open with an old, broken fishing rod and hoped for a summer breeze.

CHAPTER TWO

Charles Winetrout lived way out off South Willamette Street in the fashionable rural area where the names of the side streets end in 'Hollow' or 'Creek' or 'Ridge'. The mansions sit at the back of five acre minimum lots and the addresses require five digits instead of the three or four you find in the city.

I arrived at the Winetrout estate around three o'clock, punched in the pass code (only then realizing the significance of the numbers) and waited for the overkill wrought-iron security gates to swing open. From that vantage point, the house itself was hidden behind a grove of oak trees at the top of a knoll. The weedless, dandelion-free, freshly mowed lawn seemed to go on forever, like God's own golf course. I wouldn't have been surprised to see a moat and drawbridge. As I drove up the winding asphalt driveway, I speculated on the source of Charles Winetrout's wealth. He was what passed for a local tycoon and had extensive real estate holdings besides the ramshackle trailer I rented and the mansion he lived in. If you believed everything you heard or read about the man, Charles Thurgood Winetrout, or more accurately some shadowy companies he controlled, owned half of Lane County and had stakes in several businesses throughout the rest of the Willamette Valley. According to local gossip, Winetrout was a silent partner in some less savory enterprises as well: The Oregon Liquor Control Commission had once named him as a person of interest during an investigation of a seedy strip club that was alleged to have allowed minors to grin and bare it on the premises.

Charles Winetrout's mansion was as far from the Hot Body Club – or my shabby trailer, for that matter – as you could get, in more ways than one. I took a minute to eyeball the place before I climbed out of my ten-year-old workhorse Cherokee. I might have been amused at the contrast between his million-dollar mansion and my two hundred thousand mile heap if the heap hadn't been mine.

The bottom third of the main building, which stood two stories high, was volcanic rock masonry and the upper two thirds was rough-hewn timber. You couldn't get a more typically Pacific Northwest motif if you wanted to. The ground-level windows were protected by heavy wrought iron grating that roughly matched the driveway gates. A dozen windows flanked by green storm shutters interrupted the second-floor planks at regular intervals across the front. The ambience was more Fortress Winetrout than drop-by-Charlie's-for-a-beer.

A brick path led from the parking area to a pair of oversized, iron-studded oak doors I could have driven through. The path was guarded by a statue of a jockey in polished black boots, tight white pants and a red and white diamond-checked shirt. An eternal grin of greeting divided his shiny black face. The sweet smell of freshly cut grass reinforced the bucolic, rural atmosphere.

At the near edge of the broad manicured lawn, a muscular twenty-something kid in raggedy-kneed jeans and a tight, sleeveless tee-shirt maneuvered an electric Husquvarna trimmer across the top of an English laurel hedge. Behind the hedge was a two-story garage. Parked in front of the hedge was an aged blue Ford pickup adorned with several Christian-themed bumper stickers on the tailgate:

Christians aren't perfect – they're forgiven
I'm ready for the Rapture
Honk if you love Jesus

There was also a sticker for the Church of Redemption, a non-denominational outfit in the Whitaker neighborhood I'd driven past numerous times:

Jesus Saves Anyone Anytime

The stickers looked crisp and new, like they hadn't yet weathered an Oregon winter. I wondered if the kid, who I took to be Jimmy, was a churchgoer or if he'd just bought the truck already adorned.

I slipped my travel mug into the cup holder, stepped out of my car and slammed the door and waited for the kid to turn and acknowledge me, which he did, finally, reluctantly.

"You must be Jimmy, am I right?" I had to shout over the noise of the Husky.

The garden boy nodded once without smiling and said "My name is James". A stylized tattoo of Jesus nailed to the cross straddled his left bicep. Crimson blood from the stigmata dripped down to his elbow. Beneath the crucifix, in Gothic font, were the words: 'Piercings Saved My Life.' Suspicions confirmed.

"Hunter. Jack S. Hunter." I held out my hand. Jimmy – or James – stared at it like he'd never seen a human hand before. "I'm here to see Mr. Winetrout."

"He ain't out here." Jimmy turned his attention back to the hedge. "Try the house."

"I thought I might talk to you for a minute or so first."

Jimmy switched off the trimmer and looked nervously over his shoulder at the mansion. "'Bout what?"

"Mr. Winetrout's daughter, Summer Rain. Mr. Winetrout says she hasn't been home for a while. Have you seen her around?"

Jimmy narrowed his eyes and stared at me and then turned back to the hedge without saying a word.

"How well do you know Summer Rain, Jimmy?"

Jimmy put the trimmer down, took off his Saints baseball cap, ran his fingers through his surfer-blond hair, and pulled the cap back on. "Look, mister, whatever your name is, I ain't the one you should be asking these questions to. This here's a good gig and I ain't about to screw it up on your account. And like I already told you, my name is James, not Jimmy."

"Mr. Winetrout told me I could talk to you and somebody named Consuelo."

"Did he now."

"So why would talking to me about Summer Rain get you fired?"

"Do me a big favor, OK? Just leave me alone and lemme do my job."

I took a card from my wallet and held it out to the kid, who looked at it like it was anthrax. I wrapped a Hamilton around the card and said, "If you think of anything, give me a call. James."

Jimmy looked over my shoulder toward the front doors of the mansion and then slid the card and money into his hip pocket.

"Nice tat you got there," I said. "Looks new. Where did you have it done?"

"You leave Our Lord out of this. He ain't got nothing to do with it."

I would like to have asked what it was Our Lord had nothing to do with, but we were interrupted by a shout.

"Hunter!" I turned to see Charles Winetrout standing on his front porch with his hands on his hips. He was dressed in khaki Dockers shorts and a different unbuttoned, vivid aloha shirt. His massive white belly hung below his shirt almost to his crotch. "What took you so long? You're late. Get your ass in here and let's talk. Something's come up and I gotta be in town in an hour. Jimmy," he shouted, "get the Hummer ready to go. Pronto!"

Jimmy jumped at the sound of Winetrout's voice and stood at attention. Apparently 'Jimmy' was still acceptable coming from his boss. I half expected him to salute. I doubt he even heard me say 'good bye'.

I followed the old man into the foyer and down a long hall to an oversized study. The stench of Winetrout's cigars permeated the place like cheap perfume in a Motel 6. An executive-sized, polished black oak desk dominated the room. On the cluttered desktop were two Radio Shack cordless telephones, an intercom, some kind of electronic controller, a collection of remotes and an eighteen inch monitor. On one corner was a framed, signed *HUSTLER* magazine cover. Two long bookshelves haphazardly crammed full of books, magazines, videos and DVDs, a DVD player and a VHS player lined the wall behind the desk. A jumble of wires disappeared into a hole in the floor. The desk faced a large plate glass window that overlooked a redwood deck complete with an uncovered, steaming hot tub. Beyond the tub was a sparkling, kidney-shaped swimming pool.

Flanking the window were two fifty-inch Panasonic monitors, both of which were up and running. On one screen, Jimmy was easing the freshly-scrubbed red Hummer out of the garage. The other screen featured a naked blond woman with enormous pneumatic breasts energetically and noisily kissing and sucking a disembodied long, thick black penis, the owner of which was off-screen. Winetrout clicked a remote and froze the porn mid-stroke. A glistening string extended from the end of the man's penis to the tip of the blonde's tongue like a suspension bridge. Winetrout's alleged involvement with a strip club, as well as some of the other rumors I'd heard, seemed more plausible by the minute. On screen one, Jimmy continued putting the final touches on the Hummer.

"Coffee?" Without waiting for an answer, Winetrout shouted in the direction of the hallway. "Consuelo! Dos coffees! Pronto!" Back to me, "Cream and sugar?"

"That would be fine."

"La crema y el azúcar!"

I waited for Winetrout to settle his bulk into his chair. "Make yourself comfortable, Hunter," he said, gesturing toward a collection of padded straight back chairs. I did.

"Tell me why you think you need to hire someone to search for your daughter."

The old man looked at me like I was a golden retriever who'd failed to retrieve a stick. "Like I told you in the trailer, Summer's been gone for about a week. Consuelo says she left with her gym bag stuffed full and two bulging shopping bags in her other hand."

"Maybe she's staying with a friend?"

Winetrout shook his head impatiently. "I don't think so. Whenever Summer takes off, which she does every so often, after a few days there's a million phone messages for her on her home line." He fumbled in a desk drawer and found a mini cassette that he slid into a recorder. "These are from the last go around. Don't ask me why I bothered to save 'em, but here you go." Winetrout stabbed the play button.

'Hey, babe, don't forget the party tomorrow night.'

'S'up, girlfriend, Chloe here, pickup. Where are you hiding? I missed you in French.'

'Rainy, it's me, call me. You dead, or what?'

Winetrout stopped the playback. "You get the picture. Summer Rain is a very social creature, if you know what I mean."

"No calls from her school? If she's missing and skipping school, somebody—"

"Yeah, but they come in on my house line, not hers."

"What school does she go to?"

"South Eugene High. Why?"

"No reason in particular. I'm just trying to build a picture." I knew I shouldn't have asked. I felt myself being sucked into a teenage drama.

"Summer Rain doesn't have a cell phone?" I asked.

"Of course she has a cell phone." Winetrout didn't need to add the word 'idiot'; it was in his voice. "She lives on the damn thing, probably die of brain cancer before she's legally old enough to drink. But she doesn't have the charger."

"I don't get it."

"I got control of the charger." Winetrout leaned back in his chair, laced his fingers behind his head, and settled his chins on his neck. A heavy gold chain disappeared into the thick carpet of reddish hair on his fleshy chest. "Her battery only lasts a day or two as much as she gabs. She's got to come home to recharge it or her lifeline dies."

"Maybe she's using a friend's charger."

"Not likely." The old man guffawed, rippling his jowls. "Summer just had to have this fancy-ass model that does everything. You know kids these days. Wired. Hers even takes movies. Cost me over three hundred bucks. Catch is damned thing's got its own special charger." Winetrout slid open a drawer and grabbed a charger by the cord, dangling it like you'd hold a mouse by the tail. "None of her friends have one that fits. She screwed herself royally."

I wondered why Summer Rain didn't just buy herself another charger. Maybe she had but didn't want Winetrout to know about it. Maybe she needed to feel tethered. I already knew the answer to my next question, but I asked it anyway, just to be sure. "Let me guess. This time, no one has called her."

"Only calls from the school office on the house line asking if she was sick."

"And what did you tell them?"

Before he had a chance to answer, a pretty, chubby Latina, maybe mid-thirties, dressed in a white uniform and wearing her thick, black hair pulled back from her face and coiled in a tight bun, came in carrying a tray of coffee, cream and sugar, which she set on the edge of Winetrout's desk. I reached to pour myself a cup but the old man stopped me. "Let Consuelo do it. That's what I pay her for."

Without saying a word or looking at my face, the housekeeper fixed me a large cup of delicious Mexican coffee that I tried to keep from gulping down. Winetrout took his black.

"Muy delicioso," I said in my best Spanglish. Consuelo nodded once without smiling. She started to remove the tray but Winetrout stopped her.

"Aqui, aqui," he said, slapping the desktop with his palm.

"Si, Señor," Consuelo said and backed out of the room.

I considered the situation for a moment before I continued. When Winetrout had stormed into my office/trailer that morning, my first inclination had been to tell him to be patient. A teenager being away from home for a few days didn't strike me as urgent, especially since it evidently wasn't the first time. I wondered if she was attending her classes on a regular basis, which was something I might be able to check on. But Jimmy's strange behavior when I arrived and now the maid's quiet chilliness felt out of kilter, something the cops would no doubt characterize as hinky. The vibes in the Winetrout household seemed discordant and unharmonious. Now I questioned why the old man had waited almost a week before he came to see me.

"OK. Let's start with her friends. Does she have a boyfriend?" I realized that by starting a conversation, asking questions, I had crossed the line and agreed to take the case. I was not altogether pleased by the prospect; trailing runaways wasn't really my forte, but I couldn't see my way out of it. What with Winetrout being my landlord and me being behind on the rent, turning down a job, any job, wouldn't be appropriate. On the other hand, curiosity is an occupational hazard in my line of work, or maybe a prerequisite. And I was curious.

"How the hell should I know? Kids these days, they hang around in groups, run in packs. If you know what I mean. There's a gang she's a part of, boys and girls, but how can you tell who's paired up with who? Christ, sometimes you can't even tell them apart. They seem to like it that way." Winetrout slurped his coffee, splattering a few drops into his shaggy chest hair.

"I'm sorry but I have to ask you, is your daughter sexually active?"

"She's her mother's daughter."

"Meaning?"

"Meaning Summer's been on the pill since she was a kid. If she remembers to take the damned things."

Since she was a kid? What did that make her now? A spinster? I started to say, 'That's a good thing' but thought better of it. Instead, I said "You mentioned you had some photographs."

Winetrout rocked forward and removed a manila envelope from the top drawer of his desk. He cleared a space and shook four photographs onto the glass and arranged them in a sequence. The first one, slightly overexposed, showed a skinny child of around eleven or twelve in a bathing suit with straight yellow hair and a smile full of braces. In the background was a motley accumulation of trailer houses resting on railroad ties and beyond them a few scraggly trees and a muddy lake. In the next photo, Summer Rain had grown up a few years and pouted insolently for the camera, sans smile. She had put on some curves. Her hair was a messy bun of pink and purple and she wore denim short shorts and a tight white tank top with NIN imprinted in tall, silver letters. She was leaning against the hood of an aging Dodge pickup with a cracked windshield and a mismatched fender in a Wal-Mart parking lot. The third picture was of a group of punk kids loitering around in front of a tattoo parlor, apparently unaware they were being photographed. They were all dressed in the Goth uniform of the day; dark-colored cargo pants and hoodies, chains, studded leather, here and there a

17

flash of lace. I couldn't determine which one was Summer Rain. I rotated the photo so it was top side up for Winetrout.

"This here is Summer, believe it or not." Winetrout stabbed a tobacco-stained finger on a sullen girl dressed all in black, her hair chopped at odd angles and also black. I held the photo under the desk lamp and squinted. Her lips were outlined in black and her eyes were made up into dark shadows, making her look a little like a raccoon. She wore a studded leather belt slung low across her wide hips. Summer Rain had a silver stud in her left nostril and a row of silver rings up her left earlobe. I wondered, but didn't ask, who had taken the photo.

The last photograph was a professionally taken portrait, neutral blue curtain background, probably from a class picture day. Summer Rain, sans jewelry or makeup, looked directly into the camera, not smiling, not frowning. She was wearing an open-necked, plain white blouse. It could have been a police mug shot if there had been a profile next to it. I held it up. "Can I keep this one for the time being?"

Winetrout nodded his assent and I slipped it into my pocket. I didn't see any resemblance to Winetrout in any of the photos, but then, how much resemblance could there be between an overweight, middle-aged slob like Charles Winetrout and a Goth teenager like Summer Rain?

"That's quite a difference. Your daughter has gone through some changes."

"The worst part is the music. You got no idea what crap they listen to these days."

"How about other friends? Anyone in particular she was close to?"

"Those kids in that last picture are her gang." Winetrout gestured with his cigar. "The only friend of hers I know by name is a girl named Chloe, but I couldn't tell you which one is her. I just know because she's the only one who ever leaves her name on the machine."

"That doesn't give me much to go on."

Winetrout ignored my hesitation. "I want the girl found, Hunter, and I'm willing to pay damned good money to get her home."

This was my last chance to opt out. Did I really want to get involved looking for my landlord's wayward Goth daughter, who probably didn't want to be found anyway? On the other hand, what else did I have going at the moment? Not much, certainly nothing that would lead to mucho dinero.

"I'll need some cash up front, Mr. Winetrout. I don't know what I'll run into." Which was the truth. My private investigation business is specialized; most of my clients are suspicious husbands and wives. This would be the first time I'd looked for a runaway. My standard operating procedure for all cases, however, is to get a cash retainer at the beginning. Generally speaking, untrusting spouses are unhappy with whatever I do or do not discover. Reporting a clean bill of matrimonial health suggests that I haven't been a sufficiently diligent sleuth; confirming an angry husband's or sobbing wife's worst fears is worse, especially if I have photographs. Either way, once I finish my investigation, it has the potential to be a lose-lose situation. Once, I'd been subpoenaed to testify in a particularly messy divorce. It was a truly unpleasant experience and I had decided that in the future, any court appearances would be billed at twice my normal rate.

The old man swiveled out of his chair and lumbered to the bookcase. He swung out a section of dusty classics to reveal a hidden wall safe. He twirled the knob and opened the heavy steel door. I took the opportunity to pour myself another cup of coffee.

"Hell of a note," Winetrout muttered. "You owe me money and I gotta pay you."

"You want me to look for your daughter or not?" I was careful not to say 'find'.

"How much?"

"Two thousand now and if I need more, I'll tell you. I'll keep receipts."

"You do that." Winetrout handed me a short stack of Franklins and slammed the safe shut. He remained standing. "Consuelo!" He bellowed. Apparently, we were finished talking. I quickly slurped half the cup.

"By the way, that coffee went right through me. Mind if I use your bathroom?"

"Take a leak in the bushes on your way out. The plumbing's all stopped up. I think it's something with the septic system. I got a plumber coming out to take a look at it."

I stifled a chuckle. A million dollar castle and you couldn't flush the toilets. As I turned to go, my eye caught the framed *HUSTLER* cover on the old man's desk.

"One last thing, sir. I have to ask you, who's the looker on the cover?"

"That," said Charles Thurgood Winetrout icily, "is the soon-to-be-ex Mrs. Winetrout."

His wife was a HUSTLER centerfold? I couldn't resist the obvious question. "And you have a picture of her on your desk because…?"

"Just find Summer for me, Hunter. That's all I'm paying you to do. Consuelo!"

As if by magic, the Mexican housekeeper appeared from nowhere. She escorted me out and shut the studded oak doors behind me. It took a moment for my eyes to adjust to the hot, bright sun after the cool dimness of Winetrout's office. I realized I hadn't had a chance to interview the housekeeper and I wondered if she would have been more forthcoming than Jimmy had been. I made a mental note to make another trip out Willamette Street to follow up.

Jimmy didn't acknowledge me when I drove past him, but in my rear view mirror, I could see him standing motionless in the middle of the driveway, staring after me. I was glad I hadn't stopped to take a piss in his hedge.

When I got back to my office, the faint stench of cigar smoke still hung in the air. El Gato was sitting on my desk glaring at me and the red light on my message machine was flashing.

CHAPTER THREE

The mutilated, naked body floated face down in a shallow, slack water eddy at the edge of the Willamette River across from the University of Oregon millrace. At that point, the North Bank bike path winds through the trees and thick foliage only a few feet from the water's edge. It's a favorite camping spot for the homeless. The area was cordoned off with a wide, yellow POLICE DO NOT CROSS ribbon, which I ducked under. Looking at her bloated bluish flesh sent a shiver down my spine. I turned up the collar of my jacket, wishing I'd worn something warmer. Gray clouds were rolling in from the west.

The dead girl's arms were bound behind her back at the elbows with a thick, studded black leather belt and her wrists were locked together by adult bookstore-style handcuffs. Wide abrasions marred the insides of both ankles. An elaborate, multicolored filigree tattoo extended like a thong around her hips and into the crevasse between her buttocks. Her body, from her neck to her feet, was crisscrossed with deep, ugly, purple welts.

"Jesus Christ." I knelt by the edge of the water and stared at the corpse. A sickening feeling began to form in the pit of my stomach.

"Don't touch her, gumshoe," Detective Lucas Leonard said. "We have to get photos." The plain-clothed officer continued writing notes in a spiral notebook without looking up.

"How'd you find her?" I asked. Lucas and I were more than casual friends, bonded by professions that occasionally overlapped, an affinity for old film noir movies of the Philip Marlowe, Sam Spade variety and a shared love of fly-fishing. Normally when we met at a river, it was a happy experience. This was not going to be one of those times.

"Someone called 911. Said to check out this location and hung up quick."

"You get a trace on the phone?" I asked.

21

"You know I can't tell you that."

"Come on, Luke, maybe we can help each other."

"By the way, Hunter, what are you doing here, anyway?" For the first time since I arrived, Lucas concentrated his full attention on me, holding me with his unblinking, pale blue eyes.

Lucas and I have roughly the same build, but he's about five inches taller than I am. For some reason, I always think of myself as skinny and Lucas as buff or trim, maybe because I'm pale and dark-haired and weigh in at only about one-forty-five and he's blonde and a little wider across the shoulders. He comes from sturdy Aryan or Scandinavian stock whereas I look like an East European refugee. At his age, somewhere in his late forties, he could be excused for having a paunch, which he doesn't. He works out in the police gym, which is something I would be doing if I could afford a gym membership somewhere.

I looked around at the uniformed cops searching the area. A police photographer was documenting the body from every possible angle. I took a step closer to the detective and lowered my voice. "I got a call, too. Looked like a mobile phone prefix."

"You recognize the voice?"

I considered this for a moment. "No, it sounded scratchy and muffled. I need a new cassette."

Lucas Leonard stared at me for several more beats before he answered. "You open your mouth about any of this and your license is history." He handed me a Ziploc bag with a cell phone inside. "Friend or no friend."

I inspected the phone without opening the bag. "This is a high-end unit, Luke. Internet, e-mail, video, GPS, the whole enchilada." I handed the bag back and forced myself to return my attention to the macabre corpse floating in the muddy water. I tasted the three slices of pepperoni pizza I'd wolfed down for lunch on my way to the river working their way back upstream. The first few light raindrops of fall dimpled the Willamette. This was one hell of a way to end what had been a gorgeous Indian summer and I said so.

"Tell me something I don't know," Lucas said.

"What's the connection with the phone?" I asked.

"I'll have to wait for the records to be positive, but my guess is that both calls were made from it."

"I still don't get it."

"That phone was right there when we got here, gumshoe." Lucas pointed at a log that floated partially submerged at the edge of the river. "According to 911, the call came from within twenty feet of this location. I'll bet your call did, too, right?"

"I couldn't tell you without checking. My call came in to my land line, not my cell. I don't know if my message machine records incoming phone numbers. You'd think whoever made those calls would have turned off the GPS first. They could have called from somewhere else, for that matter."

"Or not," Lucas said. "Maybe they wanted to make sure we found the body."

"Maybe it wasn't their phone and they didn't know how to do it." I regretted my words the moment they left my mouth. Not much gets past Lucas Leonard.

"If it wasn't the caller's phone, gumshoe, then whose was it?"

"That's a good question." I dodged the question. "It could be hers."

"*Her* phone?" The detective looked at the dead body bobbing gently in the water. "Enlighten me, if you don't mind."

I squatted and looked at the spiral of silver rings in her ear, the filigree tattoo around her hips. "Trust me, amigo. It's her cell phone. A Lincoln says there's a stud in her nose." It was hard to look at her, so young, so naked and so very mutilated. You'd think, being a private detective, I would have seen lots of dead bodies, but I haven't. I felt sick to my stomach.

"Hunter, you better tell me everything you know or you're gonna be on the outside of this mess looking in." Unexpected gruffness from someone I considered a friend, although outside did sound like the best place for me to be.

We were interrupted by the photographer, who had sloshed his way up the bank and stood between us with rivulets of muddy water trickling off his rubber boots. "I'm finished for now, Detective. You can retrieve the body any time you want to."

"Don't go anywhere. I'm gonna want some shots of her front side."

"I figured as much."

"Jesus, Luke, can't you leave her a little dignity?" Again, I wished I'd kept my mouth shut. Homicide cops don't investigate accidental drownings. There was no way the damage we were looking at was accidental. Of course the diligent detective would want frontal photographs.

"A little late for dignity, gumshoe, don't you think?" Lucas turned the plastic bag with the cell phone over and over. "Let me rephrase that. What *do* you think?"

I took a deep breath of the fresh, chilly air, wishing for the first time in months that I still smoked. "I think whoever did this did it somewhere else, brought her here and dumped her, called from here and then vamoosed before we arrived." I was stating the obvious, struggling for objectivity.

Lucas looked at me squarely in the face. "Would you mind sticking around?" It was not an invitation. I had no idea what he had in mind. Usually, Lucas plays it by the book. Occasionally, he bends the rules, but not by much. He does whatever he needs to do to solve a case, making sure to cross his '*t*s' and dot his '*i*s' so everything is courtroom-proof. Lucas doesn't let a case get out of his grasp until he's as certain as he can be that twelve random citizens at the other end of the process will agree with him. His stubborn tenacity about the minutest of details can be exasperating, but he has one of the best conviction rates in the state. Or so I've heard; he'd never make such a claim himself.

The detective and I watched two uniformed cops wearing black surgical gloves sideslip down the bank and grab the dead girl's ankles.

"Don't drag her!" Lucas shouted. "I want her lifted and carried out."

Two more uniforms spread out a black tarp and then waded into the river. The four cops carried the dead girl's body out of the water and laid her down. Streams of pinkish water drained off the tarp into the wet soil.

"Turn her over," Lucas said. "Carefully.

It was Summer Rain Winetrout.

The bile I'd felt when I first saw the body floating in the Willamette was now a raging, acidic bulge in the back of my throat. The front of her bloated, bluish torso was a mass of dark intersecting whip marks. Her tattoo encircled her hips and reached up to her naval. One of her nipples hung by a thread, nearly severed by the vicious beating. Her other nipple was pierced by a thick chrome ring with a black bead. Naked, Summer Rain was plumper, thicker around the middle than I would have guessed from the photos Winetrout had given me. The most arresting details, though, were what made me finally give up my lunch: Summer Rain's pubis was crudely shaved and her labia and mouth had been sewn shut with black thread.

"Holy Mother of God," I muttered between heaves. "This is unbelievable."

"You know who she is?" Lucas asked.

I nodded.

"You gonna tell me who she is – or was – or do I have to search records to ID her? You can save me a lot of time if I can skip that step and start looking for who killed her." Lucas appeared unfazed by the brutality at the water's edge. Or the effect it was having on my digestive system.

I took a deep breath. The taste of retch burned into my throat and set my tongue on fire. It was all I could do to keep from rinsing my mouth out with river water. "Her name is Summer Rain Winetrout.," I sputtered. "She's the daughter of—"

"I know who he is." Lucas cut me off, as if he didn't want to hear the name spoken aloud. "This is his daughter?"

"I'd be willing to bet." I fished Summer Rain's high school photograph out of my windbreaker and handed it to him.

Lucas glanced back and forth between the photo and her face. "She's put on a few pounds. How is it you happen to have this?"

"Winetrout hired me to find her. He said she'd been missing for about a week." A second surge of partially digested pizza boiled up.

The drizzle had begun to penetrate the thick canopy of leaves. All that water and no way for me to rinse the acrid taste from my mouth.

"You gonna be OK, gumshoe? You must have seen plenty of stuff like this in your line of work." There was the hint of a smirk in Lucas' voice as he handed back the photo.

I clenched my teeth and struggled to suppress the taste of vomit. "Not hardly. The naked bodies I see are usually still alive and kicking."

Lucas exhaled a humorless laugh. "Welcome to my world."

"I'm not sure I want to be in your world, Luke."

"You already are, gumshoe, you just don't know it,"

CHAPTER FOUR

It should have been – and would have been if I'd been thinking clearly the next day – the ideal time to let the whole missing-now-murdered girl case drop into the lap of the Eugene Police Department. Summer Rain Winetrout may have been many things, but she was no longer a runaway nor was she unaccounted for. She was a cadaver, a memory in the minds of those who had known and loved her, including, presumably, her mother in Portland. All that remained for me to do was to pay a visit to Charles Winetrout, break the news of his daughter's death, account for the cash he'd advanced me, and get back to doing nothing at my office in Glenwood. Some quality time with a good book or a Bogart movie and El Gato curled up on my lap was called for, or maybe a day or two on the McKenzie with my fly rod. If there had been a lady in my life, which there hadn't been for a while, a drive to the coast or up into the Cascades would have done a lot to restore my sanity, if not my faith in the humanity of my fellow man.

It had not yet dawned on me that I was the logical person to break the news to Summer Rain's mom, Krista. Instead, for reasons that remain a mystery to me, I gathered up some rain gear and drove downtown and parked near the mall, stopping for a double shot mocha at a Dutch Brothers coffee kiosk on the way. There are many Dutch Brothers kiosks in western Oregon and although I tend to favor stand alone businesses to chains, I've become addicted to their double (and sometimes triple) shot mochas. The clash of rich coffee and bittersweet chocolate keep my edge sharp and my mind focused. I've filled up more tenth-cup-free blue windmill punch cards than I can count.

It didn't take me long to find the tattoo parlor that was in the background of Winetrout's photo. Sure enough, a collection of eight or nine pale-faced kids, decked out in dark, damp hoodies, low-slung pants and enough metal to bring a smile to the face of a scrap

27

dealer, were milling around in front, sharing cigarettes, carrying on and being noisy. I walked down the opposite sidewalk, trying to organize my thoughts. The leaking clouds had socked in the sky; a solid gray ceiling made it impossible to tell what part of the day it was. The only color came from the vivid ink art displayed behind the parlor's brightly-lit glass and the green and blue neon OPEN sign.

I slowed my pace so I'd have to wait for a red light, nursing the dregs of my coffee. I wanted a moment to size up the situation, determine my best approach. It occurred to me that in my Thinsulate muck boots, Gortex windbreaker and Oregon Ducks rain hat, I'd fit in with the crowd of kids about as well as a baby seal hunter at a PETA meeting. It also didn't help that I had a good twenty or more years of life experience on any of them. But this had been her crowd; these were the people Summer Rain had hung out with. That much I was certain of. What I didn't have a clue about was whether or not they knew she was dead.

The light changed green and I crossed, chucking my cardboard coffee cup into a recycling bin. I didn't have a specific plan in mind as I sauntered up to the group.

"Hi, my name's Jack Hunter. Be OK if I asked you folks a couple of questions?"

They barely acknowledged my presence. One tall boy treated me to a sullen stare and then turned back to his friends. One of the girls mumbled something and he started laughing. Someone handed him a cigarette.

"I'm trying to find someone and I thought you could help me." I felt around in my inside pocket and brought out Summer Rain's portrait photo and showed it around. "Her name is Summer. Summer Rain Winetrout." None of the kids held out a hand. *Were they afraid to touch it?* There was a general chorus of shaking heads and a few 'nos' and 'naws'. One kid coughed and turned away to spit. Not a single person made direct eye contact with me.

"She used to hang out down here on the mall. Lots of leather, lots of metal, lots of black." I said.

A couple of the girls slipped away from the group and disappeared into the tattoo parlor. The rest were quiet, unfriendly. More coughing and shuffling of feet.

"OK, well thanks anyway. Sorry to interrupt your party." I put Summer Rain's photo away and zipped up my jacket.

The tall kid finally looked at me with a hopeful smirk.

"You got any spare change, brother?" This was followed by subdued tittering from the remaining girls.

I met his vacant gaze for a beat or two and then extracted all the Washingtons I had in my wallet – maybe six or seven – and wrapped each around one of my business cards. I handed them out one at a time to the group.

"Her name is Summer Rain," I repeated. "If this jogs anybody's memory, please call me. Could be more where that came from." I'd caught myself just in time; I'd almost said 'was'. Thank God and Dutch Brothers for caffeine.

CHAPTER FIVE

"Pickup the goddam phone, dickhead. I ain't gonna leave you no fuckin' number." A deep, sickly cough was followed by the sound of horking. "You're gonna wanna talk to me."

I rolled over, inadvertently squishing El Gato, who had cuddled up next to me, and fumbled unsuccessfully for the digital clock radio on the floor. The red LED on the answering machine blinked. 2:53 AM. A light patter of raindrops tapped on the tin roof of my trailer. I'd fallen asleep part way through 'The Postman Always Rings Twice'; the last part I remembered was the car going over the cliff. With a growl of complaint, El Gato rearranged himself further down the bed. He doesn't like to be disturbed when he's sleeping, and he doesn't like rain. I picked up the phone. The answering machine kept running.

"Who is this, anyway? It's three o'clock in the morning."

"Meet me in the Whit behind Club 69 in thirty minutes. Bring five hundred bucks."

"I'm not meeting you anywhere with any five hundred dollars until you tell me who you are and why I should," I said.

"You wanna know about that little bitchlit, right?"

Bitchlit? "Which little bitchlit would that be?"

"Don't fuck with me, dickhead. You know who I'm talking about." More coughing. More spitting.

"What do you know about her?"

"What I know's gonna cost you, dickhead. Five hundred in cash. Thirty minutes." Click.

I squinted at the caller ID screen: PRIVATE UNAVAILABLE. Traceable, maybe, but not at three AM. At least I had a recording of the call.

The last place I wanted to be at three-thirty in the morning was in the Whiteaker neighborhood. I may be a private investigator, but I'm not the roughest, toughest guy on the block. I'm like my cat. I come down on the side of flight over fight whenever I'm physically confronted and have a choice. The Whit is where you go in the short hours of the night when your darker urges overcome your better sense. If you want to rent a porn video, buy a loaded Saturday night special with filed-off numbers or a quickie in the back seat of your car, or you have the urge to snort a couple of lines of white powder on a mirror, the Whit is where you want to be. Every city I've ever been in has a seedy, low rent, wrong-side-of-the-tracks cesspool of sin and neglect. In Eugene, that part of town is the Whitaker and Club 69 is the epicenter.

I shivered my way to the kitchen and put a cup of leftover coffee in the microwave. Then I slipped on a black turtleneck, Levis, a pair of Nike cross-trainers, and slid a full clip into my Glock 17. I hate carrying a gun, but sometimes it's plain stupid not to. Flight or fight, I'd be ready either way. The nuke dinged. I snapped the lid on the to-go mug, gave El Gato a cursory belly rub and was out the door in fifteen minutes flat.

On my way downtown, I stopped at the Wells Fargo ATM near the U of O campus, ironically just across the Willamette from where Summer Rain's body had been discovered, and withdrew five hundred dollars. I was thankful that I'd had the cajones to ask Winetrout for an advance and the brains to bank it. I put the receipt in the glove compartment, wondering if whatever the caller was offering would qualify as a normal business expense. I couldn't afford to fork over five Franklins on some wild goose chase, even if it was Charles Winetrout's money. The old man's trust would only go so far and I doubted I'd be getting an invoice tonight. But a big voice in the back of my mind shouted louder: *You're running low on options, Hunter. You can't afford not to check this out.* It was exactly the sort of lousy choice you make at three o'clock in the morning. The short hours can be brutal.

I turned into the potholed, unpaved alley off Blair Boulevard and splashed slowly through the puddles toward the weedy parking lot behind Club 69. A sodium streetlight, one of the few in the Whiteaker that hadn't been broken, illuminated a dismal slumscape of crushed beer cans, bottle caps, broken glass, condoms, and here and there a hypodermic needle. An ancient, destroyed couch with torn mauve velour was propped on end against an overflowing Royal Refuse dumpster. Overhead, the telephone wires had been decorated with several pairs of dirty, worn-out sneakers hanging by their laces.

I backed into the shadow of the dumpster and switched off my headlights. By force of habit, I glanced at my watch. It was 3:45. I was a couple of minutes late but I wasn't worried. There had been a cracked huskiness in the phlegmy voice on the other end of the line and I knew instinctively that money would be more important than minutes to the tortured soul who owned it. There weren't a lot of reasons someone needed five Franklins in the middle of the night and even fewer places to get it. Whatever the caller was selling had a target market of one: **Jack S. Hunter, Private Investigator.** I slid my Glock from my coat pocket to the seat, under the sports section of the *Register Guard*, which, by odd coincidence, featured a story on hunting. I'd give the caller half an hour.

Five minutes later a figure slouched out of the shadows behind my car. In the dim light, in my rearview mirror, I could just barely make out dark, baggy cargo pants and a black hoodie. I felt under the newspaper for my gun. No part of this did I like.

The troll-like creature rapped on the passenger door window with a Bic lighter and I rolled it open a few inches.

"You bring the cash, dickhead?"

"What are you selling?"

The junkie flicked his Bic and held it in front of a mass storage device suspended on a lanyard. Under the hoodie, all I could see was a pair of dark glasses and a wispy blond mustache and beard. In better light, I could have counted the hairs.

"Yeah, big deal. So what's on your flash drive that's worth five Franklins?"

"You're gonna have to pay to play, my man, pay to play."

"And what if your idea and my idea of what's worth that kind of money aren't the same?"

"Then you can meet me back here with another five big ones, dickhead." The voice in the hoodie tried to laugh but quickly deteriorated into a deep, phlegmatic cough.

Against my better judgment, I slid the short stack of crisp Jacksons through the window. The junkie fanned the bills like a poker hand and then flipped the flash drive onto the passenger seat and faded into the gloom. I waited for a moment before I eased out of the alley. A police cruiser, with only its running lights on, slowly made its way down Fifth toward Blair.

I was back in my trailer by four-thirty. El Gato looked up, yawned, and went back to chasing imaginary mice. For a human, four-thirty AM is a miserable time because it's too early to get up and too late to go back to sleep.

I poured myself a Dewar's White Label on the rocks, booted up my aging Dell and plugged the flash drive into the USB port. I began to feel nauseous as soon as the image filled the monitor. Fifty-five silent seconds later, I wished I'd stayed in bed and not answered the phone. I wished I'd never met the tweeker in the alley. I badly wanted a cigarette. I wished there was some way I could avoid showing the movie to Detective Lucas Leonard. This messy case was moving sideways and downward and dragging me along with it. I felt like I was watching the fuse burning on a stick of dynamite duct taped to my dick. All the rain in Oregon wouldn't be enough to douse that fuse.

CHAPTER SIX

I spent the better part of the next day driving around Eugene, aimlessly, trying to bring the Summer Rain Winetrout mess – or at least some part of it – into focus. I couldn't put the imagery of that bone-chilling video out of my mind. I'd only been able to stomach watching it once and I'd found it impossible to go back to sleep afterwards.

I drove out Willamette to Winetrout's mansion but when I got there, I couldn't come up with any reason to go in, so I turned around and came back. Usually I think better when I'm in motion – drive for a while, stop for a double mocha, drive some more, wait for an inspiration, a parting of the clouds – but this time it wasn't working. What I really needed was to get out of Dodge for a few days, camp out by the McKenzie or the Umpqua, watch the water flow and maybe hook a big steelie. I doubted I'd be able to relax, but just trying would be worth the effort. Instead, I drove to the top of Skinner's Butte Park and tried to doze off, perplexed and depressed that the peaceful city below could be the cauldron of the mayhem in the river and on the flash drive. A light drizzle had started, a perfect parallel for my mood.

Who was Summer Rain Winetrout really and why would someone want her dead? Why was Jimmy – James – so hostile? And what about Consuelo? Was she just shy or did she have something to hide, besides the fact that she was probably undocumented? Would I be able to get either of them to open up?

Of course, the big question was: Why was I still involved? I felt like the flash drive was the key, but I couldn't find the lock. Finally, I went home, opened a twenty-two ounce bottle of Ninkasi IPA, made a ham and cheese sandwich and waited up for the late night news. El Gato meowed and looked up at me expectantly, so I shoveled some kibble into his dish and topped it with a few slivers of ham.

There was no mention of Summer Rain's body being found in the Willamette on any of the local stations. Before long, Jay Leno was cracking jokes, doubling up on the punch lines in his annoying way, shoving his hands in his pockets. I wanted to shout, 'we get it the first time, Jay, you don't need to repeat yourself.' Eventually, I passed out in my Lazy Boy, the sandwich only half eaten but the beer history.

It felt like I'd just gotten to sleep when the phone rang. I thought about letting the machine take the call until I saw the time and who it was: Lucas Leonard at 9:00 AM.

"You better come down here and talk to me, gumshoe." Lucas' voice was emphatic. It was not an invitation, it was a command.

"What do you want to talk about?" I asked.

"The fall run of Coho in the Rogue. The price of tea in China. The going rate for courtroom-quality eight-by-ten color glossies. We got lots to talk about."

"I'm sure we do, Detective."

"Don't keep me waiting." Lucas hung up without waiting for a reply.

Forty-five minutes later I was sitting across a cluttered desk from Detective Lucas Leonard. He isn't the type to waste any time with niceties.

"You know a guy by the name of"— Lucas flipped a couple of pages on his spiral notebook—"Marcus Binkelman?"

"The name doesn't ring a bell. Should it?"

"Crack head goes by Binky on the street?"

Binky? "Sorry, Luke. I'm drawing a blank."

"His body was found over in the Whiteaker, in an alley off Van Buren." Lucas handed me a sheaf of police photographs. A crumpled figure in dark clothing had been stuffed like a sack of garbage between a dumpster and a chain link fence. I took my time with the photos. I could see right away who it was. I just didn't know what I had to say about it.

"What did he die of?" I asked.

"I'm waiting for the lab report, but if I had to guess, I'd say he OD'ed."

"What's that got to do with me?"

"You tell me." Lucas slid a sealed baggie across the mess on the desk. Inside was a business card: **Jack S. Hunter, Private Investigator. (541) 729-2251.** On the back of the card a single word was written: 'Charity'. Below were the letters 'H B C'.

"We found that in his pocket."

I stared at the card trying to buy more time before I answered. "Anything else?"

"About what you'd expect. Bogus ID, crack pipe, cheap cell phone. Less than a dollar in change. Tell me about the card."

"Anybody could have my business card." I felt a chill go up my spine. The only thing I could think of that the initials H B C could stand for was the Hot Body Club. I didn't want to know what I knew. A sequence of events ricocheted around my mind. I wasn't ready for anyone, including Lucas Leonard, to watch Binky's disturbing video. I wasn't sure I could stomach seeing it again myself.

"Anybody could have your number show up on their recently-called list, too, right?"

"I get a lot of calls."

"At three in the morning?"

"In my line of work, people don't pay attention to the time. You ought to know that, Luke. Some poor slob in the middle of the night doesn't know where his wife—"

"You got any idea who Charity is, gumshoe?" Lucas turned the baggie over several times.

"Maybe she's Amish."

Lucas didn't smile. He was clearly in no mood for humor.

"It doesn't sound like a real name," I said. "Sounds more like a name a hooker or a stripper would use."

"Listen, Hunter, I may not be Sherlock Holmes, but I'm not the dullest tool in the shed, either."

"I never said you were, Detective."

"So, fill in the blanks for me. The only daughter of a scumbag big wig turns up floating in the Willamette River. She's been raped, tortured, and her body mutilated. Who just happens to arrive at the crime scene? Why, none other than Jack Hunter, Private

Investigator. Next thing you know, a teenage tweeker ODs in an alley in the Whiteaker. What do we find in his pocket? Surprise, surprise! Said gumshoe's business card with a girl's name on the back and a cell phone with his number still hot to the touch."

"None of which proves anything."

"I can get a search warrant if I need to."

"You know you don't have to do that, amigo, you're welcome anytime."

I hoped against hope the detective wouldn't call my bluff.

"I just might take you up on that, gumshoe." Lucas stood up, his invitation for me to leave. At least for the time being, I was off the hook.

My head was spinning. The more I knew, the more I realized I didn't know. Or maybe didn't want to know. Garden-variety infidelity didn't seem quite so complicated anymore; somebody thinks the grass is greener and jumps the fence for some out of bounds grazing. The only thing I was certain of was that it was only a matter of time before Lucas Leonard took me up on my offer to visit my office. I needed to either show him that flash drive or get it out of my trailer and somewhere else ASAP.

Anywhere else.

CHAPTER SEVEN

The music hit me in the face like a blast of heat from a wood-fired pizza oven. The thick, insulated door closed behind me. I waited for my eyes to adjust to the dim lights and my ears to adjust to the blare of hip-hop. The music morphed with the times, the dancers came and went, but the Hot Body Club itself never changed.

"Two bucks cover." A huge, muscle-bound giant with a neck tattoo and gauged earlobes blocked the curtain to the inner sanctum.

I reached for my wallet. "Can you tell me if Charity's dancing tonight?"

"She's up now." He jutted his chin in the direction of the stage.

I handed Goliath two Washingtons and went inside. The night was early, only about eight o'clock, and the bar was sparsely populated. A bored-looking barmaid was racking pint glasses in the dishwasher. A rotating, mirror disco globe reflected shafts of red and blue light onto the stage. In spite of the recent ban on smoking, a haze clung to the ceiling.

In the center of the raised stage, a slender girl swung around a gleaming brass pole. She had long blond hair which, if she were to stand still, would probably have reached the small of her back. Other than a microscopic pink thong that left almost nothing to the imagination and thigh-high red platform boots that added a good five inches to her height, she was naked.

I surveyed the dozen or so beer taps, ordered a Ninkasi IPA and took a seat at the edge of the stage. A short, padded wall separated the dance floor from the counter. On my left, a couple of Latino men were yakking away in Spanish and pretending to ignore the dancer. I wondered idly if they would tip her. On my right, a few seats away, was a huge, blubbery guy with a dinner-sized plate of French fries, a soup bowl of ketchup and what appeared to be a tall rum and coke. His attention was so rapt that he was oblivious to the red smudges on his chin and the front of his shirt. His hand was like a conveyer belt shoveling dripping fries into his mouth. Every so often, he stopped chewing just long enough to take a sip of his drink. A stack of bills fanned out from under the edge of the Heinz bottle.

I folded a Washington lengthwise and arranged it on the padded wall like a barracks tent. The stripper pranced across the stage, turned around and gyrated her buttocks inches from my face. Luscious lips pursed in a kiss were tattooed on her right cheek. She pinched the bill into her cleavage and then spun around.

"Thanks, mister."

"No problemo." I waited until she was hanging upside down from the pole with one leg curled around it and the other sticking straight out with the thong hanging from her big, pink-lacquered toe before replacing the bill with another. If the Latinos heard me respond in Spanish, they didn't acknowledge it.

Four dollars later, the music screeched to a halt. My throat was no longer dry, but my ears were ringing.

"How about a big hand job for Charity, guys. Charity is now available for table dances. This is your chance to enjoy some private time with a very beautiful young lady." The DJ paused for a moment and then announced the next dancer to the stage. "Gentlemen, please give up a big Beaver State welcome to Montana. She's come a long way to strut her stuff for you, so dig deep and be generous." A chesty redhead bounded into the arena and wiped the brass pole with a spray bottle of Windex and a towel before she started her gyrations.

"So, mister, how about a table dance? Charity'd love to give you a private show." The skinny girl had put on her thong and string bikini top and seated herself on the cracked Naugahyde seat next to me. She plunked a tiny sequined clutch purse on the counter.

"Sure," I said. "Can we go to a private booth?"

She eyed me suspiciously. "Whatever. Long as he can see us." She nodded to the hulk standing by the front door.

"Charity, right?"

"You got it." The girl threaded her way through the tables to a darkened booth at the far end of the bar. I drained the rest of my beer and followed her. She slid in behind the table and patted the seat next to her.

"It's fifteen bucks for one song and twenty for two."

I extracted a Jackson from my wallet. "I don't really want a dance. I just want to talk, if it's all the same to you."

Charity folded and unfolded the bill, fidgeting. "Your money, honey. You get two tunes. Charity can talk or she can dance." She laid a hand on my thigh and gave it a little squeeze.

I laid Summer Rain's high school photograph on the table. "Do you know her?"

A flicker of recognition crossed the stripper's face, so brief and faint that I almost missed it in the darkness. Almost, but not quite.

"Nope, never seen her before." The corners of Charity's mouth curved down in an exaggerated frown.

"You're absolutely sure?"

"You like a cop or something?" She removed her hand and slid away from me on the bench.

"Trust me, I'm not police. I just need to find someone who knows this girl."

"Why? What's her name?"

"Summer Rain Winetrout."

"You sure you're not a cop?" Charity's mascaraed eyes darkened as she shifted her gaze between the photograph and me. "Legally you gotta tell a girl the truth, if she asks you. You know that, right?"

"I do and I'm not." I flipped my business card onto the table next to Summer Rain's photo.

Charity inspected the card and then concentrated her attention on the photo for a minute and bit her lower lip. "That's funny. She danced here once. Maybe twice. Her stage name was Winter. She wore a furry white camisole and a white ski hat and gloves."

"Was?" I asked.

"She used to hang out here, but she hasn't been around for a while." She looked up at me. "Why are you looking for her?"

"Her father is worried about her. She seems to have disappeared."

Charity's eyes narrowed and her voice hardened. "Her so-called father sent you? Forget about it. I've already told you too much." She looked over toward the door. Goliath was checking IDs from a mixed crowd.

I felt like a grunt in the jungle who'd stumbled over a land mine trip wire. "What do you mean, Charity?"

"Look, mister, whatever your name is." She glanced down at my card and then held it up to the light. "Jack S. Hunter. No way am I gonna help you get her back home with that...that bastard." She glared at me and practically spat her epithet on the table.

"I didn't say I was trying to take her home. I just want to know where she is."

Charity returned her attention to the photograph and my business card, her eyes flitting back and forth between like a starling about to take flight, as if she were deciding whether or not to trust me. I sat still. She took a deep breath. "OK, mister, listen up. Here's the deal. I'm gonna tell you some shit and then you're not gonna ask me any more questions. You got it?"

The waiflike girl's eyes were slits and the earlier sultriness in her voice had evaporated. A clatter of drums gave way to a brief dead spot in the music.

"Your time's half up, mister." Her voice sounded too loud in the sudden silence. She clicked a painted fingernail on the table. "Tick. Tick. Tick."

I nodded. "Your ball court, Charity. Your rules."

Charity waited for the music before she continued. "OK. Me and her were tight, you know what I mean? In this business, it's hard to make friends, real friends. There's always some bitch trying to horn in on your regulars, fuck with your shit, but me and Rainy hit it off right away." Charity stopped and shook a cigarette and a book of matches out of her purse. A beer in a bar was always the hardest time for me since I quit smoking. An IPA without a cigarette was like a double mocha without the...mocha. She glanced over at Goliath before she lit up. The music had started up again and I had to lean in close to hear her.

"Do you have any idea where—?"

41

"Hey, you're gonna shut up and I'm gonna talk, right? That's the deal."

I mimed closing a zipper over my mouth and folded my hands on the table.

"OK, now we got that straight." Charity blew a flume of smoke out of the corner of her mouth. "One night after work me and her went out to Shari's for breakfast and she like really opened up. What that old fucker done to her wasn't right. He didn't act like he should've. You know what I'm saying?" Charity took a long drag on her cigarette and sucked the smoke past her lip into her nose. My mouth watered.

I started to say 'go on', but I nodded instead.

"Rainy was phat. She had fake ID, so she could've worked in any club she wanted to. She was out there and dudes knew it. I remember one night she was like really high and she got more tips and table dances than all the rest of us put together. Her big dream was she wanted to go down to LA and do fuck flicks for major bucks."

Some dream, I thought. Hard core pornography in California? It sounded more like a nightmare than a dream. Whatever happened to true love, family, babies, careers, peace, eliminating world hunger, all the dreams a high school girl was supposed to imagine in her future? And what was a high school-aged girl doing in the Hot Body Club in the first place, let alone pole dancing?

"And Summer Rain's father?"

Charity took a final deep drag on her cigarette and flicked the ashes onto the floor and then flattened the butt under a platform boot. "Let's just say his interest was more like a horndog, not a father. You hear what I'm saying? That's all I'm gonna say. She told me shit that wasn't right."

I waited for Charity to continue, but she had apparently said everything she was going to say. The only thing passing her lips now was smoke. The second song clashed to a close. I could see, or rather hear, why Charles Winetrout hated the music.

"Charity, if you think of anything else, would you call me?"

"I'm not gonna call you 'cause I already told you more than I should. This girl's up next and she's got to get ready. We're short tonight." Charity tacoed my card into the Jackson and tucked the bundle into her little purse as she got up. She started to go and then turned back. There were tears in her eyes. "Look mister, you see her, you tell her to call me, OK? Susan. She's got my number."

"What if she's lost it?" I wanted Charity's number for myself. Maybe she'd be more willing to open up in a private setting, somewhere other than the Hot Body Club. Our conversation had that tip-of-the-iceberg feeling about it. Her moist eyes told me there was more to this story than she was letting on.

The stripper leaned over and swept her bleach blonde hair back and forth across my face and whispered. "I can't like write nothing down here, they'll fire my ass. I'll leave it on your machine."

"When I find her, I'll tell her to call you. I promise."

"One more thing, mister. Do me a big favor and split, OK?"

I cocked my head and shrugged my shoulders. "Sure, but why?" I was more than ready for another pint of Ninkasi.

"You seem like a cool dude. I don't wanna think about you sitting in the front row with the rest of the droolers checking out what I had for lunch, understand?"

Checking out what she had for lunch? "Sure. You got it."

"Thanks." Charity gave my forearm a little squeeze as she stood up.

"Wait. Before you go, tell me about your kiss tattoo."

"That is for my ex-boyfriend. When I left him, I told him he could kiss my ass good bye." And then she was gone, prancing on her platform boots up the three stairs to her arena.

"Please welcome back to the main stage charming Charity! Guys, dig deep—"

I shut the bone-jarring music behind the heavy door and stepped into the clear, cool, quiet night.

CHAPTER EIGHT

The next morning I drove out Willamette Street to Charles Winetrout's mansion. I needed more pieces to the puzzle and I didn't know where else to look. Maybe I could pry more information out of the old man. Maybe Jimmy would be more forthcoming. Maybe I could catch a private moment with Consuelo. Maybe maybe maybe.

I knew the right thing to do would have been to tell him that Summer Rain was dead, give him Lucas' extension number at the Eugene Police Department, and account for the funds he'd advanced to me. That should have been the end of my involvement. Which had been my intention until I'd watched Binky's horrific video. Those fifty-five seconds of recorded torment had changed everything for me, rearranged my psychic furniture. For the umpteenth time, I wished I had just ignored the phone that night, turned over and gone back to sleep. But I hadn't and now I was, however reluctantly, stumbling into an evil, gloomy mess I couldn't seem to avoid. I couldn't let Summer Rain's murder go. For some inexplicable reason, I felt like I owed something to a young girl I had never met and probably wouldn't have liked. And then there were Susan's tears.

Go figure.

Jimmy was nowhere in sight. I pulled right up to the black jockey, not bothering with the parking lot. The moment Consuelo swung the doors open, I brushed past her and headed toward Winetrout's office. Halfway down the hall, I could already smell stale cigar smoke, so I knew he was home. The housekeeper swept along behind me, protesting in Spanish, "Espera, Señor, espera por favor."

"I'm sorry I'm dropping in on you without calling, sir, but I'm going to have to talk to your wife." I stood at the door, armed with a notepad and a pen. Consuelo was doing her best to look apologetic.

Winetrout was on the phone, his back to the door. A black and silver Raiders windbreaker strained at the seams around his armpits. The security monitor screen was a still life of the Hummer in the driveway. The porn screen was dark. Through the window, I saw Jimmy cleaning the empty hot tub.

"Horsepucky! That's horseshit and you know it. You get back to me when you got a serious offer." Winetrout slammed the phone down and swiveled his chair without getting up. He seemed a little surprised to see me. "What the fuck do you want, Hunter? You find Summer?"

He apparently hadn't heard me. I took a seat. "I need to talk to your wife."

"I told you before, Crystal's gone. We're finished. She doesn't need to be a part of this."

"Crystal?" I flipped open my notebook.

"Technically, Krista Wycowski. She preferred Crystal."

"Krista Wycowski." I mumbled the name to myself as I jotted it down, guessing at the spelling. "C-r-y-s-t-a-l."

"Just plain, old Crystal by itself. She flattered herself that she was one of those superstar types who can get by with one name. Like Madonna or Beyoncé."

"You must have some idea where she is. You intend to serve her with divorce papers at some point, right?"

Winetrout stared out the window at Jimmy, seemingly engrossed with the kid's scrubbing of the hot tub. He snipped the end of a dinner frank-sized Romeo Y Julieta and began licking it.

"Look, Mr. Winetrout, if you want me to find your daughter, you'll have to help me out. I've been asking around, but so far I'm coming up with zilch. Zippo. Nada."

The old man lit his moistened cigar, took a gigantic puff, exhaled and slumped in his chair. "Last I heard, she was up in Portland."

"Portland's a big city, sir."

"If I were looking for that whore, which I most definitely am not, I'd be checking out escort services, titty bars, places like that. There's a swingers' club called Plato's Retreat. I know for a fact she

45

knows about it. She loves to fuck and she's damned good at it."
Winetrout pointed at me with his cigar. "You're a private eye, right?
You're supposed to know how to find people."

"Portland, huh?" I picked up the framed *HUSTLER* cover. "You
mind if I borrow this?"

Winetrout shook his head. He took a magazine out of the bottom
drawer of his desk. It was the same issue. "Take the whole thing.
There's a complete layout inside."

I resisted the temptation to unfold the centerfold. There'd be
plenty of time for that later. "I'll get it back to you."

"Don't bother. I got plenty more copies."

"Look, Mr. Winetrout, if you don't mind my asking, what
happened between you and your wife?" I crossed my legs and made
no move to get up.

"I do mind your asking." The old man studied the glowing end
of his stogie, reconsidering his answer. "What happened? The usual.
We fell in love. We fell out of love. End of story."

"There's got to be more to it than that, sir. You have a full ration
of bitterness, yet you keep a framed photograph of her on your desk.
Other than telling me what a good lover she was, you haven't said
one good thing about her, yet you have a stack of magazines with
her naked in them. It doesn't add up."

"None of that is any of your business, Hunter."

"Maybe, maybe not. I'm looking for anything that can lead me
to your daughter. That's why you hired me, remember? If I
understood what was going on family-wise, it might help. Are you
and Summer Rain close? Is she close to her mother? Could your
split up have caused her to run away? I'm just trying to put it all
together. You want to make it hard for me, fine. It'll just take
longer." I sat back and folded my arms and waited. "It's your dime,
sir."

Winetrout waved his hand back and forth in the stinking smoke
for a minute before he answered. "Krista and I met through a mutual
acquaintance who thought we'd get along. He was right. We really
hit it off. She was like no other woman I'd ever known."

"How so?"

Winetrout gave me his 'just-how-stupid-are-you, anyway?' look. "The woman would do anything I told her to do. You ever ass-fucked a woman who could lock her ankles behind her neck? She was like Gumby in bed. The cunt was a pro." Winetrout paused and scowled at the framed cover on his desk. "Of course, I didn't realize at first how much of a pro she was, but after a while it didn't matter. I was hooked." A sardonic smile crossed the bottom of his face but his eyes were still hard. "I guess that's why they call 'em hookers."

"When you say she was a pro, what exactly—"

"Jesus H. Christ, Hunter, do I have to spell it out for you? We met through an escort service in Vegas. She came to the Tropicana with me for the night and stayed four days. We lived on room service, Glenlivet and vitamin V. Just her and me. The bitch fucked my brains out."

I stifled a smile at the old man's inadvertently accurate phraseology. "And so you married her?"

"More like she married me. When I came back to Eugene, I couldn't get her out of my system. Believe me, I've had my share of poon, but this was something else. I met her in Reno three weeks later and that was that."

"Let me guess. No prenup, right?" My question was off the subject, but I couldn't resist getting in a little dig. As my landlord, I'd never formed much of a positive impression of the guy, but now I was beginning to actively dislike Charles Winetrout.

"Dumb shit move, I know. That's what happens when you think with your pecker."

"One more question. What specifically caused her to leave?"

"I threw her ass out. I found out she was wearing kneepads for half the town."

"You were positive? You had proof?"

"Reliable sources." Winetrout picked up the half-smoked smoldering cigar from a leather-covered glass ashtray and looked at it for a moment before he smashed it flat.

"You should have come to me, sir. That's what I do for a living, remember?"

"What the fuck for? I caught her in the act and she was in no position to deny it. Literally."

"And where was Summer Rain while all this was going on?"

"She made herself scarce, like she always does whenever there's any kind of static."

"You and Mrs. Winetrout had argued before, I take it."

"That bitch has a switch with two positions. Fuck and fight. She's not happy if she isn't doing one or the other."

Now I flipped through the *HUSTLER* until I found Krista Wycowski's layout and unfolded the centerfold. A staple pierced her belly button like a piece of jewelry. Her modified body had been airbrushed to perfection. Charles Winetrout evidently shared Larry Flynt's appreciation of Brazilian waxing and silicone enhancement.

Winetrout looked at his gold Rolex and stood up abruptly. "We're gonna have to cut this short. I have a meeting downtown in an hour. Consuelo!"

The housekeeper appeared from nowhere. "Si Señor? Por favor."

"Show Mr. Hunter out."

"Si, Señor."

As I drove past the garage on my way out, Jimmy stopped scrubbing the tub long enough to glare at me.

What, I wondered, had I done to piss him off?

CHAPTER NINE

It took three days for Marcus Binkelman's brief bio, complete with what looked to be a grade school photograph, to appear on the obituary page of the Eugene Register Guard. How much can a parent write about a sixteen-year-old son who dies from a crystal meth overdose? It both saddened and amused me to compare the sanitized version of Marcus Binkelman's short life – *interested in acting, avid skateboarder who dreamed of competing in the X games, enjoyed making video movies with his friends* – with the reality of the tweeker who met me in the alley behind Club 69. The family had chosen not to disclose the cause of death, understandable given the circumstances. A private service was planned. Instead of flowers, well-wishers were encouraged to make donations to the White Bird Medical Center or Looking Glass Youth and Family Services.

What intrigued me more, though, were the unanswered questions: What exactly was the connection between Marcus Binkelman and Summer Rain Winetrout? How close were they? Were they merely acquaintances, running with the same pack, or had there been something more? The flash drive video was the obvious link, but how did it connect them?

I laid the newspaper clipping next to the photograph of Summer Rain and her friends that Charles Winetrout had given me. It only took a few seconds with a magnifying glass to confirm that Binky had been in the crowd of people in front of the tattoo parlor, which didn't prove diddly squat. They had known each other and now they were both dead.

And what about Susan, aka Charity? I was sure she knew much more than she had been willing to tell me. I scanned the faces in the photograph a second time. Besides Summer Rain, there were only two females facing the camera, and neither of them was the dancer from the strip club. There were several figures facing away from the

49

camera, any one of which could have been Susan, so my search was inconclusive.

I didn't have many leads and unfortunately the few I had weren't leading me anywhere. It was time to pay a second visit to the Hot Body Club.

I stopped at the bar for an IPA. Susan/Charity was chatting with the top heavy redhead at the other end. A tall, plump black girl wearing only upper and lower pink dreadlocks and rings through about everything you could put a ring through was writhing around on a zebra carpet on stage to a jungle beat. I hopped up on a barstool and waited to see if Susan would notice me. It didn't take long.

She swiveled toward me, an unexpected smile on her face when she recognized me. "So, mister, you back for another table dance?" Susan had to raise her voice to be heard over the heavy drumbeat music.

"Twenty bucks buys me two songs, right?"

"Good memory, mister." She slid down off her stool and tottered for a moment on her platform boots.

"OK, I want two songs worth of talk." I folded a Jackson in half and balanced it on a cardboard tent sign advertising Corona.

"Whatever." Susan glanced at the door. "Let's grab some privacy." She scooped up the bill and took my wrist and led me back to the booths. When we were seated, she shook a half-smoked Marlboro out of a pack and lit up. "So, you find Rainy?"

I couldn't bring myself to tell her that Summer Rain was dead. Not yet, anyway. "Not exactly."

"What does 'not exactly' mean?"

"I'll get to that in a minute. Do you know someone named Marcus Binkelman?"

"Binky? Kind of a big, dumpy dude with a scraggly-assed beard? Yucky cough?"

"That'd be the one."

"He like hangs with us sometimes."

I waited for her to continue. "And?"

"And nothing." I turned my head as Susan blew a stream of smoke from the corner of her mouth. "You don't smoke, do you?"

"I quit a few months ago."

"This girl wishes she could quit. Tried to once, but it didn't last long."

"When was the last time you saw him?" I felt the same stiff tension in the back of my neck I feel when I am about to hand over proof of cheating to a sad-eyed lady. I hoped Susan wasn't the type to shoot the messenger.

"Mister, what's this bullshit about?"

I unfolded the obituary and smoothed it out on the table. The light was dim but she figured it out. Obits tend to have a particular generic sameness about them. Marcus Binkelman hadn't made it to his seventeenth birthday.

"Fuck." Susan's shoulders slumped and she covered her eyes with her hands. "I don't read the paper."

"Susan—"

"Don't call me Susan. In here, it's Charity."

"OK, Charity. I apologize. Were Binkelman and Summer Rain close?"

"Binky didn't have no close friends. He was a crackhead. Nobody trusted him." Susan held up the article in the light and squinted. "So, like how'd he die?" She asked.

"The family chose not to disclose the cause of death."

"Yeah, well you know or you wouldn't be here, would you?"

I glanced involuntarily at her smooth forearms. I don't think she caught me. "Best guess is he died of an overdose."

"Binky OD'ed? You're shitting me. That's too weird." Susan crushed her cigarette and immediately lit another one.

"That may be sad, but why is it weird? He was a tweeker. You already said nobody was close to him because he did drugs."

"What's weird is Binky never had no money. His parents like cut him off long ago. He didn't have a bitch to dance or trick to support him. So, you tell me, mister, where the fuck would he get enough money to OD?"

It was a good question but the answer would have to wait. "How did Binky support his habit, Charity?"

"Oh, you know, the usual. He'd deal a little, scam a little, whatever came along. He was a couch surfer so he didn't pay no rent nowhere."

I winced at the triple negative. "I take it he didn't have a steady job."

Susan laughed, causing her to choke on her smoke. "Binky? A job? You gotta be fuckin' kidding."

"So you're telling me Marcus Binkelman was a mall rat, didn't work, didn't have any friends, and somehow got enough money together to buy enough crack to overdose."

"Like I said, fuckin' weird, isn't it."

"That's putting it mildly, Charity."

The music stopped and we sat without talking for a few beats listening to the DJ jabber away. I enjoyed a couple of long swallows of my IPA. All too soon, the music started up again.

"Your second song, mister." Susan gave my thigh another light stroke. I was getting to like that.

"You were gonna tell me about Summer Rain." I said.

Susan eyed me intensely, her expression wavering between trust and suspicion. "Like, what do you wanna know I haven't already told you?"

"Is Summer Rain sexually active?"

"Sexually active? You could say that." Susan grinned and winked at me, coming down on the side of trust, at least for the moment. "Who isn't?"

"Is she promiscuous?"

"Mister, you sure like to use fancy words. Sexually active. Promiscuous." Susan stabbed out her Marlboro. "Rainy fucks around a lot. I could never figure that out about her. I mean, she claims she doesn't really like sex much, actually doing it, and she never does it for money like a lot of bitches on the street do. Used to drive Binky nuts that she'd give it away free but not sell it. Know what I mean?"

I nodded. "How about Binkelman? Were he and Summer Rain, um, getting it on?"

Susan had one of those faces that could instantaneously rearrange itself to reflect her emotions and now she gave me a 'you're-not-the-sharpest-tool-in-the-shed, are you?' look. "Binky? If you were a chick, would you want to do him? Get real."

I recalled our encounter in the alley and saw her point. "Was Summer Rain with anyone in particular?"

"Not really. Just some dudes from the group, wherever. Usually nobody more than once or twice." Susan giggled to herself before she went on. "She even fucked the gardener where she lived."

"James?" I was incredulous.

"Yeah, him. How is it you know Jimmy?"

"I met him when I went out to talk to Winetrout. He's a bit of a strange duck. I wouldn't have figured him paired up with Summer Rain."

"Can you believe that shit? Summer Rain getting it on with super straight, up-tight Jesus-freak James Sundquist. Like, I think she only did him to see if she could. She said it made his head spin big time. I think he cared a lot more for her than she did him."

"How's that?"

"Well, like, once a month they have amateur night here. Any bitch with a secret dream to be a stripper can get up on stage and show what she's got. One night, Rainy like got a wild hair up her butt and signed up. Jimmy was here that night – it was back before he found Jesus and became James – and when it came her turn, he tried to stop her. That didn't go over too good."

It was time to drop the bomb. The proverbial elephant in the room. There wasn't going to be a soft landing for this one.

"Susan, er, Charity, last time I was here, you said a few things about her father. Was she..."

"You sure you wanna go there, mister?" Her fingers slid off my leg.

"It's not about where I want to go, it's about what I have to do." I must have sounded grim. It wasn't the sort of conversation I wanted to have in a public place with raised voices and loud music, but there we were. I've learned to never turn down tips and clues, anytime, anywhere.

Susan lit her cigarette lighter several times, like she was lighting and dousing a beacon. "Rainy's not like OK, is she?"

"She's in a much better place than she was."

A lull in the music signaled the end of my two table dances. I tented another Jackson on the table between us. "Two more?"

Susan tried to light a cigarette, but her hand was shaking too badly. I took the Bic and lit it and saw the tears stream mascara down her cheeks.

"He made her do it. That fat fuck forced her." She looked at the cash but didn't touch it.

"Are you talking about her father?"

Susan's eyes were slits, her voice sharp. "That's what he told you? He was her father?"

It took several beats for reality to sink in. "Winetrout isn't her father?"

Susan exhaled a long stream of smoke from the corner of her mouth away from me and shook her head. "I swear to Christ, mister, you're dumber than a rock. Think about it. He met Crystal two years ago, when Rainy was about thirteen. Do the fucking math. How could he be her father?"

I jolted straight up like I'd sat on a handful of thumb tacks. I was slipping. Even the Hardy boys would have figured that one out in chapter one. "Daughter from a previous marriage." Even as I mumbled the words, I knew they weren't quite accurate.

"Wrong guess, mister. Crystal's her mom. That bastard is her step-father."

My head was reeling. I came damned close to helping myself to one of Susan's cigarettes. I'd come to the Hot Body Club hoping to find some answers and now I had more loose ends than I'd started with. Why couldn't I be working on a simple, run-of-the-mill divorce-worthy adultery case? What I had instead was a ball of string that got bigger and shaggier and nastier by the minute. Where did I go from here?

"Tell me about Marcus Binkelman, Charity. His obituary said he was into acting, making movies, stuff like that, right?"

"When he wasn't high, Binky liked to mess around with his camcorder. Silly shit, just make-it-up-as-you-go skits. We were all in 'em." Susan rearranged the ashes on the table with the tip of her Marlboro. "You gonna tell me how she died?"

I ignored her question. "Do you have any of his movies?"

"Nah, like I said, Binky never had any money, so he'd mostly record over his old shit."

"What did he use for a camera? I mean if he couldn't afford new tape or SD cards or flash drives, or whatever..."

"Binky had a sweet camcorder he'd scored somewhere. You know, something he didn't dare hock."

Something, some little piece, was beginning to fall into place. "Charity, did Binkelman ever try to make a porn movie?"

Susan looked over my shoulder toward the bar. "Not that I know of, but I wouldn't like put it past him." Sudden quiet. "Fuck." She stood up. "This girl's up next."

I was out of questions. "You think of anything else, give me a call, OK? You still owe me one song."

"Yeah, sure, your credit's good with me. You still didn't—"

The rest of her question was lost in a blast of ear-splitting noise. Which was fine. I wanted Susan to remember Summer Rain the way she'd last seen her. Not the way I had.

CHAPTER TEN

What had begun as a simple search for my landlord's runaway step-daughter had morphed into a much darker hunt and I knew at least one of the pieces of the puzzle could be in Portland. That is, if I could locate Krista Wycowski.

Lucas Leonard was a more than competent detective. He'd been around too long to take anything at face value and there weren't many unsolved homicides on his watch. Summer Rain Wycowski was a mutilated corpse chilling in a drawer at the morgue and sooner or later Lucas would track down and arrest whoever was responsible for putting her there. My line of work was trapping philanderers and cheaters, not murderers, so I should have washed my hands of the whole affair. But I couldn't quite picture my hard-nosed friend breaking the news of Summer Rain's death to her mother.

Curiosity is both a requirement and a curse for a private eye. Someone had wanted me to know Summer Rain had been raped before she was tortured to death and I wanted to know who and why. Besides which, my normal lurking and sleuthing business had slowed to an almost-dry trickle, like a mountain feeder stream in late summer, and I knew that Winetrout wanted me to stay involved since he didn't have much faith in the police. I knew it was a rationalization, but money was money and currently in short supply, so I cut myself a little slack.

For starters, I wanted to know who had taken the video. By the look on her face, Summer Rain had been aware they were being recorded. I wondered if the fat man – how I had blinded myself to the likelihood, especially after what Susan had told me, that the man in the video was Charles Thurgood Winetrout? – had also known they were not alone. His head had been out of the picture so I had no idea what his facial expression was. It was hard for me to believe he'd let someone videotape him raping his step-daughter. On the other hand, he'd been stupid enough to marry Krista without a prenup so maybe he'd been stupid enough to convince himself that sex with Summer Rain wasn't rape.

And how had Marcus Binkelman, aka Binky, gotten possession of the video? It did not seem plausible that a crackhead dropout from the Whiteaker would himself be in a position to film a rich, spoiled high school brat having non-consensual sex with a man old enough to be her father. Or grandfather, for that matter. And inside the gates of Fortress Winetrout, no less. There had to be a missing link. Or links.

The part that baffled me most was, why had I been given, sold really, the flash drive? The only people who knew I was searching for Summer Rain were her step-father, who had hired me, his gofer James Sundquist, and Summer Rain's friend Susan. And the kids on the mall. Binky must have been in that crowd, which would explain how he got my card. There were too many questions and something told me I might find some answers in Portland. If, and it was a long shot, I could track down Summer Rain's mother, Krista Wycowski.

I filled El Gato's food dish to overflowing and rinsed out and refilled his water bowl. "See you when I see you, fella." I scratched behind his ears with one hand and under his chin with the other, like he likes. He knows when he has my full, undivided attention. His motor started running immediately but his eyes stayed open. I think he understands when I cradle his head like that he might not see me for a day or so. Of course, it could just be the double rations.

*

My room at the Airport Sheraton had typical Pacific Northwest décor. There was a king bed with a multi-hued blue comforter, a photo triptych of the Oregon coast on the wall behind it, a room service menu that featured baked salmon and other regional favorites, and a mini fridge under the flat screen with a respectable selection of local wines and microbrews. There were several bottles of beer from the Deschutes Brewery in Bend, but so far Ninkasi hadn't made the hundred mile journey north from Eugene. I poured myself an Inversion IPA, a reasonable substitute, and settled in to watch jets land and take off. The screeching and the motion helped me think.

Charles Winetrout's estranged wife, as it turned out, wasn't hard to find. An ad in the back pages of Portland's alternative weekly newspaper, *Willamette Week*, pointed the way. The husky voice on Crystal's answering machine promised an evening of pleasure and romance between consenting adults and invited the caller to leave a message, which I did. My cell phone rang back within half an hour.

"Crystal here. What can I do for you?"

"I'm up from Eugene on business and I would love to have some female company for the evening." That much was true, as far as it went.

"Eugene, huh? How did you get my number?" There was an undercurrent of edginess in her voice.

"I saw you're personal ad in *Willamette Week*."

"Oh, yeah, of course." Sigh of relief. "Hang on. Let me check my calendar. What did you say your name was?"

"Jack. Jack S. Hunter."

"Hang on, Jack." I waited a full fifteen seconds on hold; Winetrout had been right, Crystal was a pro. "This is awfully short notice, Jack, but looks like you're in luck. I have a cancellation."

"That's great news. Sounds like my lucky day."

"It very well could be, Jack. I can meet you for dinner and maybe drinks afterwards." She emphasized the words 'dinner' and 'drinks'.

"That's exactly what I had in mind. I'm staying at the Airport Sheraton. Room 301."

"I'll meet you in the bar downstairs, Jack. Say eight?"

"Perfect. How will I recognize you?" I opened the *HUSTLER* magazine I'd brought with me to the centerfold and spread it on the table, speculating about what Crystal would look like with clothes on.

"How about I recognize you, Jack? Snap a pic of your face and send it to me."

I held my cell phone about eighteen inches away, took a photo and hit 'send', amazed at my own proficiency. A few seconds later,

Crystal said 'got it, see you in a few hours' and clicked off. I found an ice bucket under the sink and wandered down the hall in search of an ice machine.

*

Krista Wycowski arrived in the hotel bar wearing a red pantsuit with a frilly pink blouse that was a subtle blend of businesswoman and vamp. There was just enough supple tan cleavage showing to attract attention without being flamboyant. Larry Flynt's airbrush artist had had a good foundation to work from.

"Hi, Jack!" Crystal said, loud enough for the bartender to hear.

I stood up and gestured to the seat next to me. "Hi Crystal. Great to see you."

"My pleasure to meet you." She said in a quieter voice, giving me a visual once-over before she sat down, her back to the bar.

"Nice to meet you, too," I said.

Krista came right to the point. "I like to get details out of the way first and then we can have the evening to enjoy each other's company." She leaned across the table until her face was mere inches from mine. She must have bathed in perfume.

As discretely as I could, I slid three crisp Franklins under her cocktail napkin.

"We both understand this is simply a donation and whatever might or might not happen between us later is simply an act of two friendly, consenting adults enjoying themselves." She pursed her lips into a kiss.

"Of course," I said.

Krista blotted her lips with the napkin and deftly slid the cash into her blouse. I wondered how Charles Thurgood Winetrout would like reimbursing me for this particular business expense. He couldn't have imagined that a hefty chunk of his advance would end up in the grubby hands of a now-dead tweeker in the Whit and another portion nuzzling one of his estranged wife's silicone-enhanced breasts. Life can be funny that way.

"So, cowboy, tell me a little about yourself."

"I work for a grass seed wholesale business in the valley."

"And you are in Portland because…"

"I lied to you before about it being a business trip. I'm here on a purely recreational visit."

Krista took this in before she answered. "I'm sorry, but I have to ask you this; you're not a cop or connected with any law enforcement agency, right?"

"Not unless you count traffic tickets." I didn't feel the need to mention my friendship with Detective Lucas Leonard.

"So, what sort of recreation did you have in mind?" Krista leaned forward and executed a maneuver that treated me to an even more tantalizing view into her deep, scented cleavage. I couldn't help but flash back to the *HUSTLER* feature layout.

"I'd like to go someplace a little more private and talk, if that's OK with you, Crystal."

"Talk first, dinner after, cowboy?"

"I had a late lunch," I lied. "We can always order from room service if we want to."

"Sounds good to me," Krista shrugged her shoulders, rippling her breasts.

A short elevator ride later we were in room 301. I retrieved the bucket of ice cubes from the mini fridge and unscrewed a bottle of Dewar's White Label and poured each of us a drink. "I hope Scotch is OK with you." I relaxed into one of the two facing club chairs and gestured to Krista to do the same.

"Scotch is fine." Krista transferred the cash from her lacy brassiere to her purse, unlatching two more buttons in the process. "It's a little warm in here, don't you think?" She wriggled out of her red jacket and hung it over the back of my chair, freeing up yet another button along the way. "You don't mind if I get comfortable, do you?"

"By all means, Crystal. Make yourself at home."

"Thanks." Krista kicked off her heels and slid onto my lap.

"Can we talk a little first?" I said. "I'm kind of a slow starter."

"Fine with me." Krista shifted to the other chair and curled her feet underneath her. "What would you like to chat about, cowboy?"

"Well, for starters, tell me a little about yourself. You ever been married?"

A shadow crossed her face and she took a belt of the Scotch. "I'm married now, as a matter of fact. Separated would be more accurate. How about you, Jack?"

"Me? I've never been married. Separated for how long?"

"My soon-to-be ex lives in your hometown."

"Really." I tried to sound surprised but knew I'd failed. "Eugene?"

"Yeah. It's not a happy situation."

"Any kids?"

"I have one daughter by my first husband. None with number two or with Charlie, thank God."

"Does she live with you here in Portland?"

"No, Jack, she's still in Eugene."

"You get to see her much?"

"What is this, the third degree? Why do you want to know all this stuff, anyway?"

"Well, I find the experience to be much more pleasurable if I know the person a little bit before hand."

"Sure, cowboy. Right. I completely agree." Her tone of voice told me she thought I was full of crap.

I took a deep breath. I was going to have to level with Krista sooner or later. "I might as well be completely honest with you. I'm a private investigator. Summer Rain is missing. Your husband hired me to find her."

Krista Wycowski bolted upright in her chair. "What are you talking about?"

"Summer Rain has disappeared. I was hoping that you might know where she is." I didn't feel right about not being upfront with Krista about her daughter's murder. I didn't know how to handle this kind of tragedy. It was infinitely more difficult than presenting a wife with photos of her husband engaged in the act with another woman.

"That asshole." She got up, grabbed her purse and jacket, and stomped toward the door.

"Hang on, Crystal, we need to talk."

"You paid for my companionship, cowboy, not my life story. I'm out of here."

"I have reason to believe Summer Rain might be in some danger. I need your help."

Krista froze with her hand on the door knob. "What kind of danger?"

"If you'll come and sit down, we can talk."

By the time Krista sat down, her blouse had mysteriously rebuttoned itself. "What kind of danger are you talking about? Tell me what you know." Her voice was hard, with no trace of its former seductive tone. Echoes of Susan's reaction when Charles Winetrout's name had come up.

"I don't know much. That's why I'm up here. I was hoping you could help me."

"What do you want to know?" Her voice was marginally softer, but still brittle.

"I'm not sure, exactly. Whatever you can tell me about her."

"Where do you want me to start? When my daughter was young, she was a precocious child. Always pushing the limits, seeing how far she could go. Now, you might say she's a wild young lady."

Just like her mom, I thought to myself. "When was the last time you saw her?"

"She came up about a month ago. We had lunch together. I didn't have any appointments and I wanted her to stay the night, but she said she had to get back to Eugene. She wouldn't say why."

"How much does your daughter know about your life? Does she know what you do for a living?" I tried not to sound judgmental.

Krista turned her attention to the darkening clouds rolling in over the airport before she answered. "What I do for a living? She knows I'm an escort."

"And she knows about this, too?" I slid the *HUSTLER* out from under the Willamette Week.

Krista barely gave it a glance. "I'm sure she does, cowboy. Charlie had enough copies stashed around for anyone and everyone to see." She seemed to reconsider and opened the magazine to her feature. "You know, nude modeling is a strange experience."

"Strange?" I asked. "How so?"

"It's one thing to pose in a studio where everyone is totally professional and you just think some old fart you're never gonna meet who lives in West Palm Beach, Florida or Scottsdale, Arizona or Bumfuck, Texas or somewhere else far away is looking at a centerfold in a magazine and jerking off. Believe me, it's another story when literally everyone you know has seen a copy and stares at you like you're not wearing any clothes, like you're walking down the street in high heels, naked."

I couldn't help but ask. "But Crystal, you're an escort. How is this any different?"

"I can't exactly explain what it's like. Posing is removed. It's like it's not real. You're lying there buck naked on a couch in a fancy house and somebody wearing clothes runs over in front of the camera and moves your arms, opens your legs a few more inches. Somebody else touches up your makeup, fusses with your hair. There's a guy with a camera who keeps telling you to relax and be natural." Krista paused and smiled to herself. "Kinda like the first time I got married." Pause. "Forget about it. What kind of danger is my daughter in, anyway?"

I ignored the question. "Were you aware that your daughter was working at a strip club as a...dancer?"

"Not possible. She's underage."

"Be that as it may, she was on stage at the Hot Body Club less than a month ago. Her stage name is Winter."

"Well, she's her mother's daughter. She must have gotten fake ID somewhere."

Her mother's daughter; exactly the same words Charles Winetrout had used. "Maybe she knew someone at the club who got her in, let her work."

"I doubt it. You can get into a shitload of trouble doing that." Krista was choosing her words carefully.

"According to the grapevine, your husband—"

"Estranged husband, if you don't mind!"

63

"OK, sorry, estranged husband. Charles Winetrout's the silent owner of the club, right?"

Krista took a deep breath and exhaled puffing out her cheeks. "Charlie has a financial stake, but he doesn't get involved in running the joint. He hides behind some dummy corporation in Nevada. His name isn't on anything in Oregon. Don't ask me how it all works."

"That's where his money comes from." It was more a statement than a question.

"Not hardly. I don't think he takes a dime out of Hot Body."

"So what's in it for him, then?" I asked.

"Duh." There was a pause while she took in the blank look on my face. "The dancers, of course. He likes being a big shot. He can come and go as he pleases, drink and eat free, fool around with any of the girls he wants, you know, throw his weight around."

"You're telling me he's the silent owner of the Hot Body Club and he sleeps with the dancers?"

"Naw, I don't think he actually screws 'em, most of the time, anyway. Leering and fondling and groping are more Charlie's style."

"And the girls put up with it?" I wanted to ask Krista if she knew about Winetrout and Summer Rain but I couldn't find an opening.

"Yeah, mostly they do. They have to if they want to make any money. If you behave yourself and tow the mark, smile when he squeezes your ass, you get good shifts, Friday and Saturday nights. You kick up a fuss and piss him off and all of a sudden you find yourself stripping for the bartender on weekday afternoons."

I was astonished to think that a strip club owner, no matter how sleazy, would treat the dancers like his personal harem and even permit his under-aged stepdaughter to perform naked on stage. I couldn't begin to calculate the years and the fines. The more I learned about Charles Thurgood Winetrout, the more of a douche bag he was turning out to be. I guess I'd allowed his lax attitude about the rent to blind me.

"Do you know who any of her friends were?" It was a slip I hoped Krista would miss. I wasn't that fortunate. She was like Lucas; nothing got by her.

"Who her friends *were*? As in the past?" Krista slid forward to the edge of the couch. "What exactly do you mean by *were*?"

I wished I still smoked. I wanted more than anything to buy a few precious seconds to gather my thoughts and formulate my words. I wasn't ready for this part of the conversation. I walked to the rain-spattered window and watched a Thai Airways 747 glide in for a landing on the glistening runway.

"I'm sorry, there's no easy way around this." I turned and looked squarely at Summer Rain's mother. "Your daughter is dead."

"Dead?" Krista leaped to her feet. The sound that came from her throat was more of a scream or a cry than a word. For the first time since I'd met her, Krista's voice sounded real. No sexy escort. No hard divorcee-to-be. No cooing love kitten. Just wounded animal mother. She stood for a moment and then sank back into her chair, unable to remain standing.

"That can't be true. You're mistaken. She was just here." Tears flooded her eyes.

"A month ago is what you said."

"How? What?"

I took a final slug of my Scotch, shoveled ice into both glasses and refilled them. "This isn't easy, Krista. Summer Rain was murdered about a week ago. The police are still conducting a forensic investigation. I don't know a whole lot and I doubt the police will share whatever they discover with me."

"Murdered?" Krista was not going to let it go until she had the whole story, or at least as much as I knew. I couldn't blame her. I'd want it, too. She gulped some Scotch, spilling a little.

"Her body was found floating in the Willamette River. It wasn't pretty."

Krista sat rigidly with her hands knotted in her lap waiting for me to continue.

"You should leave this alone. Trust me, you don't want me to go into the details."

"I damned well do want you to go into the details." Her words flew around the room like shrapnel. "This is Summer Rain you're talking about, my daughter, remember?"

I took a deep breath and described the scene at the river's edge. By the time I got to the last part where Summer Rain's mouth and vagina had been sewn shut, Krista's hard eyes were again shiny with tears.

"Who did it?"

"That's what we're trying to find out."

"We? If you're a private dick, what are you doing here, anyway? Why aren't the cops investigating? Isn't this their job?" Krista drained her glass. "Where do you fit in, Jack?"

"Believe me, the police are all over this. You're hus— Charles Winetrout hired me to find her. At that time, she was only missing, not dead. When her body was discovered, I assumed I was done looking, but he wanted me to stay on the case, regardless."

"I can't believe my daughter's gone." Krista's head jerked up, her eyes narrowed to slits. "How can you be sure it's Summer you found in the river? Maybe it's not her. Maybe it's someone else. You never met her face to face in person, did you?"

I filled in as many of the details as I could, including the piercings and the tattoos, but omitting the fifty-seven second video. Finally Krista's shoulders slumped and I knew that she had accepted the brutal truth. Her only child was dead.

"You know, if this is too hard for you, we could talk about it another time."

"No, if I know anything that can help find the bastard, I want to tell you now. Just pour me another Scotch and I'll be fine."

Krista didn't look like she'd be fine anytime soon. I emptied her melting ice into the sink and filled her glass with fresh cubes and Scotch. "Do you know who any of her friends were? Does the name Marcus Binkelman ring any bells?"

"No, I never heard that name. What with me living here and her down there, I sort of lost track of her friends. She ran with a pretty rough bunch, that much I do know. The chains-and-leather kids, mall rats you might say. But, I swear to God, Summer is a good girl, underneath the ink and the attitude." Krista swallowed half her drink and a sad little smile formed on her painted lips. "Dancing at the Hot Body Club." She shook her head. "You should have seen her when she was a little girl. You'd have figured her for a choirgirl or a Girl Scout standing in front of Safeway selling cookies. You know, wholesome-like. That is, on those rare occasions when she wasn't getting into trouble. Are you absolutely one-hundred percent positive it's Summer? There couldn't be some mistake?"

I visualized the photos Charles Winetrout had spread on his desk. It'd been hard to see the transition from the skinny girl with the big shiny smile to the sullen Goth groupie in the last shot. I mentally replayed the horrific video I had paid Marcus Binkelman five hundred dollars for. Finally, I tried – unsuccessfully – to purge the image of Summer Rain Wycowski's mutilated corpse from my mind.

I shook my head. "I'm sorry. There's no doubt. How about a girl named Susan. You might have known her as Charity."

"Now that you mention it, that name rings a bell. Summer mentioned having a friend named Susan, but she came up here alone so I never met her. How do Susan and this Brinkman character figure into Summer's life?"

"Binkelman," I corrected. "I don't know exactly. I was hoping you could help. Susan is a dancer at the Hot Body Club."

"I might have guessed. Charity sounds like the stage name a stripper would use."

"Tell me about your marriage."

Krista took another gulp of her fresh Scotch. "I don't see how that's any of your business. Or relevant. Why do you want to know?"

"Look, Krista, I'm grasping at straws here. I don't have much to go on. Your daughter started out missing and now she's dead. So far, the police haven't come up with any leads and neither have I. You're ex hasn't been much help, I might add."

"How about DNA? If Summer was molested, raped, shouldn't there be some, you know, evidence?"

"Maybe, maybe not. For one thing, she had been floating in the water for a while before she was found. And then, too, the DNA would only be a match for someone already in the system with a criminal record. So far, there's nada. If they come up with a suspect later, they can compare whatever DNA they find with that person, but even if there is any, it wouldn't be much use at this stage."

Krista took a deep breath and closed her eyes before she started. "OK, I'll lay it out for you. Here's the story. I met Charlie the same way you found me. I was working in Vegas at another agency, *The Pleasure's All Yours*, and I got a long distance call from Eugene. It was Charlie, although I'd never heard of him at the time. I was pretty busy back then. The *HUSTLER* spread had just come out a few months before and enough high-roller johns made the connection the phone wouldn't stop ringing."

"Seems odd, going from the cover of a national porn magazine to an escort service."

"Not really when you stop to think about it. It's all part of the same business. I've worked in the sex trade one way or another since I was fourteen. It was a perfect time to up the ante, which a girl's gotta do every chance she gets, while she can, right? I mean, what man doesn't want to screw a *HUSTLER* centerfold? You have the rest of your life to slide down the backside of the hill."

I decided to let the matter drop. "So go on about your relationship with Winetrout."

"OK, to begin with, you gotta understand a few things. I was a single mother trying to support myself and my daughter, no help from her loser dad, of course, who knocked me up when I was fifteen. I never finished high school so it's pretty hard to land a decent job. What I do have going for me now are these" – she cupped her hands under her cantaloupe-sized breasts – "and what goes with 'em. Believe me, I make a lot more money doing what I do than I would asking if you'd like fries with that."

I thought of the Franklins Krista had tucked into her bra and smiled. "How did he find you?"

"Charlie? Somehow he'd gotten my number, which right off the bat was a tip off that he knew somebody who knew somebody. Later, I connected the dots, but by then it didn't really matter."

Krista was covering ground like a broken field running back. I was doing my best to keep up. "So, what convinced you to come to Eugene?"

"Charlie liked to flash cash around. And believe me, he had plenty. Even in Vegas, he got noticed. I got the impression he was a big fish in a small pond back home. When he left Vegas, he told me he'd be in Reno on business real soon and he invited me to come up for a few days. I figured, what the hay, I'd never been north before and I could use a breather."

"And from Reno to Eugene?"

"That part took me by surprise," Krista said in a tone of voice that implied not much surprised her. "Charlie showed up at the Atlantis armed with rings and things. He wanted to marry me! I hardly knew the guy, so I said no. I wasn't so sure it was a good idea, but he wouldn't take no for an answer. Finally, after a few days on the town, Winetrout-style, I caved in and said OK. We got married in the drive through at the Chapel of the Bells. It felt like he'd ordered a Big Mac to go. Turns out I should have stuck with my first answer."

"And Summer Rain was OK with…everything?"

"I've never tried to hide anything from my daughter. I mean, she was bound to figure things out sooner or later. What'd be the point? She's all I got." Pause. "Had."

"Yeah." Even though I made my living off people's sexual indiscretions, all this was way over the top even for me. Somehow, I'd started off looking for a runaway teenager and now I was sitting in a hotel in Portland with a high-end hooker/*HUSTLER* centerfold talking about her murdered daughter.

Krista must have read my mind. "Look, I don't feel quite right about this, OK? You didn't come up here to get your rocks off, so I really shouldn't take your money." She extracted the cash from her purse.

"Keep it," I said. "I'm on an expense account."

"Expense account?"

"It's Winetrout's money. I'm on his ticket."

Krista tried to laugh but couldn't quite make it. "In that case…" She returned the money to her handbag and snapped it shut. "If that's the case, I ought to charge you double."

"Hate him that much, huh?"

"What do you think? We were married over a year and he threw me out on my butt."

"And why was that, exactly?" I already knew the answer, or at least I'd heard Charles Winetrout's explanation, but I wanted to hear Krista's version. For the umpteenth time, I reckoned I was getting far too involved in this case, but I also knew there was no going back. "What happened?"

Krista was quiet for a moment, a faraway look in her eyes, then she shook her head as if clearing it. If I had to guess, I'd guess she was grieving her loss. Who wouldn't be?

"Everything was fine in the beginning. Charlie was very, very generous. He liked having me around as arm candy and I enjoyed being a pampered pet, the trophy wife. You tell me, Jack, how many fat old guys get to strut around with a *HUSTLER* centerfold? There are worse things in life; I could be chopping up chickens in Alabama." She stopped to take a sip of her drink. "Most importantly, Summer seemed happy." Her eyes got shiny at the thought of her daughter.

I gave it a moment before I asked, "So, what went wrong?"

"After we got back from Vegas and I got to know Charlie a little better, I realized I didn't really like him that much as a person. Charlie is all about sex, but in a yucky kind of way. He isn't the handsomest specimen on the planet, although he does have plenty of money and that makes him a little more attractive, if you catch my drift. But his sexual tastes were weird and once we were married and he figured I wasn't going anywhere, they got weirder and weirder."

"Like how?" I squirmed in my chair and took a big swallow of Dewar's. I could feel where the discussion was headed, but I hoped against hope that Krista's answers would lead elsewhere.

"Charlie liked to party hardy. He was determined to get into the swinger scene, so Charlie being who he was, it didn't take long before he was inviting couples over for sex parties with me as the lure. At first it would just be another couple, but as time went on the parties got bigger and bigger, more and more people. Far as he was concerned, I was great bait; he made sure everyone knew about the

HUSTLER spread. Sometimes he'd bring a girl or two up from the bar to fill things out, you know, even up the numbers."

"So you were running a swingers' club?"

"You could say that. But here's the strange part. For all his interest in sex, for all his pornographic videos, much as he liked to hang out in his strip bar and fondle the merchandise, Charlie didn't actually like to fuck that much."

Fondle the merchandise? "I don't get it."

"I didn't get it either. At first, I thought he was just having a bad night, or had too much to drink, or whatever. Men at his age, sorry, but you probably already know this, can't always raise the flag on demand, although you'd think with half a dozen naked girls prancing around in front of you there for the taking, you couldn't help but get it up. Especially when you got the magic blue pill to help things along. What I came to realize, though, was what got him off more than doing it himself was watching other people screw. You might say he's a voyeur."

I remembered the porn that had been playing on the huge flat screen TV the first time I'd been in Winetrout's office and realized with a jolt the woman had been Crystal.

"Charlie especially liked to watch me get it on with another guy." Krista paused for a beat. "Or guys."

"You sure you want to be telling me all this?" Although I admit to a prurient curiosity about the intimate life of the first *HUSTLER* centerfold I'd ever met, I had to wonder if this conversation would produce any useful information that might eventually lead me to Summer Rain's killer. Or killers.

"Well, cowboy, you asked so I'm answering." There was a detached, matter of fact tone in Krista's voice, like her body was not a part of her, but simply a tool she was just using to make a living, like her referring to dancers as 'merchandise'. She poured herself more Scotch. "What really got his juices flowing was watching me take on two or even three guys at once. Charlie paid the bills and in his book that gave him the right to call the shots, like I was bought and paid for. I don't think the women, some of them anyway, were as enthusiastic watching me getting double-teamed as he was, but what the hay? What did they expect? It was a sex party, right? They'd come up to his house knowing in advance they were going to a major fuck fest. Anyway, whatever they thought wasn't my problem."

"And Winetrout wouldn't have sex himself?" I thought of Binky's video, wondering what the old man might look like without clothes. It wasn't a pretty sight.

"Oh, yeah, once in a while he would. But he was pretty picky about who he screwed. Charlie likes 'em slender with big boobs, like me I guess, but mostly he goes for the younger stuff. Once in a while if some new, young couple showed up or if he'd handpicked a new girl from the club, he'd get all excited and even get a hard on. Especially if she had what he called a 'trophy rack'. But more often he'd just sit in his big leather chair smoking one of his stinky cigars, maybe getting a blow job, and watching everyone else getting it on."

"And where was Summer Rain while all this was happening?"

"We, me that is, always tried to arrange the parties for when she was sleeping over at a friend's house. I felt it was somehow, I don't know, Jack, over the line for her to be there."

"How was it that swingers' parties were over the line and dancing in a strip club wasn't?"

"I never said her dancing at the Hot Body was OK, 'cause it isn't. I never said it was. Think about it, cowboy. I was younger than Summer when I got pregnant. Call me a lousy mother, if you want, but nobody gave me a manual."

"So, Summer Rain was never around on party nights?"

"Maybe once or twice, but for the most part, no. She ran with her own crowd."

"Can you tell me what finally led up to your separation?"

"That's the part I can't figure out. It doesn't make any sense. I still don't understand it, but whatever." Krista paused for a moment like she was arranging the memory in her mind. She took a small sip of her Scotch, but when I held out the bottle she shook her head.

"During the time Charlie was having these sex orgies, I'd gotten to know a couple of dudes pretty well. Charlie was not, you could say, a great lover and like I told you, I wasn't all that attracted to him in the first place. I mean, you've met him, right? And a girl's got needs that have to be taken care of too, you know. So anyway, one night Alex called me from somewhere, sounded like down at the club. His story was that his current girlfriend and one of the other girls – Elton's old lady – had gone to Portland to shop and were spending the night up there and he and Elton were at loose ends and wondered if they could come over."

"Alex? Elton?" I asked.

"Alex Trippitt and Elton Miller. Players. Friends of Charlie's. Long time party regulars."

"And they thought there was going to be a party that night?"

"Something like that. Party of three, you might say. Alex said Charlie was going to be out of town. I wasn't doing anything, so I said sure, come on over."

"Did you already know your husband was going to be gone?"

"Yeah, but so what? I'd already been with these two guys. Charlie had watched me with Alex and Elton lots of times, so I figured what's the difference if we did it with an audience or without? Besides, I kinda liked Alex. I always wanted him in the back when we did threesomes. He went in slow and gentle. And Elton," Krista's mouth made a full, toothy smile at her private memory, "Elton was, like, very well hung."

"And Charlie didn't see it that way?"

"Hell no! He came home unexpectedly and walked in on us – we had the music cranked up so we didn't hear him drive up – and he was furious. He kicked them out."

"What happened next?"

Krista clenched her jaw before she answered. "What happened next was he raped me."

"He raped you?"

"I was plenty pissed at that point by the way he was ranting and raging around, throwing things, chasing me. He wouldn't let me get dressed. No way did I want to have sex with him." Krista narrowed her eyes and her voice turned hard. "You might not know this, but if a husband forces his wife to have sex against her will, legally that's considered rape."

"I'm sorry, I didn't mean to suggest—"

"Forget about it." She finished the half finger of Dewar's left in her glass. "Of all the times for that son of a bitch to get a woody, that had to be the night. Just my luck. He worked me over six ways from Sunday and the next day he kicked my ass out, too." Krista paused and laughed out loud. "You want to know the funny part?"

"There's a funny part?"

"Charlie asked me if Alex and Elton had used condoms. I told him of course we did."

"Why is that funny?"

"I can't remember Charlie being concerned with condoms. Ever. He never used them himself and I had to remind him to leave a bowl full on the coffee table when we partied."

"Krista, I'm sorry I have to ask you this, but I need to know exactly how Winetrout raped you that night."

"I told you. He raped me. Rape is rape."

"No," I said, remembering the brutality of the video, "I need the specific, exact details."

Krista tossed back the rest of her Scotch and slid the glass across the table to me. I poured a couple of fingers. Charlie-sized fingers.

"OK, if you have to know the details. He dragged me by the hair into the kitchen and tied me to the table. He raped me hard in the butt until it bled. No lube, no foreplay, no nothing. He just rammed it up my ass. He tore me up pretty good. It hurt like hell to sit down for a week."

"And you let him do it? You didn't fight back?"

"It wasn't the first time he'd gotten rough with me. He was super pissed about Alex and Elton, and I figured if I let him have his way, he'd finish quick and chill out afterwards. I wanted things to smooth over."

"And he didn't chill out?"

"Not hardly. If anything, he got even madder. I don't think he came. Here's something else. He suited up first. Only time I can remember him using a rubber."

"Then what happened?"

"He got even rougher, slapped me around for a while, and then he told me to pack up and get out. Like right now."

"So you moved to Portland and Summer Rain stayed in Eugene?"

"You do what you gotta do. A girl's gotta eat. Besides, Summer could take care of herself. She didn't stay at home all the time, anyway. I wanted to call her on my way to Portland, but my cell needed charging." Krista got up and dumped the rest of her drink into the sink and helped herself to fresh ice cubes and more Dewar's and lit a cigarette. "And now she's dead."

That didn't jibe with what Winetrout had told me. "Your husband said Summer Rain couldn't stay away more than a day or two because her cell phone died and he had the charger. Some kind of a special phone, couldn't use just any charger."

"I wish you'd quit calling him my husband."

"I'm sorry. Winetrout said—"

"Charlie's a control freak. There was a whole scene when she got that phone. Maybe she picked up another charger somewhere. Or another phone."

We sat quietly for a minute, similar images no doubt bouncing around in both our minds. Oddly, the Dewar's didn't seem to be having any effect on Krista. She was holding her liquor better than any woman I'd ever known. Any woman or any man, for that matter.

Finally, she broke the silence. "You getting hungry at all?"

"Sure. You want to go out or have room service bring something up?"

"Up to you, cowboy. Either or."

I could sense Krista retreating into her professional role as Crystal and I decided to let the shift take its course. She'd been through the ringer in the past hour or so. If there's one thing I've learned in my line of work, it's that everyone deals with heartache and tragedy in their own private way. What works for one person might outrage or offend someone else. I do know it's a mistake to confuse stoicism for indifference. If it was easier for Krista to deal with the death of her daughter by giving herself a little distance from it, who was I to object?

CHAPTER ELEVEN

I had a lot to think about on the two-hour drive back down I-5 to Eugene, beginning with my lengthy conversation with Krista Wycowski Winetrout. I'd ordered steaks and baked potatoes with all the trimmings from room service and I still felt stuffed. I'd saved a few slices of lean beef as a peace offering to El Gato so he wouldn't be too pissed at me for staying away overnight. He's easy to bribe.

Krista had had far too much Scotch to risk driving home so I insisted that she spend the night. She'd slipped out in the short hours before dawn and I woke up alone, still dressed, with a splitting headache, a mouth full of cotton, and only a fuzzy recollection of the latter part of the evening. A stop at Starbuck's on my way out of town had been marginally helpful. What I needed was a triple shot mocha from Dutch Brothers, but there wasn't a blue windmill in sight.

She'd left a note on hotel stationary: *Jack – Under the circumstances, it doesn't feel legit for me to keep this $$$, even if it is Charlie's money. Thanks for coming to Portland and telling me in person about Summer Rain. I couldn't have handled it on a phone call. You have my number if you need me. Please let me know when you catch the bastard. I hope he fries. – Krista.* Under the note were the three Franklins I'd given her.

I felt sorry for Krista; a woman in her line of work has a notoriously short shelf life and she'd been around the block a few times. I hadn't detected anything resembling a back up plan for when her looks began to fade and gravity took over, although she seemed to have a savvy enough take on life to realize what the numbers were and that her's weren't all that good.

Speculation about her eventual retirement was beside the point. I'd been the bearer of the worst news any parent can get; the death of their only child. Maybe Krista hadn't been the best mother in the world, and maybe her daughter hadn't been a model child, but flesh and blood was flesh and blood, no matter how you sliced it. I winced at the image; Summer Rain had been plenty sliced up.

The bottom line was that although Krista Wycowski had filled me in with some details about family life in the Winetrout household, I wasn't any closer to discovering who murdered Summer Rain or why. I hadn't learned much new from Krista beyond confirmation of her estranged husband's predilection for swingers' parties and his capacity for violent sex. Charles Winetrout would have been a prime suspect, if not for the fact that he had hired me to find the girl in the first place.

Somewhere around Salem, it occurred to me that I had not yet questioned Consuelo. On his first visit, Winetrout had invited me to talk to her and to Jimmy, but I couldn't figure out how I was going to interview the housekeeper without him knowing I was there. If she knew anything that might help unravel the mystery of Summer Rain's murder, it didn't seem likely she would do so with her employer and benefactor overhearing us. With no car, probably no driver's license or green card, she had to be a virtual prisoner in Fortress Winetrout. As for James Sundquist, he'd made it clear that he didn't want to talk to me. That kid was clenched tight as a bull's ass in fly time.

I knew I couldn't face the old man again without telling him that Summer Rain was dead. I seriously doubted that he would keep me on his payroll once he learned the truth. Paying me to follow a trail that could lead to him made no sense.

The next question I had to deal with was whether to break the news of Summer Rain's death to the old man before or after I paid a visit to the Eugene Police Department. The police wouldn't have known who to contact to positively identify the body; Charles Winetrout was not blood kin and Krista Wycowski had left town.

All this was a lot more challenging than hiding with my Canon in the bushes outside a motel room window somewhere.

The off ramp into downtown Eugene, ironically, ran right through the Whitaker, past the alley where Marcus Binkelman had sold me the video and later turned up dead. It was still early enough that the Hot Body Club had not yet come to life; there was no flashing neon to dress up the basic seediness of the neighborhood. I thought about Susan, coming to dance there every night, going home at three in the morning. I wondered where she lived, if she had a husband or boyfriend, what her life outside of her job was like. She'd gotten under my skin. I worried about her.

The parking lot at the Church of Redemption was empty as well. No saints, no sinners. I was back in Eugene and it was depressing. Instead of going straight to my trailer, I detoured to the police station.

"About time you turned up, Hunter. I've left a dozen messages for you on your machine."

"Nice to see you, too, Luke."

"Where the hell've you been?"

"Portland."

"Let me guess. You went up to do a little sturgeon fishing on the Columbia."

"Boy, are you one smart police officer, or what? No wonder they promoted you so fast. The shad are running up the river. The sturgeon are ravenous."

Lucas sat upright with a 'don't-mess-around-with-me' look on his face.

"I paid a visit to Summer Rain's mother," I said. "I didn't want Krista to read about her daughter in the papers."

"How did you find her?"

"Winetrout told me she was working as an escort. It wasn't hard to track her down."

"And?"

I filled Lucas in on my conversation with Krista Wycowski. When I got to the latter part of the evening, I dragged it out a little.

"You can skip the personal details, gumshoe. I don't care what might or might not have transpired between the two of you."

"Whatever you're thinking, it didn't happen, Detective."

"Did she tell you anything that might help with our investigation?"

"Nothing beyond what I've already said."

Detective Leonard stood up. He seemed to be hesitating or debating. "Well, you think real hard and if anything else comes back to you, you let me know, right?"

"That's it? You guys haven't found out anything yet?"

"Not much. Nothing I can share, anyway."

"So why did you call me? Why am I here?"

Lucas didn't answer, but looked at me hard, like he was trying to makeup his mind.

"Come on, Luke. You've had two days," I nudged. I expected a little quid pro quo.

Lucas closed the door and pushed the button on his intercom. "Cheryl, no interruptions for a while." He turned back to me. "I'll tell you what we know, but so help me, if I find out you've been holding out on me, you won't be a happy camper."

"Luke, you know me better than that." I realized I'd have to show him the flash drive sooner rather than later. The longer I withheld it, the worse it would be.

The detective lowered his voice. "We got the forensic report back. Summer Rain Wycowski was sexually molested in every way possible."

I nodded, not surprised at all.

"We found traces of ejaculate in her vagina, her anus, and her throat."

"Let me guess. You got DNA samples which don't match with anything here or in Salem, right?"

"Correct. We have nothing other than a crazy theory that the killer wanted us to have his DNA."

"How do you figure that?" Dumb question the Dutch Brothers could have prevented.

Lucas looked at me like I was a freshman flunking Forensics 101. "Remember how we found her? Mouth and vagina sewn shut? Whoever raped and murdered this girl didn't want his evidence leaking out of her."

"Maybe the rapist and the murderer were two different people."

Now it was Lucas' turn to look blank. "That's quite a jump, gumshoe."

"Maybe she wasn't raped at all. Maybe the sex was consensual and the only crime was the murder."

"Summer Rain Wycowski was only sixteen. She was legally incapable of consensual sex."

"Come on, Luke, get real. Legally or not, teenagers have sex all the time. We both know that girl ran with a fast crowd. I'm just throwing ideas out here."

"Go on."

"Let's say it wasn't a crime of passion. Let's say someone wanted her dead, for some particular reason. Given her lifestyle, what better way to divert attention than to have her look like the victim of some perverted sex crime?

Lucas clasped his hands behind his head, leaned back in his swivel chair and stared at the ceiling. After a moment of contemplation, he shook his head. "I don't buy it. Ninety-nine percent of the time the simplest explanation of a crime is the right one. I think we have one very sick person on our hands. Some twisted guy raped her, beat her to death, and sewed her up for some crazy reason only he knows."

"You're probably right."

"Besides which, nothing has surfaced in the way of a motive to support the theory this was a premeditated murder." Leonard leaned forward and rested his elbows on the table and stared at me. "You wouldn't know something you're not telling me, would you?"

"I talked with a girl named Susan. She was one of Summer Rain's friends." I hoped I didn't show how uncomfortable I was dodging Lucas's question. "She dances by the name 'Charity' at the Hot Body Club."

"And?"

"There may have been something going on between Winetrout and Summer Rain."

"Go on."

"Look, amigo, I'm trying to fit the pieces together. Give me a little time. I haven't been home since I got back."

"Pieces? A little time? I get the feeling there's something you're not telling me."

Tom Arnold

I shook my head. I couldn't bring myself to utter the word 'no'. I tried to convince myself that I wasn't lying if I kept my mouth shut. Marcus Binkelman's flash drive had assumed the potential to land me in jail for obstruction of justice. I wished it was no longer in my office. In fact, I wished I'd never gotten it, seen it, or even knew about it.

CHAPTER TWELVE

When I got home early that afternoon, the message light on my answering machine was blinking incessantly, like a naughty reminder that I'd stayed out all night without permission. El Gato wove figure eights through my legs, trying to purr and meow at the same time. I clicked through three calls from Detective Leonard before I came to an unexpected message. Susan's smoke-damaged voice was unmistakable. 'Hi. This is Susan St. Marie. Charity from the Hot Body Club. I need to talk to you but not at the club. I'm off tomorrow, but I'm gonna sleep in 'cause I work late tonight so don't call me before noon.' And she had left a number.

I unwrapped El Gato's steak treats before I picked up the phone. It worked; I was instantly forgiven. He tried to chew and purr at the same time. "Don't talk with your mouth full," I told him as I dialed Susan's number.

'Hi, I can't take your call right now. Please leave a message and I'll call you back.'

"Susan, this is Jack Hunter and I just—"

"Hi, I'm here. I'm glad you called." She paused for a yawn and a cough. "Can you meet me at Dutch Brothers? The one downtown?"

"Sure, what time?"

"Gimme an hour. I just got up."

I glanced at my watch; one-thirty in the afternoon. But then, she did work until two AM. "Two-thirty. I'll see you there." I was pleased that she'd chosen Dutch Brothers. There are dozens of coffee kiosks in Eugene and after a while you begin to develop favorites. Dutch Brothers is one of mine.

Susan was sitting on the deck under the blue windmill, bundled up in a black cloth coat with white fur sticking out of the neck and sleeves. One gloved hand held a tall, covered cardboard cup and a cigarette and the other palmed a cell phone against her ear.

83

"OK, he's here. I'll call you later." Pause. "Yeah, me, too. Bye." She snapped the phone shut.

I ordered a double mocha with an extra shot and sat down. "So, what's up?"

"Not much. I was just wondering if you found Rainy's mom or not."

"Krista's in Portland, like you said. She's working as an escort."

"Yeah, that figures."

"You didn't call me down here to ask if I'd found Krista."

Susan took a sip from her cup, leaving a faint, pink-veined outline of her lips on the plastic lid, and scanned the parking lot. "I want to tell you something about Binky."

"I'm listening."

"You gotta promise to keep your mouth shut." Susan flicked her half-smoked cigarette into the street.

"I've been a private investigator for over fifteen years."

"Yeah, I know. I like checked you out on the Internet. Domestic relations. You mostly chase cheaters, if I read it right."

"Some of my clients are people who believe their spouses are having affairs."

"Must be a pretty interesting job."

"It has its moments."

"So. Have the cops come up with any ideas about who killed Rainy?"

"If they have, they haven't told me."

Susan St. Marie took a deep breath. "Well, Jack Hunter, here's what I'm gonna tell you. You just listen, OK?" She waited until I nodded. It was the first time she'd called me anything but 'mister'.

"You asked me if Binky ever wanted to make a porn movie and I said no. Well, after I thought about it, I realized that wasn't completely true. He did try to make a sex flick once, but it wasn't really, like, real porn. I don't know how it came out 'cause I never saw it. I doubt he recorded over it like he did everything else, though."

My interest was immediately piqued. "Tell me about it."

"I told you about Rainy and her stepfather, right? That bastard used to make her, you know, do him. She hated him but she let him 'cause she didn't want her and her mom to have to split. Their life was pretty sketchy before Krista's centerfold spread in *HUSTLER* came out. That led to her meeting the old bastard and then all of a sudden life was, like, wonderful. You've been to his house, right?"

"I've been there." I said.

"Well, you know. It's like one minute you're living in the back of your car burning gas to keep warm or staying in some crappy one-room motel shit hole eating Top Ramen and peanut butter while your mom is turning tricks. All of a sudden you make the big time and the next minute you have your own room, flat screen, cell phone, whatever you want. Like winning Powerball."

"So you're telling me Summer Rain had sexual relations with Charles Winetrout so as to not rock the boat?"

Susan rolled her eyes and gave me a 'well, duh' look. "Something like that."

"And her mom went along with this?"

"I don't know if Krista knew about it or not. Rainy told me like it was a secret nobody else knew. She made me swear not to tell anyone. I guess, now that she's dead…"

"So, where does Marcus Binkelman come into this?"

"I'm getting to that." Susan lit a Marlboro and took a deep drag. "Rainy hated her step-father and all the sick shit he made her do. You could always tell when he'd forced her to do something weird 'cause she hated him a little more."

"What kind of sick shit?" I was thinking of the video.

Susan looked at me like I was an idiot. "Think about it, Mr. Brilliant Private Detective. How many ways are there?" She paused for a minute, presumably so I could count to three. "Plus, he was into bondage. He liked to tie her up."

I tried to keep a straight face because I was sure this was leading up to the flash drive. "Getting back to Binky…"

"Like I said, as time went on, Rainy despised him more and more. She came up with the idea that if she had proof of what was going on, she could force him to give her money to keep her mouth shut. That way, her and Krista could still be living the sweet life and she wouldn't have to put up with his perverted bullshit."

"Blackmail," I said. "It makes perfect sense."

"Yeah, I guess you could say blackmail. She didn't call it that, though. Anyway, she got Binky to agree to come up to the house and video them through the window."

A piece of the puzzle fell into place with a thud. "Did you ever see this movie?"

Susan shook her head. "No."

"Do you have any idea where it is?"

"Nah. I don't even know for sure what Binky did with it, whether he kept it or gave it to her or what."

"Maybe he recorded over it. Didn't you tell me he never saved anything?"

"I seriously doubt it. After Rainy'd set the whole thing up, she would have killed him if he'd done that. Like, that video is somewhere, believe me."

In the split instant before I remembered Marcus Binkelman had overdosed, the thought flashed across my mind, *somebody did kill him.*

I nodded, eager to change the subject. I knew exactly where that somewhere was. The details were piling up faster than I could process them. Now there was a suspect who had a motive. My next thought was whether it was necessary, or perhaps the word was advisable, for Susan to see Binky's video. I needed a moment to think. "So your last name is St. Marie, huh? As in Buffy St. Marie?"

"Wow, you're right. I never would have thought of that." The look on Susan's face told me that only about a million people had already made that connection. I felt stupid.

"OK, I'm slow. I'm the first to admit it."

"You never have told me what the 'S' in your name stands for, Jack S. Hunter."

"I'll tell you sometime."

"Right now is sometime."

I shook my head. "I will, I promise. Just not right now."

"I'm not gonna let you off the hook, you know."

"I don't doubt that for a minute."

Susan cocked her head and studied my face. "You're holding something back."

"Yes, I know."

Susan St. Marie was a sharp observer. There was no way around it; I was going to have to show her the video.

CHAPTER THIRTEEN

I dreaded my next conversation with Charles Winetrout but I knew there was no way around it. There had been at least a dozen cops at the river where Summer Rain's body had been discovered and it was only a matter of time before the story leaked out. There'd be hell to pay if he read about Summer Rain's death in the paper or saw it on TV before I told him. I had the delicate task of breaking the news to him without letting on that I knew he'd sexually abused his stepdaughter and had a video to prove it. It promised to be a balancing act worthy of Philippe Petit's stunt walking between the World Trade Center towers. I drove through Dutch Brothers for a mocha espresso with an extra shot. I needed to be as clear headed as possible.

"I want to ask you some questions, Consuelo. Preguntas, por favor."

Consuelo tried to shut the door, but I blocked it with my foot. "Consuelo. If you do not talk to me, you will talk to the police."

I pushed past her into the hallway and shut the door behind us.

"No! No police!"

"Do you know where Summer Rain is now? Donde está Summer?"

"Yo no sé."

"How many days has Summer Rain been gone? Quántos dios no Summer?"

"Cinco." Consuelo held up an open hand.

"Has she come back for anything?"

Consuelo shook her head.

I repeated my first question. "Consuelo, do you know where Summer Rain is now?"

Again, Consuelo shook her head. "Yo no sé. No esta aqui."

"Tell me about Summer Rain and Señor Winetrout."

Consuelo trembled, clearly frightened. "Yo no sé, Señor."

In spite of the language barrier, we were both tiptoeing around something, like you'd step through a dog owner's front yard full of turds. She wanted to tell me something, but she was scared shitless.

"Yes, you do know." I tried to think of appropriate words in Spanish. "Molestar? Did Señor Winetrout violar Summer Rain?"

The housekeeper lowered her eyes and tears trickled down her cheeks.

"Consuelo, answer me." I gripped her by the shoulders and shook her and she began to sob. "Molestar?"

"Si." She was incapable of uttering more than that one syllable. We stood there for several beats, her sniffling and me waiting for her to stop. Then she took a step back from me and did something that caught me completely by surprise: Consuelo interlocked the tips of her fingers and pushed her belly forward.

"Qué?" I asked

"Embarazada," Consuelo mumbled, as if she were afraid of the word.

My Spanglish didn't include the word she used. "Embarrassed?" I guessed.

"No, Señor" Consuelo shook her head. "El bebé. Summer embarazada." Consuelo rubbed her hands around her extended abdomen. "Comprende? El niño. Embarazada."

I felt like I was running down a dark street, focused on a dim light that was receding as fast as I could move, and then I smacked face-first hard into a lamppost. I hadn't seen it coming. Summer Rain had been pregnant. The next thoughts came faster than I could sort them out. Whose child was she carrying? Winetrout's? Jimmy's? Why hadn't the autopsy revealed her status? Or had Lucas known and kept it to himself?

"Consuelo, the police will come to ask you questions. Do not be afraid."

Consuelo dropped to her knees and wrapped her arms around my legs, crying. "Por
favor. No police. Por favor, Señor."

"Do not be afraid," I repeated. "No INS, I promise." I crossed my heart.

"I no like go Guatemala."

"Don't worry. You won't go to Guatemala." I wished I could be as sure as I tried to sound.

Any lingering doubts I might have had about the authenticity of Binky's video were gone. It was time to show it to Detective Lucas Leonard.

As I started to get back in my car, I saw Jimmy coming around the corner on a riding lawnmower. Maybe with Winetrout gone, he'd be more forthcoming. I stood up and slammed the door shut.

"James!" I shouted.

"I told you last time you were here, I got nothing to say to you."

"I think you do, James. Summer Rain is dead. The cops are going to be asking everyone who knew her a lot of questions. My guess is you'll be right at the top of their list."

Jimmy's face went rigid. "What do you mean dead?"

"Dead, James, as in no longer alive. Her body was found floating in the Willamette."

"Summer drowned swimming in the river? That water is way cold." Whatever emotional reaction Jimmy was feeling, he kept bottled up. His lips were tight and unsmiling, his ice-blue eyes were hidden underneath unblinking eyelids, but the veins in his neck were throbbing.

"She didn't drown. It's a lot worse than that." I didn't know for a fact that Summer Rain hadn't drowned, but I could see by his body language that the kid could be pushed. "Tell me about you and her." I was still absorbing Consuelo's admission that Summer Rain had been pregnant.

"I ain't got nothing to tell. She lived here and I just work here. I never got much reason to go in the house. I seen her around, but that was it. I'm real sorry to hear she passed away."

"Never saw her in town? On the mall?"

"I quit hanging out on the mall. It's better for me to stay away from her."

"Why was that?" I asked.

Jimmy wiped the back of his forehead with a gloved hand, leaving a streak of grime in the sweat. "Summer was bad news. I tried to have as little to do with her as possible."

"I heard you didn't stay quite as far away from her as you could've, at least on one occasion."

Jimmy looked over his shoulder as if to confirm that we were truly alone. He lowered his voice. "Look, Hunter, whatever your name is. I used to lead a sinful life. There wasn't much I didn't do. Whiskey, drugs, women, you name it. But that life is all behind me now. I've totally cleaned up my act. Mr. Winetrout gave me a chance and I grabbed it."

"With the help of Jesus Christ, right?"

Jimmy took a deep breath and squared his shoulders and stabbed a finger into my chest. "Don't dis the Lord. He held His hand out to me and I took it."

"What about the time Summer Rain held out her hand?"

"I never said I was perfect. I'm sorry she's gone, but that girl is Delilah, pure temptation. I slipped and fell, but I prayed long and hard about that night and I truly believe in God's eyes I've been forgiven."

"You're telling me all you and Summer Rain had was a one night stand?"

Jimmy hesitated, and then nodded, reluctantly, like someone who isn't telling the whole truth. In my line of business, I've come to know that look. Consuelo didn't have it.

"Look, buddy—"

"What do you know about her relationship with her stepfather?"

"I don't know nothing about her and Mr. Winetrout. Or anyone else, for that matter."

"And I suppose you don't know anything about Mrs. Winetrout or the parties she and her husband threw here or the Hot Body Club, right?"

"I mow the lawn. I wash the car. I clean the pool. I don't go to the Hot Body Club no more. With Jesus' help, I lead a clean life now. Mr. Winetrout has been very good to me. I mind my own business. What anybody else does is their own business." Jimmy swung his leg over the seat of his riding mower. "Look, buddy, I gotta get back to work, if you don't mind."

"Do you have any idea where Mr. Winetrout is now?"

"He ain't here. It's Saturday. He always goes to work on Saturdays."

"Work? On Saturdays?"

"The Club. Saturdays are busy and he has to keep an eye on things."

"Please tell Mr. Winetrout I was here and I need to talk to him ASAP."

"Why don't you call and leave him a voice message?"

"Sure. You bet. I'll just leave him a message on his answering machine that his step-daughter is dead."

"Well, if I see him, I'll tell him you want him to call you. He closes up Saturday nights and gets home pretty late. I hope you see him first; I ain't gonna be the one tells him the bad news."

"You think of anything else, James, you call me. You still have my card."

Judging from Jimmy's face, it would be a cold day in his hell before he'd ever dial my number.

CHAPTER FOURTEEN

It wasn't until the next morning that I connected with Charles Winetrout. I woke up to the blinking red light on my machine; I must have slept through the short message he'd left a few minutes before three AM. I was on his doorstep at nine. Not because I wanted to be, but I wanted to talk to him before Lucas Leonard did and before he read about Summer Rain's death in the paper. It was only a matter of time before her murder would be on the front page of the *Register Guard*. I also wanted to get to him before Jimmy did.

"Señor Winetrout sleeping. I no like wake him up." Consuelo stood in the doorway like a defensive lineman trying to stop a quarterback sneak. She spoke in hushed tones, as if she was afraid her voice would carry throughout the huge house.

"Wake him up, por favor. Muy importante," I said as loudly as I could without shouting. Consuelo backed peddled down the hallway a few steps, her dark eyes wide, before she turned and hurried away.

It took about ten minutes for Winetrout to appear, disheveled, wrapped in a stained bathrobe and a foul mood.

"This better be good, Hunter. I had a late night."

"I gathered that. You left a message for me at three this morning."

"I had a late meeting. What do you want?"

"Can we go into your office and talk?"

Without answering, Winetrout turned and shuffled down the hall, apparently expecting me to follow him.

"Consuelo! Coffee! Pronto!" he shouted. Then he seemed to remember me and without turning, asked, "You want coffee, Hunter?"

The housekeeper appeared out of nowhere. When she saw me, she put a finger to her lips.

I nodded. "Thank you, yes."

Winetrout turned his head to Consuelo, pointing his thumb over his shoulder at me, "Crema y azúcar."

I followed Winetrout into his office and we sat down. Thankfully, both monitors were black.

"So I assume you have some news about Summer or you wouldn't be here at this hour."

"I do, sir." I wasn't sure how to break the news, so I just plunged ahead. "I'm afraid I have some bad news. Summer Rain is dead. I'm deeply sorry."

Winetrout's head snapped around like a steelhead that had taken a Caddis Fly with a line attached to it. "Dead? How?"

"I'm terribly sorry," I repeated. Consuelo arrived with a tray of coffee cups. I waited until she had poured the coffee and left the office, grateful for the interruption.

"Go on, Hunter."

"She was found floating in the Willamette."

"Summer drowned?" Winetrout's tone of voice told me he registered only the information, not the sentiment.

"The cause of death has not been established." Lucas would kill me if I let all the details out.

"I take it you don't believe she drowned."

"I don't believe anything without proof. The police are doing forensic testing as we speak."

"Forensics? So you're saying Summer was murdered? This wasn't an accident?"

I was watching Winetrout carefully, looking for any hint or sign that he was not surprised. The old man's face was a mask.

"I'm not saying anything at this point, sir. You hired me to look for her and I'm afraid that search is over."

Charles Winetrout rotated around and stared at the silent monitors, his hands teepeed in front of his face. It was the first time I'd seen him without a cigar jammed in his mouth or stuck in his fingers. It was impossible for me to tell if he was grieving or scheming. Finally he turned back to me.

"Listen, Hunter, I want you to stay on this."

"I beg your pardon?" That was the one reaction I hadn't expected.

"You heard me."

"I don't understand, Mr. Winetrout, Summer Rain is dead. You hired me to find her. She's no longer missing. Exactly what do you want me to do now?"

"I want you to look for her killer." He didn't say 'duh' but I could hear the sentiment in his voice.

"I'm sorry, but it's not a runaway child issue any more. It's a police matter."

"I know that, Hunter, I'm not stupid. But the cops, you know, their hands are tied. There's things they can and can't do, places they can and can't go. You're a snoop. You can go places and ask questions they can't."

"Sir, I don't think—"

"Our deal stands, goddammit. I'm paying you good money. I want you to stay on the case. Talk to whoever you need to, go wherever you have to go. Whatever it takes. You got it?" There was anger and finality in his voice. He didn't ask if I had any other professional commitments. He didn't care. Charles Thurgood Winetrout was not someone who took no for an answer.

I nodded. I was not completely unhappy to still be 'on the case', as the old man put it. I'd already made up my mind to keep digging around on my own, at least until something more lucrative came my way, and Winetrout was offering to pay me to do it, so why not? Too many years as a private eye had made me overly curious and I couldn't help but wonder who'd murdered Summer Rain. I also wanted to know about the video, why it had been given to me, how it fit into the bigger picture. The more I knew, the less sense it made.

"You listening to me, Hunter? I want to know everything you find out and I want to know everything the police find out, too. I'm sure you have contacts with the police department, don't you? Everyone in your line of work has an inside source with the cops."

"You've been watching too many cop shows, sir. I'm just another civilian." I didn't want my friendship with Detective Lucas Leonard known to Charles Winetrout.

"I don't give a rat's ass how you do it, but I want to know everything they know when they know it, and I want to know everything you find out before they do."

"That's a tall order." I decided to change the subject. I took a big gulp of Consuelo's delicious coffee. I wondered, briefly, where she got it. "I paid a visit to your wife in Portland."

"Oh yeah? How did that go? You get laid?"

Did I get laid? I didn't know what to say. Here was a man who had just been informed of his stepdaughter's death under suspicious circumstances and five minutes later was asking if I'd had sex with his wife, the victim's mother. I struggled mightily to keep a straight face.

"No, sir, it was a professional visit." I paused. "Krista told me about the parties. She told me about Alex and Elton. She—"

"I told you she was a slut." Winetrout smiled smugly like he'd just solved Fermat's last theorem.

I took a deep breath, well aware that I was headed into dangerous terrain. I could feel that fuse hissing in my groin. "So, explain something to me, sir. I'm just trying to square you and Krista hosting no-holes-barred swingers' parties with you throwing her out for having sex with men you'd already seen her, uh, having sex with. The two of you had an open relationship but you dumped her for fooling around. It doesn't add up."

This time around, if Winetrout was offended at this intrusion into his private life, he didn't show it. "At a party, in front of my face with my permission is one thing. Cheating on me behind my back is something completely different. Don't try to understand too hard." Winetrout stood up, signaling our conversation was finished. "You let me know anything you find out."

"Mr. Winetrout, I just want to say again how deeply sorry I am."

"Thanks. Consuelo!"

I wasn't looking forward to what I had to do next. I pulled to a stop at the foot of Winetrout's driveway and stabbed the speed dial on my cell.

CHAPTER FIFTEEN

"Luke, can you meet me for a cup of coffee?"

"What's up, gumshoe?"

"Not on the phone, Detective."

"The usual? Starbuck's downtown?"

"No, it would be better if you came by my office."

"You have something for me?"

"You could say that."

"You going to give me a clue what it is?"

"I'd rather wait 'til you got here."

"This has to do with Summer Rain Wycowski, I assume?"

"It does."

Thirty minutes later, Lucas Leonard pulled up outside my trailer. He opened the door and then edged forward a couple of feet so that he could get out without stepping in a puddle.

"What's so secret I had to come here to get it?"

"First off, you have to keep this between us. At least for the time being." I waited for Lucas to agree. "Secondly, I know you're going to ask a bunch of questions afterwards. Some of them I can answer and some of them I can't answer right now and that's got to be OK with you."

"You know I can't agree to conditions like that."

This felt like a no-blink contest in a high-stakes poker game. "Well, I guess I dragged you out here for nothing."

"Look, Hunter, if you're hiding evidence in an ongoing investigation, you're obstructing justice."

"We're both trying to find out who killed Summer Rain, aren't we, amigo? Why don't we work together instead of against each other?"

"We'll catch the killer or killers, with or without your help."

"Absolutely. You guys are professionals. There's no better cop in Eugene. I just might be able to save you a lot of time and energy is all."

"And taxpayer dollars," Lucas deadpanned.

"There is that." I shrugged my shoulders and feigned surprise.

Lucas paused for a long minute, his eyes boring into mine. Did the detective have an ace in the hole? Finally, he nodded his assent. "OK, let's see what you have."

"You agree?" Nodding wasn't enough. I had to have verbal confirmation.

"I agree."

"How about a cup of coffee?" I wanted to do something to ease the tension, but Lucas wasn't having any.

"I'm fine. Get on with it."

"Take a seat, amigo. Believe me, you'll be better off sitting down for this." I switched on my computer, which flickered to life far too quickly to suit me. I wasn't eager to watch Binky's video again. I took a deep breath and plugged the flash drive into the USB port.

The camcorder image is steady, suggesting the cameraman has used a tripod or some other fixed rest. A ghostly image clouds the high-resolution movie, as if it has been shot with a filter or through a window. In fact, this is my third viewing and I now notice that a window frame roughly corresponds to the edges of the screen. A digital clock ticks off the seconds in the lower right corner. There is no date.

The video shows a large, fat old man having sex with a naked young girl. His trousers are bunched above his knees. His huge, stretch-marked belly jiggles grotesquely like purple-veined, pink Jell-O against her plump pale buttocks. An intricate, filigree whale-tail tattoo wraps across the girl's lower back and disappears under her trapped hips.

The man's head is cut off at the neck at the top of the screen. His Adam's apple is bobbing like a float at the top of the window, tantalizingly in and out of camera range. The girl lies bent over a Formica kitchen table. Her wrists and ankles are bound to the chrome legs with duct tape. Next to her on the table are a riding crop such as a jockey might use and a short black whip, the tails of which dangle off the edge. The girl's face is turned away from the camera. Part of her head is hidden behind a blonde wig that has jostled out of position. Watching is a solely visual experience; the vivid video is accompanied by an eerie silence. Whatever sounds the copulating couple is making do not penetrate the glass.

After twenty-five seconds of vigorously thrusting into her from behind, the man grabs the riding crop and begins lashing the girl across her shoulder blades. As the intensity escalates, the girl turns to face the window. These are not gentle love swats; the man's hand disappears over his head out of view at the top of the screen and reappears in viscous, full-arm swings. With each stroke, the girl flinches and her mouth opens in a silent scream made more terrible by the helplessness of the viewer.

Suddenly the man drops the crop and rears back. He pulls the captive girl against his pelvis by the supple flesh around her hips, lifting the front table legs a foot off the floor, revealing her ravaged back. The whip slides off the table. Her head is now at the top of the screen; whoever is operating the camera isn't keeping the scene centered, confirming the use of a tripod.

At the moment of his presumed climax, the girl twists her neck and looks directly into the camera. She shakes her head a few times until the blonde wig falls to the floor, exposing black makeup and messy black hair. As the man grabs a handful of hair and yanks her head back, a painful grimace escapes from her clenched jaws, followed by a sardonic smile. The auto focus has triggered and the camera zooms in, centered on the girl's face. The perimeter of the image is blurry and unsteady. Something shiny flashes on the man's wrist. The screen goes blank at fifty-seven seconds.

When it was over, Lucas asked to see the video again. Every time I've watched it, I feel a little bit queasier. I've taken many photos and videos through windows of people engaged in the act; surreptitiously documenting clandestine sexual encounters is what keeps beans on my table, but I'd never witnessed anything with this level of brutality. I wondered if it had the same effect on Lucas

Leonard. I slid the mouse to him so he could replay it himself and excused myself to pour a cup of coffee. I'd had enough.

"Sure I can't get you something, Luke?"

Lucas ignored me, his full attention on the monitor.

A minute later, he turned to me. "Where did you get this?"

"Can we hold off on that for the time being?"

"How long have you had it?"

"A couple of days." I didn't want to be any more specific and I hoped Lucas wouldn't press the issue.

"What's your take on it?" Lucas asked.

"I'd bet you a weekend salmon fishing on the Rogue the girl is Summer Rain Wycowski. It would appear to be non-consensual sex, but I wouldn't put a Franklin on it."

"She's taped up to the table, gumshoe," Lucas said. "Leaving aside the question of her age, that's not much of an argument for consensual sex."

"I'd agree with you except for the ending. You noticed how she looks directly into the camera?"

Lucas backed up and reran the final ten seconds. "So you think the whole thing was staged?"

"I don't know what to think, Luke. That's why I wanted you to see it."

"Any idea who the man is?"

"I'm awfully tempted to believe it's her stepfather, Charles Winetrout, but without seeing his face, there is no way to be absolutely sure."

"Does he know about this video? Does he know you have it?"

"I don't know if he knows about it or not. I haven't told him I have it. Anyway, the whole thing doesn't add up."

"Why not?"

"Because Winetrout hired me to find Summer Rain when she first went missing. That was reasonable. But when I told him she was dead, he ordered me to stay on the case and try to find the killer."

"He told you to do what? Doesn't he realize homicide is a police matter?"

"It doesn't make any sense to me, either. Listen, amigo, I'm ninety-nine point nine percent sure the girl in the video is Summer Rain Wycowski. Let's assume the man is her stepfather, Winetrout. She was taped to the table so we can further assume it was non-consensual. That makes him a prime suspect for rape and maybe murder, too. Why would he be willing to pay me to find the killer if he was guilty?"

"Don't forget kidnapping," Lucas said. "Technically, having her tied up qualifies as kidnapping. He doesn't have to take her anywhere."

"Let's say that Summer Rain was into it, that it was consensual. Who knows, maybe she was into bondage. But that scenario doesn't make it any better. It's still statutory rape, sodomy, unlawful penetration, sexual exploitation of a minor, you name it. The question remains, why hire me?"

"To deflect suspicion, would be the obvious answer."

"Maybe he thinks the crime will go unsolved."

"Consensual doesn't make it much different. He'd spend the rest of his life in prison either way." Lucas looked at me and pursed his lips. "I'll take that cup of coffee now, gumshoe."

I picked out a Eugene Police Department coffee mug that was emblazoned with the motto: 'Quality Policing Through Partnerships' and poured a cup. The mug had been a Christmas present from Lucas a few years back. He smiled a little smile when he saw it. I handed him a spoon.

"I'd like to know who was at the other end of the camera. You wouldn't have any idea who that might possibly be, would you?" Lucas dipped the spoon in the black coffee.

"I have an idea, but nothing you could take into a court of law."

"And your idea is?"

I shook my head. "Luke, let me look into that on my own. I think we'll get further that way."

Lucas sat and stared at me, slowly stirring his coffee, brooding, for nearly a minute before he stood up. "You sure know how to screw up a cop's day, don't you, Hunter? You show me a movie of a man raping a girl who is probably under aged and who subsequently turns up dead and you refuse to tell me where you got it, when you got it, who you think shot it, or anything else."

"I'm sorry. My only other option was to not show it to you at all."

"And you certainly don't want to be caught obstructing justice, do you?"

"Not if I can help it, Detective."

"You know I'm going to want answers to those questions. Sooner rather than later." Lucas took one more sip of his coffee, stood up, and carried the half-full cup to the sink. He poured it out and rinsed the cup.

"I know that, Luke, and believe me, I want answers as badly as you do."

"Don't keep me waiting. You know how I hate to wait."

"Indeed I do," I said. "Indeed I do."

Lucas was out the door and halfway to his cruiser when I yelled after him. "Luke, there's more."

Lucas stopped, seemed to consider for a beat or two, and then came back to the door. He had that look on his face, the same one he'd had by the side of the Willamette when Summer Rain's body had been found.

"How thorough an autopsy did your team do?"

Lucas chose his words carefully. "Are you asking if we knew the girl was pregnant?"

I was flummoxed. "You knew and you didn't tell me?"

"How long have you been sitting on that flash drive?" Lucas shot back.

"Luke," I started, but I didn't know what to say.

"You don't have to say a word, gumshoe. I came out here with a dead girl, no suspects, no motive, no murder weapon, no nothing except for her badly battered body. Now I have two motives, a possible suspect, whips and duct tape for murder weapons."

I stood on my porch under the leaky overhang, watching the rain drip off of Lucas' EPD baseball cap, speechless.

"We were going to work on this together, right?" He said. "That's what you said at the river."

I nodded. "From here on out, amigo."

Lucas didn't smile. "From here on out." He stepped over a puddle that had formed and hopped into his car.

"Luke," I called after him, "when this is all over, we need to—"

But he was gone.

I watched Lucas' Crown Vic bounce slowly down my street, splashing through the potholes. When I turned to go back inside, El Gato was sitting outside the door, not moving a muscle, watching with his big, yellow eyes. There was little doubt in my mind that he understood more about what had just happened between Lucas Leonard and me than I did.

CHAPTER SIXTEEN

"Susan? Jack Hunter." She'd answered on the sixth ring so I'd probably woken her up. It was raining steadily. I felt lousy asking her to come to my office.

"Nice to hear from you, mister. You calling to tell me you found out who killed Rainy?"

"Not quite yet, but we're getting closer. I was hoping you could help us."

"Us? Who's us?" Susan asked.

"The police, of course. You didn't think they'd be involved?"

"I don't mind talking to you but I don't want to talk to no cops."

"You won't have to, Susan, at least for the time being. Can you come by my office? There's something I want you to see."

"I just got up and I gotta be at work at four today. It's like pouring out."

"This won't take long." About fifty-five seconds she'll wish she'd never experienced, I thought to myself. "It's important. It could be a clue, a big clue, to who killed Summer Rain."

"No cops, right?"

"No cops. You have my word on that. I live in Glenwood." I gave her directions.

An hour later Susan knocked on my door, dripping wet. Her hair cascaded out from under a sodden wool beanie. "Sorry if I sounded paranoid on the phone, mister. It's just that—"

"You don't have to explain, Susan. Come on in." I helped her out of her coat, hung it on a hanger, and took it into the bathroom so it could drip into the tub. I hunted around in my hall closet until I found a clean bath towel.

"Coffee?" I called out.

"Tea, if you got it."

"Cream and sugar?" I handed her the towel.

"Thanks. Just a little sugar. This girl's lactose intolerant."

"Are you hungry? Have you had breakfast?"

"Tea'll be fine." She toweled her hair for a minute and then wrapped it up and twisted the towel over her forehead and let it hang down her back. It seemed like an awfully domestic gesture for someone who'd never been in my house before, but I liked it.

I rummaged around in the back of the pantry and found an old box of Bigelow bags. I hung one in a mug, filled it with water, and put it in the microwave. I poured myself a cup of coffee and stirred in a little cream and sugar.

"I've got honey, if you'd prefer," I said.

"That'd be perfect."

"No trouble finding the place?"

"Not really. I've never been to Glenwood before."

"Nobody has who doesn't live here."

When the nuke dinged, I squeezed a spoonful of honey out of the bear, stirred it up and handed the cup to her. "Nothing special," I said. "All I had."

"Thanks." Susan wrapped her thin, pink-tipped fingers around the hot mug. "This'll be fine."

"Sorry if I nuked it too long and it's too hot."

"So what's so important I had to like come all the way over here?"

"There's something I think you ought to see. Sit down and watch this."

I rolled a second chair next to my desktop monitor for Susan. El Gato appeared out of nowhere and began rubbing her shins until he realized her leggings were soaking wet. He took a seat next to her ankles and began licking himself dry.

"Cool. You have a kitty." She reached down to pet El Gato, who consented to having his head scratched. "What's your name, puss?"

"El Gato."

"You named your cat *the cat*?" She looked skeptical.

"He already had that name when I got him."

Susan cocked her head and looked at me quizzically. "How did you get him?"

"He turned up at the back door one day, scrawny and dirty, meowing. I gave him something to eat and a bath and after that he just stuck around."

Susan didn't ask how I managed to give a stray cat a bath or how I knew what his name was, obvious questions that would have been at the top of my list. Instead, she studied him for a bit and then asked, "Does El Gato catch mice?"

"When he first moved in, he brought me a few presents, but nothing lately. I think he's cleaned up the neighborhood."

"Cats know where to go when they need help, don't they?" She looked at the heavy rainfall outside and tried to sip her tea, but it was too hot. "Bummer people aren't that smart."

There couldn't have been a more appropriate lead in.

"Can I get you to sit over here?" I centered Susan in front of my computer and plugged in Binkelman's flash drive. My fingers hovered over the mouse. "Susan, I have to warn you, this is disturbing. It almost makes me puke." I clicked PLAY.

Susan watched the video without blinking. She didn't say a word. El Gato stopped his grooming and hopped up onto her lap and curled up. Without looking down, she scratched behind his ears and soon he was purring. Like I've said, El Gato sizes up folks pretty well.

"Mister, that is fucked up. That is one fucked up—" she paused, shaking her head, her lips curled somewhere between a snarl and a frown. Tears glistened in her eyes. "I don't even know what to call it."

I put my arm around her to comfort her and she collapsed against me, sobbing. "I'm sorry, mister."

"It's Jack. My name is Jack Hunter. You can stop calling me 'mister'. OK?"

"I'm sorry, Jack Hunter."

I waited with my arms around her until she felt cried out. "Do you want to see it again?"

"Shit no." Susan pushed herself out of my clumsy embrace. "I didn't want to see it the first time." She pulled a cellophane bag of

Kleenex out of her purse and blew her nose. "That's what you called me for? To watch some disgusting homebrewed porn?"

"I'm sorry, Susan."

"We're off to a great start, me and you, telling each other how sorry we are." Her tears had made a mess of her makeup. I thought she looked beautiful.

"I'm just trying to fit the pieces together, Susan, figure out what happened. That's Summer Rain in the video, right?"

Susan gave me her you're-dumber-than-a-rock look. "No shit, Sherlock."

"And I assume the other person is her stepfather, Charles Winetrout?"

"Couldn't see his face, but yeah, that's gotta be him. That bastard. He's got that fancy-ass gold watch."

"Ok, Susan, hang in there with me. I'm just trying to make sense out of it. We both know Summer Rain wasn't normal, or maybe typical is a better word, when it came to sex." I took a deep breath. "Do you think this was rape or do you think it was consensual?"

"Consensual?" Susan looked at me like I was out of my mind to ask such a question. I probably was. "Give me a freakin' break. That old bastard has Rainy tied up to a table and he's fucking her in the ass. This girl sure as shit wouldn't ever consent to nothing like that."

"This is Summer Rain we're talking about, not you. And she did look right at the camera."

"Still don't make it right. Or consensual. " Susan stood up and fished a pack of Marlboros and a lighter out of her pants. "Sorry, I gotta have a smoke."

Now the second person in less than a week was lighting up in my trailer. Without permission. I wondered if that sort of temptation happened to everyone who quits. El Gato, who hates smoke, bolted for the bedroom at the other end of the hall.

"Who do you suppose made the video?" I asked. I was pretty sure it was a Marcus Binkelman production, but I wanted Susan's untainted opinion.

"Looks like Binky's work to me." She dipped an experimental tongue into her tea, but it was still too hot so she blew across the top instead. "Had to be him. Coming off a high."

"What makes you say that?"

"Kinda obvious, if you ask me. The camera's too steady, like it's resting on something, like he couldn't hold it still."

Susan was observant, stringing together details that I hadn't noticed. She would have made a good private eye.

"I think this is the video Summer Rain intended to blackmail Winetrout with," I said.

"Yeah, too bad you can't see his face. I recognize that watch, though. He likes to flash that man bling around when he comes in the club. You know, always checking the time." Susan gave up on the tea and set it on the desk and concentrated on her cigarette. "Can a girl get an ashtray around here?"

"In the cupboard over the fridge." I nodded in that direction, then thought twice and hopped up and got it for her. While I was up, I freshened my coffee.

Susan sat on the couch and rested her forearms on her thighs. Instead of tapping her cigarette to knock off the ashes, she rolled the end in the ashtray.

"Where did you get this video, anyway?"

I told her about Binkelman calling me in the middle of the night and meeting him in the alley in the Whiteaker.

"You're where he got the money that he OD'ed on, right?" Whatever Susan St. Marie might have lacked in formal education, she more than made up for in street smarts.

I'd just about managed to deny my complicity in Binky's death to myself. As a private investigator who's carved out a niche doing adultery cases, I've learned to focus an objective lens on the foibles of others. Like everybody else, though, I'm not as courageous when it comes to scrutinizing my own actions. I didn't think in the great scheme of things the world would suffer the loss of one lowlife tweeker, but I didn't like knowing I had provided the means for his demise. Marcus Binkelman did have a mother and father who presumably loved and missed their son. Somebody had sanitized his obituary, after all.

Susan sensed my discomfort. "Don't beat yourself up over it, Jack Hunter. If it hadn't a been you, it would a been someone else. Or something else. Come here and sit down." She patted the couch next to her.

"Yeah, sure." I sat down, not too close and not too far away.

"Really, you gotta believe me on that one." This point of moral culpability seemed important to her. "No way was Binky gonna make it to old age."

"I'm doing my best."

Susan's tea had finally cooled enough for her to take a sip. "You make it strong like I like it." She took another sip, more like a gulp.

"Tell me what kind of tea you like and I'll have it here next time you come." I hoped I didn't sound presumptuous.

Susan smiled, warily at first, and then she just smiled. "Chai. I like Chai tea."

"Any particular brand?"

Susan shook her head. "As long as it's tea, I'm not that picky. I can't stand coffee, though." She took a sip. "Why would Binky want you to have the movie? That don't compute."

It was my turn to feel smarter. "Let's say Summer Rain planned to blackmail Winetrout and recruited Binky to make the video. She'd have to cut Binky in for his help. With her dead there'd be no money coming his way, from her anyway. He somehow found out that I was looking for her and figured I'd be willing to pay for the video. Binky didn't dare go to the police, or to Winetrout either, for that matter, but he knew the video was worth something to somebody and I was the logical person."

Susan considered this. "Makes sense. Sort of. Weird, though."

"Yeah. That and more." It made sense to me, too. Perfect sense.

"Hey, this girl's gotta go and get ready for work." Susan stood up, slipped her lighter and pack of Marlboros into her pocket, fumbled with her keys, and finally turned to face me. "Look, Jack Hunter, I'm still not sure I trust you. I mean, I guess I do. I don't know. But thanks."

109

"Thanks? What for?'
"I just want to say that. Thanks."
I wasn't ready for her to leave. "Can we see each other again?"
She smiled. "Sure, I'm up for that." Susan turned toward the door. In a lower voice, she said, "You know where to find me." She sounded sad.
And with that, she was out the door into the rain. El Gato reappeared, scanned the room, and padded over to the front door and settled himself down. Like he was waiting for her to come back.

CHAPTER SEVENTEEN

"So, what have you found out so far?" I was sitting in Detective Lucas Leonard's office, a place I was becoming way too familiar with. Lucas' desk was littered with papers, folders, phone messages, like it always was. He was reading a lab report. "You called me in, remember?"

"We got the preliminary forensics report back," he said.

"And?"

"Again, I have to tell you none of this—"

"Come on, amigo, you don't have to remind me every time we talk."

"Yes, in point of fact, I do." Lucas paused and looked hard at me without blinking, like he was making up his mind. Eventually, he leaned forward and rested his elbows on his desk. "OK. The deceased had sexual intercourse with two men prior to her death. The body lacerations occurred pre-mortem but the sutures on her lips and labia were post-mortem."

"You're saying Summer Rain was raped and beaten, then killed, then mutilated? In that order?"

Leonard gave me his 'listen up, dummy' look. I'd been getting a lot of those lately. More and more I was feeling like I was in over my head. "That's why you're a gumshoe and I'm a cop."

I didn't say anything to that, waiting for him to elaborate. You can't say anything stupid if you keep your mouth shut.

"We don't know if the whipping occurred before, during, or after the sexual intercourse. We don't know for sure it was forcible rape. There is evidence of anal tearing. The labial sutures mask any vaginal lacerations there might have been. We don't even know for certain yet what the exact cause of death was. The coroner is still working on that. There was very little water in her lungs so it's doubtful she drowned, although that remains a possibility. She could have died from the whipping, loss of blood, but that's inconclusive since there was minimal blood on the riverbank."

"You don't know much, then, do you?" My chance for a little payback.

Lucas ignored me. "Our working assumption is that everything that was done to her was done somewhere else. We think Summer had been dead for a while before she was dumped in the river."

"A while?" I asked.

"Several hours."

"What about a drug overdose? We know what kind of a lifestyle she had."

"We're looking into that. Those tests will take a while longer to determine."

"And what about the man who…" I had to pause. If Lucas wasn't sure what the crime had been, I had no idea what to call the man who was responsible.

"We sent the evidence to Salem. The samples taken from her vagina and anus were from two different men. That much they figured out at the lab here. So far, Salem hasn't matched the DNA up with any known sex offenders. But they aren't finished yet; too many databases to check. Someday, they'll have them all merged—"

Cheryl's voice came over the intercom. "Detective, there is a call for you from Salem. Do you want me to take a message?"

"No! I'll take it now."

I got up to go, but Leonard snapped his fingers and pointed to my chair. He was silent for a minute, said 'thank you' and hung up the phone.

"OK, here's what we know for sure." He paused for a minute, waiting for my acknowledgement that he was sharing confidential information. I nodded.

"Summer Wycowski had sexual relations with two men. I already told you that. One entered her vaginally and one anally. There was a bare trace of lubrication, water soluble, so if the rapist used more, it probably washed away in the river. The penetrations were most likely simultaneous or very close to it. There was significant damage to the perineum. There was pre-ejaculate in her throat as well. The throat sample matched the anal sample."

"And? Any matches with known perverts?"

"Nothing. The DNA search came up empty, at least for sex offenders registered in Oregon."

"You got to be kidding. No records at all? Nothing?"

Lucas shook his head, slowly.

"So, we have two sickos with no track record acting together to rape and mutilate and murder a young girl. It doesn't make sense, Luke."

"No, it doesn't. Possibly a crime of opportunity, but that is highly unlikely. A crime like this is not the work of a first-timer. Usually, a sex offender works up to something this horrific from lesser aggressions. And that's only one of the monkey wrenches. Think about *two* men with no criminal records collaborating on something this grisly."

"It boggles the mind," I said, thinking of Krista's two boyfriends, Alex and Elton.

"We can't dismiss the possibility that the victim knew the men. Things could have started off amicably and gotten out of hand."

"Summer Rain did have an out-of-left-field attitude toward sex." I was remembering what Susan had told me, how her friend didn't really enjoy sex but liked to use it to manipulate men. I thought of her convoluted relations with Jimmy.

"How so?" Lucas asked.

"From what I've been able to determine, Summer Rain used her body to control and manipulate men. She wasn't into sex for her own enjoyment. It was a tool, a means to an end," I said.

"And consider this," Lucas said. "It would have to be premeditated for the events to have taken place in two different locations."

"*Two* locations?" I asked. "You've narrowed it down to two?"

"Good point." Lucas grimaced. He didn't like even minor points to escape him. "At least two. What happened to Summer Rain Wycowski started somewhere else and ended up in the Willamette River. There could have been some stops along the way." He swiveled and stared out the window, musing out loud to himself. "Virtually no blood, no signs of a struggle, no evidence accidentally left behind at the river."

"What about the cell phone?" I said. "That was evidence."

"Evidence, yes. Accident, no. Wiped clean, no prints. Left in plain sight on a log." Lucas turned back to face me. "Whoever left that cell phone by the river wanted us to find it."

"Was I right?" I asked. "Was it her phone?"

"We checked the serial number. The contract is registered to Charles Winetrout, so you could say it belonged to her."

Wonder of wonders, I thought to myself. I got something right. I got up to go.

"That's it?" I asked.

"That's it for now," Lucas said. Reluctantly, he added, "You got any ideas?"

"There are a couple of things to check out. I'll let you know if I come up with anything."

"You do that, gumshoe." Lucas tried to smile, but smiling didn't come naturally to the man. I wondered if he had smiled as a child, before he became a homicide detective.

CHAPTER EIGHTEEN

Alex Trippitt had relocated to Portland but Elton Miller was easy to track down. Most alcoholics have regular haunts. Their home away from home is anywhere they can drink and socialize, maybe cage a drink or two on credit at the end of the month. A call to Susan got me pointed in the right direction.

I wondered if Krista's relocation to the Rose City had been solely to get away from her husband or whether Alex Trippitt had anything to do with it. That was another question I wanted to ask Elton Miller, who I was due to meet later in the afternoon.

"So, what's this all about? Why am I here?" Miller sat across from me in The Shamrock, a dive out on Highway 99 that served green beer for the two week period spanning St. Patrick's Day, where we had agreed to meet. The Shamrock was the kind of bar where most of the patrons were regulars. I've never liked the place, but it'd been Miller's call. It was early but the room was already crowded.

Elton Miller was a mousy little man with shaggy, reddish-blond hair, a droopy, tobacco-stained walrus mustache, and the beginnings of spidery, broken blood vessels in his cheeks that advertised a history of hard drinking. He wore a tie-dyed Grateful Dead tee-shirt and his arms were covered with faded blue tattoos. He had been reluctant to come to my office but I had hinted that if he didn't want to talk to me, he wouldn't have a choice when the police got around to him, so we'd compromised on The Shamrock. I offered to pick up the tab for a few drinks and that cinched the deal. A pack of Salem's lay on the stained table and one dangled from his lips. His eyes skimmed the room, stopping for a moment whenever he came to a good-looking woman. Hard to figure what Krista had seen in him.

"Get you something to drink?" The bartender asked, looking at me.

"I'd like an IPA. Ninkasi or Ten Barrel, or whatever else you have on tap.

"We have Boneyard."

"That'll be fine."

The bartender turned to Miller. "The usual?"

"Yeah, Seven and Seven. Fact, make that a double," he added, no doubt remembering the drinks were on me.

"Kinda early, isn't it Elton?" Asked the bartender.

"Not in New York it ain't." Miller shot back.

I handed the bartender a Jackson. "Let me know when we bump up against the top of that."

The bartender looked at Miller. "Won't be long," he said.

I waited until he left before I asked, "So, tell me about Summer Rain Wycowski."

"Summer?" Miller abruptly stopped his survey and looked at me with narrowed eyes. "Summer? Ain't much to tell. Only ever met her a couple times."

"You were a regular visitor at Winetrout's mansion."

"Yeah, well, lotta people are regular visitors up to Mr. Winetrout's. Big flipping deal."

"How well do you know Summer Rain?"

"She wasn't never there."

The bartender arrived with our drinks, putting mine on a coaster but handing Miller his.

"So, when was the last time you saw her or spoke with her?"

"Tell me again what this is all about."

I focused my full attention on Elton Miller's face. "Summer Rain is dead. She'd been missing for a while before that. Winetrout figured she was a runaway and he hired me to find her. Once she turned up dead, the police got real interested."

"Dead?" Miller looked genuinely shocked, his tumbler stalled half way between the table and his mouth. That was the primary reason why I had asked him to meet me; I wanted to see his reaction, the look on his face, when he got the news. I needed to do it in person and I needed to do it before it came out in the news. "How is she dead? Car crash or something?"

"No, her death wasn't accidental. At this point, the police don't have many details and I know even less." I made a mental note that Miller hadn't jumped to homicide right off the bat.

"What happened? How did she die?"

I've had considerable experience observing how folks react to big news. People want to know if their spouses are cheating and by the time they hire me, their suspicions are usually correct. Miller looked shocked.

"Sorry, I can't give you any of the details. Obviously, it's an ongoing investigation."

"If the cops don't know who killed her, how's it you fit in? You ain't no cop."

"Like I said, her father hired me to find her. That was before he knew she was dead."

"And you're still on the job? Thought occurs to a person if she was murdered it would be a police concern, strictly speaking. Mr. Winetrout wouldn't be needing your services no more."

"He wants me work alongside the police, approach the matter from another perspective."

"You're on the clock right now, as we speak, I take it."

I nodded.

"Take the money and run, huh? Smart move." Miller tapped his forehead and grinned.

I winced, which served to remind me that somehow I'd become more subjectively involved than I normally did with a case. "It's more than that."

"You got that right. She was definitely eye candy, you want my opinion. I'm real sorry to hear she passed away."

"Tell me about her mom. Better yet, tell me about you and Krista."

Miller stabbed out his cigarette in an ashtray already full of butts. Not all of them were his, which tells you something about the place.

"Crystal? Ain't much to tell, really. Me and her met a few times at Mr. Winetrout's parties. Crystal's kinda on the trampy side, but I like her. Fact, that's prob'ly *why* I like her. Face it, a person don't go to swingers' parties looking to make lifelong friends, huh? Me and her hit it off, though. Crystal has a great set of jugs, even if they are plastic. Loves to give head. A real pro in that department, know what I mean? She has a thing about big dicks." Miller winked at me and lifted his glass and toasted his memories of Crystal in the dusty mirror behind the bar. "Truth be told, I was happy to oblige." Miller slid his empty glass to the edge of the table and waited to catch the bartender's eye. "Man'd be a fool not to enjoy what he can get when he can get it."

"And then what happened?"

Miller seemed to be waiting for the bartender to bring him another Seven and Seven.

"What happened? I'll tell you what happened. One night me and Alex, that's my old wing man who moved to Portland, we went up to her house to party. Mr. Winetrout was out of town on a business trip to Las Vegas or somewhere, but we'd both already had, a man could say, intimate relations with her plenty a times and he knew all about it. Fact of the matter is, he'd been there. Mr. Winetrout'd watched us lay waste to his wife." Miller paused while the bartender brought us fresh drinks. He drained a third of his glass and then went on. "We thought he wouldn't give a rip about the three of us having ourselves a private little party." Miller took a big swallow and wiped his mouth with the back of his hand. "Wrong."

I waited for him to continue.

"Mr. Winetrout, he came home early, unexpected like. Heard him slam the front door and assumed – you know what 'assume' means, right? Makes an ass out of you and me –we assumed the man would come in, light up a stogie, kick back and enjoy the show, like he usually did. Way wrong. He was majorly pissed off. Kicked us out, which wasn't hard, seeing as how me and Alex knew he owned a shitload of artillery. He kicked Crystal out, too, but not 'til the next day after he'd had a chance to work her over, you know, smack her around some. She high-tailed it to Portland, too."

"That have anything to do with Alex moving up there?"

"Nah. He scored a better gig. Buckets of ducats."

"You think he's seeing Crystal?" I didn't know what bearing any of this could have on my search for Summer Rain's killers, but you never know what you might stumble over going down a blind alley, and I was anxious to keep the conversation flowing.

"I most seriously doubt that. I hear she's gone pro. Ol' Alex, he would never pay for it."

"Can you think of anyone who would want Summer Rain dead or any reason why?"

Miller fumbled a Salem into his mouth and managed to drop his lighter on the floor, from where he said, "Like I told you before, only ever met her once. Or maybe twice."

"What was her relationship with Charles Winetrout like?"

"Got no clue about that. He was her stepfather. You know how that shit goes. A man doesn't know nothing, he's got no business saying nothing."

I mulled over Miller's answer, trying to decipher the ambiguities in his language. I decided to take another tack.

"Do you know James, Winetrout's gardener?"

"Gopher Jimmy?" Miller stifled a laugh, then coughed some smoke which made his eyes water.

"What can you tell me about him?"

"Oh, Jimmy," he said, once he had recovered his voice. "He used to be a wild one. A real player." Miller dropped his chin to his chest and raised his arms high. "Here comes Jimmy! Lock up your booze and hide your wimin."

"We're talking about the same Jimmy?"

"Not hardly. You prob'ly only just met him. I'm talking about the Jimmy I knew before he got religion, before he found Jesus and became James. Nothing you could drink or shoot or screw was safe around that kid."

I remembered the tattoo of Jesus on Jimmy's arm. "And then?"

"Yeah, well, he got into some trouble, don't know exactly what. Some sort of hassle with the bouncer down at the Bod. Jimmy don't look like no scrapper, but from what I hear the bouncer most definitely got the short end of that stick. Wish I'd been there to see it. Must have been on a Saturday night, seeing as Mr. Winetrout was there. Some way or another, he managed to chill everyone out. Didn't want the cops busting down the place."

"It's a long stretch from being a drunk in a brawl in a titty bar to being a born again Christian gardener."

"Yeah, well, you know how that crap goes. Mr. Winetrout has a persuasive manner about him."

"How so?"

"He made Jimmy an offer. Straighten up and fly right and I'll give you a job. Otherwise I'll file a complaint and the bouncer'll sign it and the cops'll be on your ass like stink on shit. Rumor was Jimmy had some priors."

"An offer he couldn't refuse."

"Yeah, that'd be a good way to put it." Miller finished his drink and held it up for the bartender to see.

"Jimmy started working for Mr. Winetrout, mowing the lawn, yard work, cleaning the pool, parking cars when he had a party, general all around girl Friday. Except he wasn't a girl. Somewhere along the way he found God. Or God found him." Miller smiled. The teeth he had left were stained brown. The bartender came with Miller's third double of the evening. I was only half way through my second beer.

"You driving home, Elton?" The bartender asked.

"Nah, I walked down. I'll walk home or maybe catch a ride." Miller looked at me hopefully.

"Where does Summer Rain fit into this?" I asked.

This time Miller didn't bother to hide his laugh. "Once Jimmy found the Lord, became Saint James, Summer couldn't help herself. She did her best to seduce him. She flounced around in front of him, shaking her booty like there was no tomorrow." Miller paused and looked at his occupied hands like he couldn't decide between taking a drag on his Salem or sipping his Seven and Seven. "Yeah, that there was Summer in a nutshell. She liked to play with the effect she had on dudes. Fuck with their heads, you could say."

"I heard one night he found her irresistible."

"Ha!! One night? More like several times on and off. Summer had a wicked sense of humor with a mean streak kinda mixed in, if you know what I mean. She'd leave the poor dude alone for a while and then out of the blue she'd wander out to the garage where he was fixing the lawnmower or washing the car, wearing something skimpy and lacy and that would be all she wrote."

I wondered how Elton Miller knew these details about Summer Rain. It was doubtful Jimmy would have been this forthcoming and Miller claimed he had only met her once or twice. Where was the connection?

"So you're saying Jimmy and Summer Rain had an ongoing relationship?"

"Nah, a body wouldn't call it a relationship. More like a game. Once Summer found out Jimmy'd become a Jesus freak, she just had to mess with his mind. Sort of like a challenge for her, know what I mean?"

"You told me you only met Summer Rain on one or two occasions. How do you know all this?"

"Hangin' out at the Bod. A man hears things. Eugene ain't that big of a town."

"Did Jimmy go there, too?"

Miller laughed. "Not since he found Jesus. Before that, yeah, a lot. You could say he was a player, a regular pussy hound."

"What about Alex Trippitt and Summer Rain? Did they know each other?"

"He prob'ly knew her better than I did. Ol' Alex's a few years younger'n me and he used to run with some of the older folks in that crowd."

"Was there anything going on between him and Summer Rain?"

"Most definitely not."

"You sound pretty sure of that."

Miller grinned and winked. "Ol' Alex would have liked there to be something going on between her and him but she shot him down. Like I been saying, that chick had a weird-ass attitude about sex."

"Tell me about that."

Miller took a deep breath and looked at me like a school teacher trying to explain arithmetic to a fourth-grader. "OK, take Alex for example. It was like he wanted it too much so she wasn't going to give it to him." He paused for a moment, lost in thought. "I don't think that chick liked doing it as much as she liked dangling it in front of some dude's face."

"Like she teased Jimmy, right?"

"Yeah, exactly. That's what I've been trying to tell you. She liked to mess with dudes' heads."

"Do you think Alex was pissed off enough that he could have killed her?"

Miller considered this for a moment and then he remembered something humorous and chuckled.

"What's so funny?"

"Remembering one night ol' Alex was trying to put the moves on her. You know, making sure her glass never went dry, her cigarettes got lit, that sort of crap. We were all at the Bod and after a couple drinks Summer announced she'd just gotten her nipple pierced. Alex was all over that like a fly on a dung heap. Wanted to see it. Had to see it. Summer played all innocent and modest for a while, but she eventually unbuttoned her shirt and unhooked her bra. She had one of those high-school make-out kinds that unclips in front. What was funny was that she hauled out both her boobs, the one with the ring and the other one, too. She could've just showed him the titty with the ring, or said no altogether, but she didn't. Come to think of it, she could a never even mentioned the ring in the first place. That's the way she was, though. Sex was a game for her, more'n anything else."

"You didn't answer my question."

"Your question was?" Elton Miller didn't have enough grey matter left for much more than a one paragraph attention span.

"Do you think—?"

"Oh. Do I think Alex could have killed Summer? Nah, seriously doubt that. Ol' Alex is used to getting whatever he wants in the pussy department, but if he killed every chick that got away, he'd've been locked up centuries ago."

"Any way I can get in touch with Alex?"

"Alls I got is his cell number. Don't know where he's staying. Ain't seen him since he moved."

I gave Elton two cards and he wrote a number on the back of one and slipped the other one in his pocket.

"Yeah, well, I'm outta here," he said. "Places to go. People to see. Say hello to ol' Alex if you manage to find him. Tell him life ain't the same down here since he left." Miller slid out of the booth, drained the last few drops of his Seven and Seven, and ambled a crooked path toward the door. He paused for a moment. "Say, you wouldn't be headed out ninety-nine, would you?"

"Sorry," I said. "Other direction. I live in Glenwood."

"No problem. See you next time." Miller swung open the door, flooding the dim interior of the Shamrock with sunlight. He paused for a minute, like a deer emerging from the forest at the edge of a clearing, wondering if it was safe, then he stepped outside and the door closed quietly behind him.

Something felt out of kilter about Elton Miller. As I watched him leave, I realized we'd only made eye contact once or twice the whole time we'd been talking. He'd always been focused on something to my right or my left or behind me.

I spread out a dry bar napkin, wrapped up a few of his Salem butts, and slid the makeshift packet into my pocket.

CHAPTER NINETEEN

I waited until I got back to my office to call Alex Trippitt. For whatever reason, I wanted my office number to show up on his screen rather than my cell number.

"Trippitt here. I'm no doubt doing something a lot more fun than talking to you on the phone. Leave a message and I might call you when I get finished."

"Mr. Trippitt, my name is Jack S. Hunter. I'm a private investigator down here in Eugene. I'd like to talk to you about a case I'm working on. Please call me back at your earliest convenience. Thanks." And I left my number.

I looked around for El Gato. He was at the bedroom end of the trailer preoccupied with an inch-wide crack where the floor was falling away from the wall.

It didn't take long for my phone to ring.

"Trippitt here. You left a message you wanted to talk to me. So talk."

"I'd rather do it in person, if that's possible."

"Anything's possible. What's this have to do with?"

"Are you going to be in Eugene anytime soon? If not, I can come to Portland."

"No plans to go to Eugene. Can you tell me what this is about?"

"It's regarding a missing person. You're on a cell, right? I'd rather not go into any more details on the phone."

"So come to Portland if it's all that important."

"When would be good for you?"

"I work nights and get up late. Afternoons are best."

"How about tomorrow? I could be there at two if that works for you."

"Fine. Call me when you get here and I'll tell you where to meet me."

"Portland's a big town."

"Take the Lake Oswego exit and call me from there. Can't tell me any more now, huh?"

"I'd really rather wait until we meet."

"See you tomorrow. I gotta go to work at six so don't cut it too close." Click.

*

I met Alex Trippitt in a Denny's just off the freeway. I could tell before he said a single word that he fancied himself a stud, one of those God's-gift-to-women types. The man stood about six three and weighed two-fifty if he weighed an ounce. Most of him was muscle. He had a narrow beard that began at his earlobes and finished in a meticulously barbered Van Dyke. His head was shaved bald. Alex wore small diamond earrings. His shirt was partially unbuttoned and a gold chain wove through his thick chest hair.

"So, Mr. Hunter, what's so important that you can't talk about it on the phone and had to drive all the way to Portland?"

"You can call me Jack."

"Fine. Jack. What's up?"

"It's about Summer Rain Wycowski. Charles Winetrout hasn't seen his step-daughter for almost two weeks and he asked me to look around for her."

"Summer? Missing? How could Charlie tell?" Trippitt laughed at his own joke.

"Do you have any idea where she might have gone?"

"Me? Why should I know where she is?" He ran his tongue inside his upper lip as if he felt something stuck between his teeth. "That girl knew tons of people. If she ran away, she could've gone anywhere. Summer. She could be in L.A. making porn movies for all I know."

Zing! That could not possibly be a coincidence. It was exactly, to the letter, the future Summer Rain had envisioned for herself, according to Susan. It took me a minute to process and recover. I felt like I was close to something but I couldn't tell what it was. "Porn movies? Los Angeles?"

125

"You ever meet our girl?"

"No. I'm getting to know her, but only from talking to people who do know her. Like yourself."

"Oh, I knew her alright." Trippitt rummaged in his pocket until he found a toothpick. He peeled away the cellophane and began probing between his teeth. "Sixteen going on twenty-six. All grown up and hot to trot. Just like her mama. Crystal."

"I gather Crystal lives here in Portland now. You ever see her?"

"Nah. She's a hooker working out of some escort service. She was a good lay when she was free."

"Meaning…"

"How much do you know and how much don't you know, anyway?" Trippitt dislodged whatever was bothering him and broke his toothpick in half and dropped it ceremoniously on the floor.

"Why don't you start at the beginning of the story and I'll tell you when you can skip over any parts I already know."

"No story to be told. I like women. I like to screw 'em. The more the better and the more often the better, too."

"And Summer Rain? Where does she fit in?"

"Back when I lived in Eugene, I used to hang out at this titty bar where I got to know the owner. Charlie. He'd married a stripper, a real looker. She'd been a *HUSTLER* centerfold. Crystal. Me being who I am, one thing led to another and before long I was screwing her at get-togethers in his living room."

I decided to let the conversation wander wherever Trippitt let it. "By get-togethers I take it you mean his swingers' parties, right?"

"Call 'em whatever you want. Six or eight couples, an occasional single broad, some single stags. You know, friends of his, maybe someone he was doing a real estate deal or some other kind of business with. Charlie always balanced off the numbers with strippers from the club. It was a kick to go because it didn't take long for me to get real popular with the women." Trippitt ran his hand over his bald scalp and winked at me with what he must have intended as a man-to-man, knowing wink. "You better believe it's easy pickings. Everyone's there for one reason. To get laid. No pussyfooting around. You see what you want and you take it. Done deal."

"When was the last time you were there at one of these parties?"

"Not since before I moved to Portland. Let's see, gotta be two months or more."

"And Summer Rain fits into this somehow, right?"

"Not at the parties. Summer danced at the club a couple of times. The first time I saw her wrapped around that brass pole I about blew my load. It was the way she did it. All the strippers like to use the pole, but if you watch 'em closely, you'll see that most of 'em don't let their pubes touch the brass. Not Summer, though, oh no. To watch her you'd think she wanted that pole in the worst way." Trippitt took a drink of water and crunched an ice cube in his back teeth. "I gotta tell you, it about killed me when I found out she was Charlie's personal property."

"Summer Rain Wycowski is Charles Winetrout's under-aged step-daughter." I said.

"Yeah, whatever. The bouncer let me know right away she was off limits."

"I thought all the dancers were hands off to the customers."

"Legally, inside the club, that's most definitely the case. You never know when some OLCC prick is gonna be snooping around, looking for an excuse to cause trouble. Believe me, Charlie's been there, done that."

"And?" I paused, waiting for Trippitt to continue. "You said inside the club. What about outside?"

"And? Well, the way it went down was if you saw something on stage you had the hots for and you were on Charlie's good side, then that particular bit of trim would turn up at his next party. Trust me, you didn't have to wait long. He had those gangbangs once or twice a month."

"Was Summer Rain ever at one of these parties?"

"Could have been, but very doubtful. I never saw her there. I think her mama hustled her out ahead of time."

"Was there something going on between Summer Rain and Charles Winetrout?"

"Again, could have been but I never saw it. Fact of the matter is, I never saw Summer anywhere besides those times down at the club. Not that I wouldn't have liked to see more of her, and I'm sure she would have liked to see more of me, but that would have meant getting eighty-sixed from the parties and the club. Numbers were all wrong."

"Numbers were all wrong?" I gave him a blank stare.

"Why trade away a whole roomful of snatch for one piece of ass? Know what I mean?" Trippitt treated me to another manly wink.

"I see your point. And Summer Rain was underage don't forget."

Trippitt frowned and arched his eyebrows like Summer Rain's age was a brand new consideration. "Yeah, well, I guess there was that, too." Suddenly he looked at me with a newfound intensity. "You sure you're private? You aren't a cop, are you?"

I laid my card on the table. "Not hardly."

Trippitt looked at my card skeptically and slipped it into his pocket. "Look, I gotta make tracks. I gotta get ready for work. You know what I mean?"

"Thanks for meeting me. You mind if I called you if I think of any more questions?"

"You called me the first time." He stood and hitched up his pants. "Give my regards to Charlie next time you see him. Elton, too," he added as an afterthought.

"I'll do that." I called out to his back.

This time I was ready. I picked up the broken toothpick with a pair of tweezers and dropped it into a Ziploc bag, wrote 'Alex Trippitt' and the date, and put it in my pocket.

*

The hundred mile drive back to Eugene wasn't long enough for me to think about everything I had to think about. A day or two of serenity on the North Umpqua River was definitely called for.

I filled my Coleman cooler with bits and pieces of leftovers and several bottles of Ninkasi and packed it in the back of my Cherokee, along with my tent, sleeping bag, and fishing gear. El Gato glared at me from the couch as if to say, 'you just got back and you're leaving again already? What about me?'

"You'll be fine, amigo," I said. I piled his food bowl with kibble and topped it with a full can of Moist Morsels.

I stopped by the police station on my way out of town. Lucas wasn't in his office, so I left my card and the Ziploc bags containing Elton Miller's cigarette butts and Alex Trippitt's broken toothpick with Cheryl. She knows me well enough, but I didn't want there to be any doubt as to where the samples came from. I wrote DNA in large letters on the back of my card and handed everything to her with my tweezers.

She grimaced. "I'll make sure Detective Leonard sees this the minute he comes in."

"You do that," I said. "I'll be out of cell range for a couple of days. Tell him not to panic."

CHAPTER TWENTY

"Where did you get that stuff?" Detective Lucas Leonard stood straight as a laser beam on my doorstep. No preliminaries, no friendly greetings, directly to the point in mach five time.

"Good to see you, too, amigo. Not even going to ask me if I caught anything?" I'd just walked in the door less than an hour earlier and I wondered how he knew I was home.

"Cut the crap, Hunter. I'm in no mood. Who are these characters?"

"I take it you got a match?" I was both surprised and not surprised at the same time: Elton Miller and Alex Trippitt both knew Summer Rain Wycowski. They were part of the same sleazy, easy-sex culture that included Summer Rain, her step-father, her mother, Jimmy (before his precarious rebirth), and maybe even Binky as well, although that would have been a stretch. Susan worked at the Hot Body Club, too, but now that I was getting to know the person inside the dancer I didn't see her in the same light. However, proximity didn't equate with commission and certainly wasn't motivation. Trippitt was a serial womanizer and Miller was a drunk, but that didn't make either of them monsters.

"Two of them, to be precise. The DNA sample from the cigarette butts matched the semen taken from the victim's vagina and the DNA on the toothpick fit the samples taken from her rectum and mouth," Lucas said. "Give me names. Now."

I was at a loss for words. Whatever suspicions had prompted me to collect the samples had long since evaporated. Until that moment.

Lucas Leonard fixed me with a hard stare. An innocent bystander would never have guessed we were fishing buddies, or even friends. "Explain something to me, Hunter. How is it you're always right there or ahead of me on this case? First, you turn up at the river where a dead body is floating around minutes after I do. Next, you come up with a video of the deceased being tortured and

130

sodomized. Now you provide me with two samples that match our DNA evidence. And all this from a licensed voyeur."

"Honestly, Luke, I don't—"

"I'm in no mood, Hunter. You've got ten seconds to name names. I'll give you a little longer to explain."

He must have missed Alex's name on the Ziploc. "Elton Miller and Alex Trippitt."

"Which is which?"

"Miller smokes Salems. Trippitt's the toothpick."

Lucas had his notebook in hand, jotting everything down. "Go on."

"At first, I thought there was something that you cops call hinky about these guys." I reminded Lucas about my trip to Portland to interview Krista Wycowski. I told him about the sexcapade with Elton Miller and Alex Trippitt that resulted in her ouster from Charles Winetrout's home and hearth and about my subsequent meetings with both men. I told him how I'd been mildly suspicious of both of them when Summer Rain's name had come up in our chats and how I had decided – on the spot with Miller and ahead of time with Trippitt – to somehow collect DNA samples from each of them.

"The more I thought about it, though, the more I decided I was off on the wrong track. By the time I handed the samples over to Cheryl, I'd have bet a Franklin there wouldn't be any connection."

"You'd have lost your bet. Where can I find these pieces of shit?"

"Elton Miller's still around. He hangs out at the Hot Body Club and the Shamrock among other watering holes. Alex Trippitt has skedaddled to Portland. He works nights but I don't know where. Some steel fabricating shop, I think. I have his cell number, if you want it."

"*If* I want it?"

"Better figure out what you're going to leave on his message machine before you call."

"Give me physical descriptions."

I described both men and offered to meet with a sketch artist.

"I got a better idea. Why don't you and I take a run up to Portland together? You arrange to meet him and when he shows up, I'll bust him."

"Luke, how can I do that? I'm not—"

"You let me worry about that."

"What about Elton Miller?" I asked. I didn't feel right about this.

"You tell me he's local. We'll worry about him later."

"Yeah, sure." I was doubtful. "Something about this isn't right, Luke."

"What isn't right, gumshoe, is a sixteen-year-old girl has been raped and tortured to death. Jack Hunter, Private Investigator, comes up with DNA evidence that super glues two viable suspects to the victim. Nothing circumstantial, no guess work, direct connection. I think I can handle things from here."

"Do either of them have records?"

"Their DNA didn't match anything local. I'm not waiting for Salem."

"Luke, these guys just don't seem like the type."

"They never do, gumshoe, they never do."

"No, what I mean is, when I gave you the cigarette butts and the toothpick, I was expecting a zero match. I mean, yes, Alex Trippitt and Elton Miller do know each other. Yes, they both knew Summer Rain. And yes, Trippitt, at least, admitted to having a bad case of the hots for her. But I don't see where this adds up to motivation. Opportunity, maybe, depending on their whereabouts when Summer Rain was killed. But motivation?"

"The DNA's a match. That's more than enough to pick them up for questioning."

"I'll be very curious to hear what you find out."

"I'm sure you are, gumshoe. With your track record, you'll probably know the answers before I ask the questions. Get your coat and whatever else you want, we're going to Portland. Bring your weapon."

CHAPTER TWENTY-ONE

I called Alex Trippitt from my cell phone on I-5 as we were leaving Eugene and told him I had a few more questions and some photographs to show him. I was not enthusiastic about helping Lucas bust Trippitt, but the detective is a hard man to say no to. Given that our professions frequently intersected, I judged it better to say yes than no.

If Trippitt was suspicious about meeting me a second time in three days, he didn't let on. We agreed to meet at the same Denny's in two hours. That would give Lucas, who was wearing civilian clothes, plenty of time to situate himself in a strategic position before his suspect arrived. Lucas' unmarked Crown Vic covered the distance in less than an hour and a half. Not a state trooper in sight.

We were sitting back to back in adjacent booths when Trippitt strode through the door. Lucas had his nose buried in a newspaper, a cup of black coffee and a half eaten slice of Marionberry pie in front of him.

Trippitt settled into the booth and stretched his arms out on the seatback. "So, what do you want to know that you didn't already ask me?"

"I want more details about Summer Rain dancing at the Hot Body Club."

"Like I told you before, I saw her there once, maybe twice. On stage that is. She hung out there more than that." Trippitt paused, closed his eyes, and tilted his head back before he continued. "Believe me, Summer was plenty hot. She got your blood flowing. Given the chance—"

"We're talking about an underage girl here, you know. Jailbait."

Trippitt visibly stiffened and his head jerked back into the here and now. His voice took on a nasty, accusatory tone. "You sure you're not a cop or something?" He started to slide out of the booth. "I'm outta here."

133

There was a rustle of newspaper from behind him and suddenly Detective Leonard Lucas was standing at our table with his service Glock in one hand and a pair of handcuffs in the other.

"You are under arrest. Keep your hands on the table where I can see them."

Trippitt froze at the sight of the gun. "I'm under arrest? You gotta be shitting me. Arrest me for what?"

"You are under arrest for the rape and murder of Summer Rain Wycowski."

The color left Alex Trippitt's face and he shifted his glare back and forth between Lucas and me. "What kind of bullshit set up is this?"

"Slide out real slow and easy and lie on the floor. Keep your hands where I can see 'em."

Trippitt slid awkwardly onto his stomach on the floor. "You got the wrong guy, man. I didn't even know the girl was dead until your buddy here told me a couple of days ago. I haven't been to Eugene in over a month."

Lucas read Trippitt his Miranda rights and handed me the handcuffs. "Put your hands behind your back."

Once I'd gotten Trippitt cuffed, Lucas holstered his Glock and together we hauled him to his feet. I wondered briefly exactly what my legal status was, given that I'm not a sworn officer of the law, but things were moving quickly and you could almost smell the adrenaline of the three of us in the air, so I shelved my qualms for a later time.

"What about my car? I can't just leave my car here."

"Believe me, you have much bigger things to worry about than your car. Let's go."

I left a nice photograph of Abraham Lincoln on the table to cover Lucas' coffee and pie.

We loaded Alex Trippitt into the back seat of Lucas' Crown Vic and headed for Eugene.

CHAPTER TWENTY-TWO

Lucas Leonard and two uniformed officers picked up Elton Miller without incident at one of his favorite watering holes later that same day and lodged him in the Lane County jail. His new home was just a few doors down from Alex Trippitt's.

I was sitting in Lucas' office, nursing my second double mocha of the day, trying to decompress from the events of the past few days. My emotions were a jumble; sadness, relief, a vague sense of completion, all in no particular order. I was tired, too. I'd been getting my normal amount of sleep, but I wasn't getting whatever recuperation sleep was supposed to provide.

"How are they taking it?" I asked. Somehow it was redundant to identify who 'they' were.

"Judging from what I hear back from the jail, Trippitt's a jailhouse virgin but Miller is something of a repeat guest." Lucas shuffled a few papers on his desk. "Maybe not a regular, but he's been there before; he knew the routine. They've both called lawyers. Not sure where it'll go from here. It's up to the D.A."

"What do you mean, you're not sure where it will go?"

Lucas treated me to his just-how-dumb-are-you look. "In case you overlooked it, there is a chain of custody problem with the DNA samples you collected. A smart lawyer could make a big deal out of that. We'll have to build a case independently of your samples. Of course, we'll get fresh DNA samples in jail, but the ones you collected make for a weak just cause case."

I was more than a little miffed. Here I'd solved the case for him, handed him two prime suspects on a silver platter, and not even gotten a thank you.

"Well, that's your problem now, amigo. I'm out of it."

"Have you talked with Winetrout yet? With the arrests, it's all going to be out in public by tomorrow."

"That's my next stop." I got up to go, not looking forward to talking to Charles Winetrout, but anxious to get out of Lucas Leonard's office.

*

I mentally prepared to wind up my involvement in the case with a drive out to the Winetrout Estate. Miller and Trippitt had been regular customers in his strip club and guests, if that was the right word, at the swinger orgies at his mansion. The same men who'd had sex multiple times with his wife, who'd been the proximate cause of the breakup of his marriage, were now in custody for the murder of his stepdaughter as well. Disgusting and onerous as it was, Winetrout's sexual abuse of Summer Rain paled in comparison to Miller's and Trippitt's crimes of rape, torture, and murder. How can you even compare or quantify such atrocities? Winetrout's perversions had stopped short of murder, but Summer Rain had likely endured him for much longer.

Summer Rain Wycowski did not choose the hand she was dealt; she got a lousy deal and made of it what she could. I felt sorry for her. It was not a comforting thought that her death probably meant Winetrout would never be prosecuted. The only evidence implicating Charles Winetrout sexually with Summer Rain Wycowski was Marcus Binkelman's video and that was problematic at best; Winetrout's face was off screen and Binky was dead. A good defense attorney could get the flash drive thrown out of court faster than it would take to view it.

Everyone's life is a story. Some of these stories are big and encompass a wide variety of people, others are small and intimate and don't involve more than the person's immediate family and close friends. Everybody I have ever known, however, has a darker underbelly of their world, a nasty part of themselves they don't share and try their best to keep hidden. Usually they fail.

Exposing and documenting the seamier intersections of those stories is what I do for a living. That doesn't make it any easier. One of the ironic connections I have with Lucas Leonard is that we are both happier when we don't have anything to do, professionally.

The old man would certainly demand an accounting of the cash deposit he had advanced me, which meant I'd have to refund most of it to him. Other than my standard fee for a week or so of my time, the only serious money I'd spent was the payment to Binky for the flash drive and the overnighter at the Sheraton in Portland. There were a slew of miscellaneous expenses adding up maybe a hundred bucks; cash to James, cash to Binky's gang on the mall, drinks with Elton Miller, dances with Charity. I figured I'd have a hard time justifying table dances at the Hot Body Club and for James' sake I didn't want Winetrout to know I'd even talked to the kid, so I was in a quandary.

I also wanted to talk to Susan. I had no idea what I wanted or needed to tell her, but disappearing into my familiar old world without some sort of conclusion or closure and then turning up at some future time at the Hot Body Club for a beer didn't seem quite right. I sensed there was something more going on with Ms. St. Marie, but I wasn't sure what. The stories cross and recross and life goes on.

A final loose end I felt a need to tie up was with Krista Wycowski. I hadn't talked with her since the night we'd met at the airport Sheraton. I was confident she would come to Eugene to arrange a funeral or memorial service for Summer Rain and it seemed logical that she would also come when her daughter's murderers went to trial or maybe for the sentencing phase.

Before I made the trip to Portland, however, I needed to parse out the parameters of visiting her again. There was a void in my life where a partner should have been, but in spite of the fact that we'd made a human connection rather than a strictly professional one, Krista Wycowski wasn't the right candidate to fill it. I felt deeply sorry for her, for her loss and her grief, for how she had to make her living, but that didn't add up to the basis for a relationship. And now there was Susan.

The arrests of Elton Miller and Alex Trippitt for the rape, torture and murder of Summer Rain Wycowski should have been the beginning of the last chapter in the story of her sad, short life. And for a day it was. The wheels of justice would grind on. Or so I thought.

I got up early the next morning and went to Dutch Brothers and Market of Choice. I'd been running in so many directions that I was getting low on some of the essentials of life, like cans of Friskies Tuna Banquet and Fancy Feast. When I got home, the red message light was flashing. I spread out a banquet of classic turkey and cheddar cheese for El Gato – his favorite treat usually reserved for successful case closures – changed the water in his drinker, and frisbeed the 'to go' lid from my double mocha into the wastebasket. When the essentials had been covered, I pushed the button.

"Hunter. It's me, Leonard. Get over here to my office ASAP." Click.

The tone of Lucas' voice was grim and urgent. Something was awry. I called him up immediately.

"What's the matter, Luke? What's up?"

"Not on the phone, gumshoe. Hustle your ass down here pronto."

"I'm on my way." I retrieved the coffee lid from the trash, snapped it on the cup, and rushed out the door. I hoped that the Moist Delights treat hadn't been for naught.

Ten minutes later I was in Lucas Leonard's office.

"What's going on?" I asked.

"Alex Trippitt was at work in Portland the day Summer Wycowski was killed. He even put in some overtime that Friday night. All verified by his boss and several of his co-workers as well. Boss says he's got initialed timecards to back it up. He's going to fax copies to me. Trippitt's lawyer is already up there taking depositions."

'You've got to be kidding."

"Do I look like I'm kidding?" Lucas said.

Since Portland was over a hundred miles north of Eugene, it was logistically impossible for Alex Trippitt to have been anywhere in the vicinity during the time frame of Summer Rain's murder.

"What about Miller?" I asked. "I can't see him acting alone. He doesn't seem together enough…maybe capable is the word…"

"The word you want is available. Capable is beside the point."

"Huh?"

"Elton Miller was in jail on a DUI, his third, by the way."

The poor bastard couldn't have known how lucky he was when he failed the breathalyzer test that night. What better alibi could anyone ask for than to be locked up in jail at the time the crime that he was accused of was committed?

Overnight, the nice tidy package that tied Alex Trippitt and Elton Miller to Summer Rain Wycowski's murder had unraveled. Both Trippitt and Miller had hired lawyers and in short order they had good, solid alibis that placed them far from the crime scene, DNA matches or no DNA matches.

None of which made a bit of sense to me, or to Detective Lucas Leonard, either. DNA matching was supposed to be foolproof. In recent years, the working assumption in law enforcement, and by extension in my line of work as well, was that if your DNA was at the scene of a crime, then you had been there, too, O.J. Simpson's 'trial of the century' notwithstanding. Witnesses could forget or lie, tape recordings and videos could be electronically altered and photos, especially digital images, could be photoshopped to 'prove' something that wasn't true. Virtually any evidence introduced into a court of law was potentially flawed, but DNA identification was offered to the public as the holy grail of proving innocence or guilt. Better than fingerprints, possibly better than retinal scanning.

Lucas was as flummoxed as I was. "This is the damnedest case I have ever seen. I have no motive, no opportunity, no means. I have DNA evidence linking two men to the crime who could not possibly have done it. You tell me, gumshoe, how can that be?" He stared out the window, shaking his head. Clearly, the foundation of law enforcement as he knew it was cracking. "How is this possible?"

"I wish I knew, amigo, I wish I knew."

"Let's talk about Winetrout and the blackmail video."

"OK, well, on the face of it, he'd be a prime suspect. Summer Rain's dancer friend at the Hot Body, Susan, claims the old man was having sex with her and Binky's video would appear to prove it. Summer Rain didn't want to rock the boat and give up the perks of living the good life, so whether it was legally consensual or not, she went along with it. She didn't exactly have a strong role model for making other choices. Even after Winetrout kicked Krista out, Summer Rain chose to stay in Eugene and not move to Portland with her mom."

"Go figure," Lucas said. "You'd think somebody besides Susan would have known if Winetrout was sexually abusing his stepdaughter."

"Not necessarily. Think about it, Luke. The only people who could have witnessed it first hand were Jimmy and the housekeeper, Consuelo. Jimmy owes his life to Winetrout; he'd be serving time in jail on an assault charge if it weren't for Winetrout's intervention. Come to think of it, Jimmy would be liable for statutory rape charges, too, except that the old man wasn't in any position to kick up a fuss. As for Consuelo, I get that frightened, caged animal sense about her. I'd bet a Franklin she's undocumented. With no green card and only marginal English, where's she going to go? Certainly not the police. Face it, neither of them is going to say a word."

"Hard to believe anyone would put up with the kind of abuse we saw on the flash drive just for some material gratification," Lucas said. "I want to take another look at that video. Maybe there's something we missed."

I felt queasy at the thought of watching Binky's fifty-seven second porn experiment again, but Lucas was insistent. "Your place or mine?"

"Funny. Very funny." Lucas slipped on his windbreaker and a Eugene Police Department baseball cap. "We'll go to your office."

Fifteen minutes later we were huddled around my monitor in silence, watching the video a third time. El Gato was curled up on my bed, oblivious. Where I wished I were.

"Freeze it right there," Lucas said. I paused the action and the detective squinted at the frozen image of Summer Rain's profiled face, squished against the tabletop, facing the camera. Her eyes looked directly into the lens. "Now, can you slow it down?"

I backed up the video and restarted it in slow motion.

"There, watch," Lucas said. "She knows they're being recorded. You see that thing she does with her mouth? That little smirk at the corners? I'd bet she set this whole thing up."

"Are we agreed that is Winetrout…" I struggled for the right word "…doing her?"

"You tell me, gumshoe. You've been out there and met him."

"Yeah, but I haven't been in the kitchen, which is where a table like that would be."

"We don't know that's where the video was taken," Lucas pointed out. He was a stickler for irrefutable factual evidence, which of course was why he was so dumbfounded about the DNA.

"OK, let's make some assumptions. Just for the sake of argument." I waited for him to agree.

"Assume away."

"Let's say that it is Charles Winetrout having sex with his stepdaughter. Let's say that she planned it all out and got her buddy Binky to video it."

"Go on, gumshoe, you're on a roll."

"Why would she want such a video? It's not Internet porn quality or length. You can buy better pornography for next to nothing at a dozen adult bookstores in Eugene or Springfield alone, plus everything there is on the Internet. Doubtful she intended to send it as an audition to a smut studio in California. There's only one other possibility; she wanted proof.

"Krista had moved to Portland and Summer didn't want to leave her gang of friends here. She figured she'd end up in the same line of work hustling like her mom. If she could prove her stepfather was raping her – and she was a sharp cookie, she would have known any sex with Winetrout would constitute rape – she could blackmail him."

"Makes sense, as far as it goes," Lucas said.

"As far as it goes?" I asked

"Somewhere along the line, something went wrong," Lucas said.

"Remember your rule, Luke. Ninety-nine percent of the time, the simplest explanation is the correct one. Summer Rain confronted her stepfather with the video and demanded money. Maybe Winetrout paid her once or twice, maybe not. Soon enough, he realized keeping the girl quiet would be an expensive lifetime commitment."

"And Binkelman kept a copy for his own insurance."

"That'd be my guess."

"That's a long way from a first-degree murder conviction." Lucas shook his head. "We'd need a lot more to go to court. Remember, Winetrout's face never appears in the video."

"That's true. Why do you suppose that is?" I asked.

"I'd have to see where it was made, see the angles through the window, you know, recreate the scene. It could just have been sloppy camera work on Binkelman's part."

"That I doubt, Luke. Binky's hobby was making short story videos. Susan told me that. If Winetrout's face was out of the field of view, it was on purpose."

"Maybe he was high on meth."

"Maybe he was playing both ends against the middle."

"You could get a search warrant and take a look around Winetrout's house."

"I could do that, maybe," Lucas said. "I'd need an idea of what I was looking for to get a judge issue a warrant. I couldn't go on a fishing expedition. Winetrout is pretty big in this town."

"Tell me about it. How about a Formica table with chrome legs and some BDSM paraphernalia?"

"Like whips?" Lucas asked.

"Like whips. Like a pair of handcuffs. Like a needle and black thread."

"Do we have any indication, anywhere along the line, that Winetrout had a mean streak?"

"I wouldn't describe him so much as mean as kinky," I said. "Other than his connection with the Hot Body Club and a prurient interest in watching other people fornicating. Winetrout may be a sleaze ball, but he's pretty much a vanilla-flavored sleaze ball."

"Sort of like you, gumshoe." Lucas grinned.

"I do it for a living, mi amigo, remember?" I said icily.

"Yeah, whatever."

"Before you show up with a warrant and a contingent of uniforms, I think I'll go out and have a look around myself." Lucas was beginning to piss me off. Something that happens in every friendship, I suppose, even in the best of times. And these were definitely not the best of times.

"Be careful, gumshoe, you may be tramping around a crime scene." Lucas' eyes drilled into me. "I know you aren't telling me everything you know and for now I'm going to let it ride. But don't press your luck."

"We do need to get out on the river, amigo," I said by way of a good bye.

CHAPTER TWENTY-THREE

Jimmy was hosing down the Hummer as I drove up the winding driveway to the Winetrout estate. The genteel atmosphere, the bucolic layout of trimmed hedge and freshly-mowed lawn, the austere mansion set against the cloudless blue sky, did not add up to a crime scene any more now than it had before. Nor was there any hint of the wild sex parties I'd been told about. The placid scene was all too wholesome and perfect. Maybe that was the problem.

The only thing disturbing the peace was the loud music. From inside the garage I could hear the rock opera *Jesus Christ, Superstar*.

"Hey, James." I had to shout over the blaring boom box. "I need to talk to you for a minute."

Jimmy scowled at me. "I told you I got nothing to say to you." He held the piston grip water sprayer like a gun. I would have laughed at the image if it weren't for the 'I'd-like-you-to-drop-dead' look on his face.

"Listen up, *James*," I shouted, "the cops are going to be out here sooner or later with a search warrant. My guess would be sooner. They're not going to play kissyface. I know you have Jesus in your corner now, but you still have a record from the good old days, am I right?" I waited for my words to sink in. "You might want to talk with me first."

The kid vacillated for a minute, looking nervously between the front door of the mansion and me. "OK, come in the garage. Do me a favor, OK? Park around the back. I don't want Mr. Winetrout to know you're here."

I drove my Cherokee behind the garage and gunned the engine a couple of times before I switched the key off. Jimmy turned down the boom box.

"So, what is it you wanna know about?"

"Summer Rain," I said. It took a minute for my eyes to adjust to the darkness. "Tell me more about your relationship with Summer

144

Rain Winetrout." The stink of gas and oil had replaced the sweet smell of freshly-cut grass.

"We didn't have no relationship. That girl was wicked."

"How do you mean, wicked? Be more specific."

"Look, Mr. Hunter, I told you all this before. I wasn't no angel. I used to lead an evil life. I used drugs and alcohol." Jimmy lowered his voice and looked at his boots. "I did sinful things with women."

"I know about all of that. I specifically want to know about you and Summer Rain."

"I used to be part of the bad crowd Summer runs – ran – with. There was me and her and some of the girls from the club and a crackhead named Binky and a few other guys. Some other people, too. Street people with no better place to go and nothing better to do."

"Summer Rain," I said. "What about her?" I had the distinct impression he was trying to avoid talking about her.

"The devil knows your weaknesses and puts temptation in your path."

"And by that you mean?"

"I truly believe in my soul she was sent to test my faith."

"How did you meet her? Did you know her before you started working here?"

"I used to hang out at a bar called the Hot Body Club. That place is a cesspool of sin. I guess I met her down there. I also knew her from the street."

"Tell me about the time you got into a hassle with the doorman at the Hot Body Club."

"You heard about that, huh?" Jimmy hung his head and combed his fingers through his hair and shook his head, as if he couldn't bring himself to speak about the incident out loud. "Things got kinda out of control that night," he mumbled. Then his head snapped up. "No, *things* didn't get out of control, *I* got out of control. I gotta take the responsibility for my actions."

"That's big of you, James. About Summer…"

"Taking responsibility is one of the rules of the program. Anyway, Mr. Winetrout turned me around. I came to realize I wasn't leading a righteous life. I quit hanging out with Summer and her friends. I stopped going to the club. I cleaned up my act and started going to meetings." Jimmy paused and clenched his teeth before he continued. "One day I was here in the garage, minding my own business, sharpening the mower blade, and Summer turns up. She was dressed real whore-like, not like a nice girl should dress." Jimmy's voice dropped an octave. "I swear to holy God, the devil sent her to tempt me."

"And you succumbed to temptation, right?"

"You gotta understand something, Mr. Hunter, living by the Lord's words is a new thing for me. I do fine so long as I'm not around sinful influences or if I can call my sponsor when I feel temptation. But there is no sponsor on God's green earth that can help you when someone like Summer comes around."

Time for a curve ball. "By the way, where do you meet God? "

"Huh?"

"What church do you go to?"

"The Church of Redemption. What difference does that make?"

"None really, just curious."

"I go to church every Sunday morning and Bible study every Wednesday night and we got men's groups two other nights."

"So you and Summer Rain," – I fumbled for the right words – "had sex here in the garage." I meant it as a question but it came out as a statement of fact. "Do you remember the date, James?"

"No. Look, Mr. Hunter, it's not something I'm particularly proud of. Not to mention I'd lose my job here if Mr. Winetrout found out."

"Not to mention you could go to prison. It's also statutory rape. Summer Rain was underage. You knew that, right?"

Jimmy sat on an overturned bucket and hung his head into his hands.

"Was that the only time, Jimmy? James?"

Jimmy was motionless and quiet.

"Time to take some responsibility," I prodded.

"No," he said finally. "There were a few other times."

"How many other times were there?"

Jimmy looked up at me. Tears blazed in his eyes. "That woman is Jezebel. That woman is evil."

"Maybe she just liked to mess with your head, Jimmy."

"I already told you before, call me James. I'm not Jimmy anymore. Jimmy was a bad person. Jimmy did bad things." James was shouting now. He stood up and stretched out his arms. The light from the window shone through his shaggy blonde hair. A thunderous baritone replaced the whiny tone of his voice. "I am James now."

"I'll try to remember that." I was dumbfounded at the transformation that had just taken place before my eyes.

"You better leave, now. If Mr. Winetrout sees you here, he'll get angry."

"Why is that, James? Why would Mr. Winetrout be angry if he saw me here?"

James lowered his arms but not his voice. "He doesn't like me talking to people. He says talking to strangers is what gets me into trouble."

"James, what was the beef with the bouncer at the Hot Body about?"

Jimmy narrowed his eyes and put his hands on his hips, defiantly. "If I tell you about that, will you go away and leave me alone?"

"Deal," I said. "If you promise to be truthful," I added.

"I do not lie. It was about Summer. She was at that place of sin that night. She shouldn't have been there because she's too young. Everybody knows her ID is fake but she gets in anyway on account of Mr. Winetrout owns the place."

"What happened?"

"Like I told you, Summer is wild. It was amateur night. That's a contest they do once a month where any girl can get up on stage and take her clothes off and do nasty things. There are cash prizes. The first place winner gets five hundred dollars."

"Let me guess. Summer Rain danced that night, right?"

"Summer was determined to win. It wasn't about the money – she's always had all the money she needed – it was about being the winner. See, what happens on amateur night is that some of the dancers from other clubs that have the night off come in. They try to mix in and pretend to be amateurs, but everybody knows who they are. They just want a chance to win the money. Anyway, I didn't want Summer to take her clothes off. I didn't think it was correct."

"So you tried to stop her?"

"The rule is that you can't touch the dancers. Putting her name on the list made her a dancer. When they called her name I grabbed her arm to keep her from going up on stage. That's when the fight started."

"That bouncer is a pretty big guy, a regular Goliath."

"The bigger they are, the harder they fall. I used to fight Taekwondo."

CHAPTER TWENTY-FOUR

Back in my trailer, I closed my eyes and tried to recall everything I knew about Charles Thurgood Winetrout, every contact I'd had with him as a landlord, as a person whose name appeared in the paper every so often and now as a client,. Was he simply an arrogant, blustery old guy with an impressive collection of perverted kinks – he was an admitted voyeur and he had almost certainly been having sex with his underage stepdaughter – or was there a murderous monster lurking beneath the sleazy surface? Where was the line between the two? Given what I knew about Summer Rain, that line for Winetrout could have been blurry.

I was creating a mental composite of Charles Winetrout, trying to fill in the blanks, when the phone jolted me back to reality. My screen read: EUGENE POLICE DEPARTMENT.

Lucas sounded grim but not dismayed. "The search warrant on Winetrout's mansion turned up nothing. No whips. No chains. Not even a needle and spool of black thread. There was a kitchen table with chrome legs, but I'd have to watch the video again to see if it matched up. There were no traces of duct tape on the legs. If Winetrout had anything to do with Summer Rain Wycowski's death, proving it isn't going to be very easy." He paused like he was waiting for me to say something, which I didn't. "At this point, I got maybe one out of three. Motivation. So far, no means. Opportunity's anybody's guess. Even motivation is weak."

"Any idea where Winetrout was the night Summer Rain was murdered?" I asked.

"He claims he was at his club, partying with the strippers."

"You believe him?"

"It's a soft alibi, gumshoe, everybody who can vouch for him also works for him. Not in the same league with Miller's and Trippitt's stories."

149

"I talked to a friend of hers, girl named Susan. She's another dancer at the Hot Body. Maybe I can find out something from her."

"I should bring her in and question her," Lucas said.

"I wouldn't do that, Luke. Let me talk with her. She's pretty down on cops. I doubt she'd say anything to you. If you freak her out, she'll clam up for sure."

Lucas treated me to one of his loaded silences. I could almost hear the wheels grinding on the other end of the line. "You could wear a wire."

"Not a good idea. I've built up a little trust with her and I don't want to take a chance on compromising it."

Lucas signed. "Whatever. But if Susan has any information, she'll end up testifying in court anyway."

"One step at a time, amigo, one step at a time. She hates Winetrout almost as much as she hates the police. If she knows anything that'll help us nail him, she's more likely to talk to me than to you."

"I'll be expecting to hear from you, gumshoe."

"I'll give her a call as soon as we hang up."

"Don't make me wait too long. You know how I hate waiting."

"Patience is an admirable characteristic of the successful angler, Detective."

"Right." Lucas slammed his phone down.

It was one-thirty in the afternoon. I took a chance that Susan would be awake. She answered on the third ring, a good sign.

"Susan? Jack Hunter here."

"Hey, good to hear your voice."

"Same here." I remember how she cried and crumpled in my arms after watching Binky's video.

"I'm wondering if I could meet you for a cup of coffee. Tea."

"Sure. I'd like that." Pause. "What about? I've told you everything I know."

"We're still trying to figure out who killed Summer Rain."

"I don't know what more I could tell you that would help with that, but for sure I'll meet you for a cup of Chai. I'd gladly do that for Rainy."

And for me, I wondered? "Same place as before? Dutch Brothers? Say two-thirty?"

"Yeah. That works for me."

I was half way through my triple mocha by the time Susan arrived.

"Sorry I'm late. It's still a little early for me."

"I didn't mean to get you out of bed before you were ready. I know you need your beauty rest."

"No sweat, I got shit to do before I go to work anyway." Susan fidgeted with a cigarette, but didn't light it.

"Susan, the police believe that Summer Rain was killed on Friday the tenth. That would make it about two weeks ago. Were you working that night?"

"I'm sure I was. I work every weekend. My regular days off are Wednesday and Thursday, but a couple of the girls quit and they haven't auditioned anyone new yet so sometimes I don't get those days off, neither."

"Do you remember if Charles Winetrout was in the club that night?"

Susan thought for a minute, her attention focused on her unlit cigarette, which she tapped against her thumbnail. "You know, this no smoking deal is fucked up. Who wants to have a cup of coffee or tea or a beer or anything without a cigarette?"

"Lots of people, apparently, or they wouldn't have passed the law."

Suddenly she straightened up and grimaced. "Oh, yeah, I do remember. He was in the club that night with some of his blubber buddies."

Blubber buddies? "Blubber buddies?"

"You know, fat old fuckers that can't get it up any more but like to eyeball naked girls anyway."

"See what they had for lunch." I remembered Susan's comment the first night I'd met her at the club.

"You got that right." Susan snickered. "The old letch was there hustling some girls for a party Saturday night."

"Did he ask you?"

151

"Hell no! He'd never ask me."

"Because…?"

"For one thing, he knew I was Rainy's friend. He knew I'd never go. Also, I'm too skinny for his taste. He likes big boobs, in case you haven't figured that out. I remember he asked Brittany to go."

"Brittany?"

"Oops, sorry. I shouldn't'a told you her real name. She goes by Montana. Henna hair with humongo hooters. She was working the night you came in." Susan giggled. "The girls call her the original brick shithouse."

"I'll bet she loves that."

"She's pretty good natured. You gotta be in this biz. Copping an attitude makes life miserable for everybody concerned."

"Do you know for sure if she was at Winetrout's mansion Saturday night?"

"I don't know, but I think so. She wasn't at the club so she was probably raking in the big bucks at the bastard's party."

"I'd like to talk to her. You think she'll talk to me?"

"I could ask her. Look, I gotta go outside for a smoke." Susan drained her Chai and bussed our cups back to the counter on her way out to the smoking deck.

"Hey Brit, it's me, Suze." Susan held her cigarette and cell phone in one hand and shut out the Seventh Street traffic noise with the other. The deck was close enough to our table that I was able to catch her side of the conversation. "Yeah. I'm talking to this guy who wants to talk to you." Pause and drag on cigarette. "No, no, no. He's OK, he's not a cop. He's a private eye looking into Sum—" Susan paused and looked at me. "Yeah, I trust him. Sorta. Don't ask me why." Another pause. "He's nice." Pause and giggle. "Don't you dare even ask me that! Not all of us are sluts!" More titters. "OK, I'm gonna give him your number. See you tonight. Bye." She flicked her half-smoked cigarette into the gutter and came back inside.

"I owe you one, Susan. Thanks."

"Nah, bullshit. You don't owe me nothing. We all of us loved Rainy."

"By the way, what were you laughing about?"

"That's for me to know and you to find out." Susan grinned. "Thanks for the tea. Gotta go."

I jotted down Brittany's number in my notebook, wondering what she might have to say and where it might lead me.

CHAPTER TWENTY-FIVE

I was getting nowhere fast in my search for Summer Rain Wycowski's killer. Or killers. I had to keep reminding myself that it wasn't really my responsibility at all. Once Summer Rain's body turned up floating in the Willamette River, it became a homicide investigation. The only reason I was still involved was Charles Winetrout's insistence that I work alongside the police, who were running into the same dead ends I was. I had no other investigations going on; the good citizens of Eugene seemed to be staying in their own beds, stemming the flow of Franklins in my direction. If Winetrout wanted to keep me on his tab and was willing to let me slide on the back rent as well, I was in no position to argue.

I had a few questions for Brittany. Perhaps she could shed some light on the tangled murder mess I was trying to unravel. We agreed to meet at Burrito Boy on West Eleventh. Burrito Boy is a Mexican taqueria open 'til midnight and it's a favorite alternative for the late night crowd to the fast food franchises that line the busy avenue. There are half a dozen or so Burrito Boys scattered around Eugene, which I suppose qualifies as a chain. Nonetheless, I like their food.

I was waiting at the order counter when Brittany strode through the door, glanced around, saw I was the only single man, and introduced herself. She was wearing blue jeans and a pink tee-shirt, both of which were a size or two too small, and pink ankle-high Converse sneakers over Hello Kitty socks. Her thick red hair was pulled back in a tight pony tail that stuck out through the opening in the back of her Oregon Ducks baseball cap. Her eyes were so green she had to have been wearing contacts. We both ordered the house specialty, chili verde wet burritos.

"Make mine spicy," Brittany said. "Mucho spiceo."

"Si. ¿Y para usted Señor?" the waitress asked.

I nodded. "Same same."

"To drink?"

"Agua," I said. I already knew what Burrito Boy's version of mucho spicy was like. Brittany ordered a large Coke. The waitress handed us thirty-two ounce paper cups and we filled them and sat down.

"Tell me about Summer Rain," I said.

"I didn't really know Summer all that well, so I doubt I'll be able to help you much. It was her and Susan who were buds."

"What do you know about Summer Rain and Charles Winetrout?"

"I suppose Susan already told you, he was doing her."

"That much I do know. I gather she didn't like it." Stupid observation on my part.

"Would you? Put yourself in her place. Your centerfold mom marries some ugly, fat over-the-hill dickhead for his money. He's twice her age, three times your age, and the old fart puts the make on you." Brittany stuck an index finger in her mouth and mimed puking.

"Sounds like a double whammy. Why didn't she do anything about it?"

"Like what? Get real. If she tells anyone, it's bye-bye gravy train."

"How about her mom? She could have gone to her."

"Oh sure, you bet." Brittany mimicked a little girl voice. "'Mommy, mommy, my new daddy is putting his peepee in my weewee!' Massive upheaval in the Winetrout household. Crystal and Summer move out or get booted out. Cops get involved, investigate, check out the old man, look at them, and guess what? Diddlysquat happens. Who's going to go after a mover and shaker like Charles Winetrout – cheesy titty bar owner or not – on the say so of his hooker trophy wife and her pierced and tatted mall rat daughter?" Brittany paused and took a deep breath and sipped her Coke. "Could be even worse. Say her mom doesn't believe her. The one person she loves and trusts pulls the rug out from under her. It's a no-win situation."

The waitress arrived with our order. I cut off a bite and swirled it in the verde sauce.

"You paint a bleak picture." My mouth was on fire.

"You want my personal opinion?"

"I'm buying lunch, aren't I?"

Brittany smiled and took a big mouthful of her burrito before she continued. "I think Crystal knew what was going on. She had to'ave." The spicy verde sauce didn't seem to have any effect on her.

"What makes you say that?"

"How could she not? Winetrout married Crystal 'cause she was a *HUSTLER* centerfold. That old fart is into porn, owns the Hot Body, hits on the dancers, has regular sexathons at his house, you name it. He let Summer dance at the club. Or made her dance is probably more like it. I don't know for sure, but I wouldn't put anything past that asshole. You think he wouldn't put the make on her? And a smart cookie like Crystal wouldn't notice?"

"Summer Rain was only sixteen," I said. "Jailbait."

"BFD. Winetrout's like every man I ever met: When he gets a hard on, he gets a brain drain at the same time. You know the old joke, right? God gave man a dick and a brain but not enough blood to run 'em both at the same time." Brittany forked another huge bite of wet burrito into her mouth, dripping a bit of sauce on her chin. She was a big girl with a big appetite and apparently a big capacity for spicy Mexican food. "That's Charlie Winetrout in a nutshell." She swabbed her mouth but missed the drip.

I took an oversized mouthful of my own chili verde and waited for the flames in my sinuses to die down. "Tell me about the parties," I croaked.

"The parties? Not much to tell. The old man likes to watch people having sex more than doing it himself. I was up there twice. I made a thousand dollars each time. Tax free. Hard to turn down that kind of cash. Sometimes I don't make that much in tips in a week dancing."

"I suppose I don't need to ask you what you were expected to do for that kind of money."

"Three guesses and first two don't count."

There was an awkward silence while I drank half a glass of water and watched her thick red lips work on her burrito. She licked a drip of verde sauce from the corner of her mouth. A rumble of thunder drew our attention to the plate glass windows facing Eleventh. Dark clouds had replaced the blue sky. It was only a matter of time before the rain would fall.

"Should have brought an umbrella," Brittany said. "I'll never get used to this weather."

"That's Oregon for you," I asked. "Do you know Alex Trippitt or Elton Miller?"

"Alex and Elton? Sure, I know 'em. They hang out at the Club and they were at one of the parties I worked at."

"What can you tell me about them?"

"Alex is full of himself. Elton is usually full of whiskey." Brittany grinned. "Alex is a good tipper, but he makes a girl earn it. Can't say the same for Elton. He's tight, in more ways than one."

"Was there anything going on between either of them and Summer Rain?"

Brittany looked at me like I had grown a second head. "You gotta be kidding. Alex had the hots for her, but he never, ever would have dared."

"What about Elton?"

"Summer isn't Elton's type."

"I had to ask. What can you tell me about James?"

By now, big, fat raindrops were dancing on the sidewalk.

"Jimmy? Now, there's a strange case. Used to be a more or less regular guy until he got born again. Now he's wound up so tight you think he's going to explode any second."

"I gather he and Summer were an item of sorts."

"An item? Not hardly. They never would have made a good match, even if they could have worked it out."

"Why's that?" I asked.

"Deep down, I think Summer liked Jimmy. She just never learned the right social skills. She didn't know how to deal with dudes other than physically. My guess is she learned everything she knows about men from her mom. You've met Crystal, haven't you?"

I nodded.

"Summer tried to get close to Jimmy, but the only way she knows how to relate was sexually. The only thing she offered him was her body and he hated himself for taking it. There was this hidden streak of honesty, or maybe morality is a better word, in Jimmy, even before his so-called conversion. Once he found Jesus, everything became black and white, right and wrong. No gray area, no middle ground. In the gospel according to Saint James, you're either a saint or a sinner."

"*So-called* conversion?"

"Jimmy's an emotional cripple. In my opinion, he just changed crutches."

"Anything else you can tell me?"

Brittany forked in the last dripping mouthful of chili verde and switched to a spoon and scraped up a few dabs of sauce and melted cheese. "Can't think of anything at the moment. By the way, speaking of items, tell me about you and Susan."

"Me and Susan? Nothing much to tell."

"Come on, guy, you can tell me. She and I are super tight."

"Then get her to tell you. And while you're at it, get her to tell me, too."

"That's all you got to say?"

"I like her. She's a nice girl," I said. "Why?"

"Oh, nothing, I just thought I heard something new in her voice the other night that wasn't there before. Probably just my imagination."

"Probably," I said. Had I missed something?

I'd eaten all I could. I stood up and took a card out of my wallet. "If you think of anything else, here's my number."

"Want me to say hi to her for you?"

"Sure," I said. I reconsidered for a nanosecond and added, "Thanks. I'd appreciate that."

"She will, too." Brittany winked and then returned her attention to the table. She looked at the uneaten remains of my burrito. "You gonna let that go to waste?"

"Have at it. I'm done."

"Cool. See ya around." Brittany grinned at me and switched plates. "Oh, yeah, thanks for lunch."

"No problemo," I said. I stopped at the self-serve fountain, refilled my water cup, snapped on a plastic lid, stabbed in a straw, and hurried through the rain to my car. I was stuck on 'She will, too'.

CHAPTER TWENTY-SIX

I got back to my trailer to find it nearly destroyed. Somebody had kicked in the door, which now hung by a single hinge, and wrecked the place. There was a greasy waffle-stomper boot print a good foot above the doorknob. My desk drawers were on the floor, the filing cabinet was overturned, papers and photographs littered the worn carpet, along with a tangled mass of wires, keyboard, video cam, and a mouse that had been my computer. It was difficult to tell if anything was missing, but I had a hunch.

There was no sign of El Gato.

My cell phone vibrated against my leg. It was Susan.

"Hey, Jack, I tried to call your home number but your line isn't working."

My land line had been ripped out of the wall and my phone was in the kitchen sink.

"Somebody broke into my trailer and trashed it. My phone is non-operational, along with everything else."

"Jesus! That's fucked up. I'm sorry to hear it."

"Yeah, it's going to take me a while to clean up and put things back together."

There was a pause during which I heard the scrape of a Bic lighter.

"How 'bout I come over and help you?"

Her offer caught me by surprise. "You don't have to do that. Don't you have to be at work?"

"They've got this girl on late shift and she has a couple of hours free."

"It'd be nice to see a friendly face." I surveyed the destruction around me.

"How about I bring you a cup of coffee? Would that help?" She asked. "Dutch Brothers double mocha, right?"

"Would it ever."

"I'm on my way."

Binky's flash drive was nowhere to be found. I regretted not following my instinct and sequestering it somewhere else. I called Lucas on my cell phone.

"Luke, somebody broke into my trailer. They completely ransacked the place."

"Are you calling to make an official report? I'll be there in half an hour."

"Not yet. Let's take this a step at a time."

"Can you tell if anything is missing? Is your weapon there?"

I checked the bedside drawer. My Glock was right where it was supposed to be.

"It's here. So far, the only thing I've noticed missing is the flash drive."

"Who knew you had it?" Lucas asked.

"You and I and Binkelman, but he's dead."

"That's it, gumshoe? No one else?"

I thought for a moment. "I played it for Susan. She told me Summer Rain intended to blackmail Winetrout."

"If Winetrout saw the video, that would be motivation," Lucas said.

"Maybe Binky kept a copy for himself before he sold the original to me," I said.

"I can't see Winetrout risking a breaking and entering bust."

"I agree. He would have gotten someone else to do his dirty work." It didn't take me long to come up with a likely candidate.

"You got any ideas, gumshoe?" Lucas asked. "And, by the way, why are we talking about this on the phone instead of my coming out there?"

"Just hang tight for now, Luke. I do have an idea. Winetrout has a kid working for him more or less full time."

"Go on."

"His name's Jimmy, or James as he prefers to be called. The story I heard is that he used to be a real badass until Winetrout stepped in and bailed him out of a nasty mess."

"Would he have crossed my radar?" Lucas asked.

161

"Possibly, but I don't know his last name."

"And you think he would have burglarized your place if Winetrout had told him to?"

"Not much doubt in my mind."

"Where do we find this James character?"

"*We* don't find him anywhere, Luke. I'm not ready to make an official report."

"So why are you calling me?"

"I'm going to have a chat with him. If you haven't heard from me by the end of the day, come looking for me." I heard a car squishing down my muddy alley. "I gotta go. Company."

I hung up without giving Lucas a chance to ask who. Susan's mud-spattered Jetta splashed to a stop outside my trailer.

"This is fucked up." Susan stood in the doorway holding a couple of steaming to-go cups, her attention focused on the boot print. I caught the same flicker of recognition in her eyes that I had seen the night in the Hot Body Club when I'd shown her Summer Rain's photo. "Somebody doesn't like you."

"Somebody who wears about a size twelve boot," I said.

"Yeah, I wonder who that could be." I could tell by her tone of voice that we had the same suspect in mind.

"A Grant says it's somebody who mows lawns and washes cars," I said.

"A Grant? That's all?" Susan was catching on.

I shrugged my shoulders.

"If you're thinking of Jimmy, you best be careful. That fucker has a hair trigger. It doesn't take much."

"Thanks for the warning," I said. "Hey, do me a favor, OK?"

"Like what?"

I got a tape measure and had her hold it up next to the boot print while I took a picture.

Susan and I spent the next two hours cleaning up my trailer, salvaging what could be saved and cramming the rest in garbage bags. When we were about done, I tried to jam the front door in a closed position, figuring I could use the back door until the front one was fixed, but the upper hinge was beyond hope. I nailed it shut as best I could. There were gaps around the edges.

"Lucky for me this dump has two doors," I said.

"You're gonna freeze your ass off tonight. No way you can keep this place warm." Susan stood in the middle of the room with her hands on her hips. "You better come and spend the night at my place. I don't want you freezing to death before you find out who killed my friend."

I cocked my head, trying to parse where she was coming from. Once you stripped away Charity's nakedness, the girl you found inside was smart, perceptive and complex. Maybe there had been something to Brittany's inquiry. In spite of my professional interest in relationships, I can be pretty dense when it comes to women. Something was going on, I just wasn't sure what. "That's a great offer. You sure?"

"I get off at two. I'll leave the key under the mat." Susan rooted around in my wastebasket, came up with an envelope, and wrote down her address, an apartment building on the west side of Eugene. "Apartment seven's off the street, on the inside of the horseshoe. You can park in any space that isn't like under a carport."

"Thanks," I said. "I appreciate it."

"You will." She grinned and gathered up her hat and coat. "This girl's gotta go and get ready for work. See you tonight. Late."

CHAPTER TWENTY-SEVEN

I awakened the next morning to a clear blue sky and a skinny girl snuggled against me. I had been half conscious when Susan came in, made herself a cup of tea while the bathtub filled, and then settled in for a soak. By the time she was done with her bath, I had already fallen asleep.

As gently as I could, I got out of bed and pulled the covers up to her ears. Susan smiled without opening her eyes, turned over, and started snoring.

I swung by my place and filled El Gato's food bowl with dry kibble. He was nowhere around. Maybe he was punishing me for spend the night out.

"Sorry, pal, the case isn't closed yet. Soon I hope," I said to his bowl.

As I drove out Willamette Street, I contemplated what approach I should take. My first choice would be to look around a bit before anyone knew I was there, but I doubted that would be possible, given the exposed layout of Fortress Winetrout. Most likely Jimmy would be engaged in one of his many outside chores and my arrival would be noticed long before I got halfway up the driveway. I had to wonder how deep Jimmy's dedication to Winetrout ran and if breaking and entering was all in a day's work for him. For that matter...

Jimmy was hosing down the very muddy Hummer when I arrived. He looked at my equally grimy Cherokee, scowled, and turned his back. I pulled up next to the Hummer and got out.

"You spend plenty of time washing that car, don't you?" I asked.

"It gets dirty on these roads around here."

I looked down the paved driveway that wove through the manicured lawn. Where all the mud came from was a mystery, but I said, "I can certainly understand that. My car gets the same way. In fact, if you've got time—"

"If you're looking for Mr. Winetrout, he's not out here." Jimmy concentrated his attention on the filthy Hummer, in no mood for humor.

"Actually, Jimmy, I came out to talk to you."

"It's James—"

"James, Jimmy, whatever. Somebody broke into my office and trashed the place."

Jimmy paused his scrubbing for a couple of seconds. It was exactly the pause I was looking for. "Ain't got nothing to do with me."

"I haven't made a report yet. I thought I'd do a little checking around myself before I got the cops involved. You know," I waited until Jimmy turned and faced me, "how they can be, poking around, checking leads, looking at records, and so on."

Jimmy shifted his weight from foot to foot. "You wanna talk to Mr. Winetrout, he's up at the house." Jimmy pointed up the walkway with his head.

"Fine. He's my last stop before I go to the cops. They'll be all over my trailer, looking for evidence, fingerprints, footprints, anything that might contain DNA. You remember the drill from the old days, right? Dusty as it is in my place, I'm sure they'll find more than they need. Shouldn't be hard to figure it out if whoever did it has a record. Any kind of record at all." I focused my attention on Jimmy's feet. "Kinda hot and wet to be wearing heavy boots, isn't it?"

"Man, you're sticking your nose into something you outta leave alone." For the first time since I'd gotten there, Jimmy looked directly into my face.

"You're probably right. If it was up to me, I'd turn the whole affair over to the police. They have a knack for figuring out things like who broke into my office, who raped and tortured and murdered Summer Rain, and so on. You better believe there are some sharp cookies down there."

Jimmy's ice-blue eyes bored into me like bullets, his mouth shut. I did my damnedest not to blink.

"Truth of the matter is," I said, "Mr. Winetrout himself asked me to stay on the case."

Jimmy fidgeted the hose sprayer from hand to hand and glanced up at the house. "Is that a fact," he said flatly.

"That is a fact, James. Anything occurs to you, you got my card." I climbed back into my Cherokee and gunned the engine.

"Hey," Jimmy shouted at me, "I thought you wanted to talk to Mr. Winetrout."

This time it was my turn to not say a word. In my rear view mirror, Jimmy stood staring at me until I lost sight of him around the first bend in the driveway.

I called Lucas as soon as I got back to what had been my office. There was still no sign of El Gato. I hoped he wasn't gone for good; the place wouldn't be the same without him.

"Well?" Lucas asked. I could tell by the tone of his voice that he was itching for me to file an official report about the break in. "Are you ready for me to make a visit?"

"Give it a little time, Luke. I'd bet a stack of Franklins Jimmy is our guy. I'm also sure there is a tie in between my office getting ransacked and Summer Rain's murder."

"You're not working on anything else at the moment?"

"No. Wish I were. I'm in way over my head."

"You sure nothing else besides the flash drive was stolen?"

"I didn't notice anything else missing yet."

"So, let me ask you something. Do you think Jimmy has it in him to kill someone? Could he have killed Summer?" Lucas asked.

"I'm not ready to go that far yet. I don't know how it all fits; I can't quite put it all together."

"There is the problem of the matching DNA."

"Something hinky is going on, but I'm not sure all the pieces are part of the same puzzle."

"OK," Lucas said, "I'm on my way over."

"Wait, Luke?" I started to tell him about the only thing I could find missing.

"Yeah?"

I paused for a moment. "The video... Never mind, nothing. See you in a few."

*

Detective Lucas Leonard stood in the debris that had been my office. "Whoever did this made a hell of a mess."

"Tell me about it."

"You're sure nothing else is missing?"

I hauled out my Glock and laid it on the desk. "Not as far as I can tell."

"How about money? Do you keep any cash around?"

"Parking meter change is about all." I picked up a plastic beer nut jar from the floor and shook the contents. Quarters and dimes and nickels rattled around. "Binky's flash drive is the only thing I can't find. And El Gato's gone."

"Did you make a copy?"

"I wish I had."

"Think of anyone who'd want that flash drive?"

"You mean besides Charles Winetrout?"

Lucas nodded.

"No, I can't." I said.

"Maybe I should go back to Winetrout's and do another search, now that I have something specific to look for."

"It's Saturday. The timing couldn't be better."

"How's that?" Lucas asked.

"Winetrout spends Saturdays at his club. It's a big night, so he's there all day and then closes up. The only one who should be in his house is the housekeeper, Consuelo."

"Latino?"

"Si. One hundred percent."

Lucas considered this for a moment. "Legal? Green card?"

I shook my head. "I don't know but a Lincoln says not. Winetrout seems to collect people who owe him."

Lucas turned to the ragged hole in the wall where the door had been ripped off its hinges. "I'll let you know if I find anything."

167

I grabbed my coat. "You don't think you're going out there without me, do you?"

"That's exactly what I think, gumshoe."

"There could be a lot of flash drives, amigo. Winetrout is into video porn. How are you going to identify Binky's if it is there? Sit and watch them all one at a time?"

Lucas considered this for a moment. "I hate it when you do this to me."

"Just trying to be helpful, Detective."

"Yeah, right." Lucas shook his head in resignation. "Come on, let's go."

I waited until we were well on the way. "Is this going to be an official visit or an unofficial visit?"

"Think about it, gumshoe." I was treated to one of Lucas' just-how-stupid-are-you looks. "Official. It's a multiple entry warrant. Any two-bit lawyer would get illegally seized evidence thrown out of court."

Just another reminder, as if I needed one, that I was out of my league.

CHAPTER TWENTY-EIGHT

When we got to Winetrout's mansion, Lucas drove right past Jimmy, who was scrubbing the gate, up to the front door. Consuelo opened the door and stood with her arms crossed blocking our way. "Señor Winetrout no esta aqui."

Lucas flashed his badge and offered her the search warrant, which was in English legalese and looked official. Consuelo's eyes got big, but she refused to step aside until Lucas reached for his handcuffs and demanded 'carte verde?' She paled and visibly cringed as he pushed past her into the foyer. Lucas tapped I-told-you-so on his forehead and gestured for me to lead him down the hall. We stopped at the door to Winetrout's office and Lucas produced two of pairs of blue rubber gloves.

"My fingerprints are probably all over the place already," I said. The latex pulled at the hair on the backs of my hands and fingers.

"Humor me," Lucas answered.

On the top of Winetrout's desk, a dead, half-smoked cigar lay in the ashtray next to a couple of stacks of legal documents. Like a sheriff in the old west checking the bad guys' campfire, Lucas touched the cigar with the backs of his fingers.

"Still warm," he said.

Half buried under a clutter of newspapers and magazines was a small HP laptop computer and a yellow, lined legal pad covered with figures. Lucas' eyes lingered for a moment on the framed *HUSTLER* cover before he picked it up for closer scrutiny.

"What's this all about?" Lucas asked.

"Winetrout's wife. Summer Rain's mom." I explained. "My prints are all over it."

"I'll bet they are."

"What's that supposed to mean?"

Lucas ignored my question and set the picture down and opened the top drawer. "See anything familiar?"

"Not yet."

The drawer of Winetrout's desk was a tangled mess of chargers, wires, headphones, DVDs, cassette tapes, flash drives on lanyards, condoms in wrappers, a cigar butt, and a coaster from the Club Paradise in Las Vegas with a phone number written on it. I gingerly poked around with a letter opener. Sure enough, in the back of the drawer, behind a filthy, wadded up handkerchief, I uncovered a 64 GIG SanDisc on a blue lanyard. It was identical to thousands of others sold at Staples and Office Max, but somehow, maybe because Winetrout had apparently tried to hide it, I knew it was Binky's.

"Hang on, don't touch it." Lucas took a couple of photos with a small digital camera. "You sure it's the right one?"

"I'd bet a Lincoln."

"Only a Lincoln? Not that sure, huh?"

"OK. I'll offer my friend Benjamin."

"Only one way to find out." Lucas booted up the desktop computer and plugged the flash drive into a USB port. The porn monitor on the opposite wall flickered to life. It only took a few seconds to confirm we'd found what we were looking for.

"I don't think I can stomach this again," I said.

"Thought this was your line of work, gumshoe," Lucas deadpanned. "Watching people engaged in the act."

"Consenting adults, Detective, consenting adults. Kids tied to tables and getting raped is your department."

Lucas ignored me, his eyes glued to the screen. "Now all we have to do is figure out how this flash drive got here."

"How about you leave that to me?"

"How about you tell me why every time I turn around, there you are telling me to butt out and let you look into it on your own?"

"Believe me, I'd gladly turn this whole screwed up mess over to you. I'd be the first to admit, it's way out of my league. You'll just have to trust me."

"Trust you? That's the part that scares me the most."

CHAPTER TWENTY-NINE

I'd driven by the Church of Redemption many times but never given it more than a cursory glance. It was in the heart of the Whiteaker, within staggering distance from Club 69 and the Hot Body Club. For a preacher on a mission to save sinners, it would be like fishing for hungry trout in a well-stocked pond. I looked up the number in the white pages to check the schedule of services. A recorded message introduced the lay pastor as one Brother Edward Beauchamp and invited anyone who wanted to know Jesus Christ through His words to attend a Bible study meeting any Wednesday night at seven. As luck would have it, it was Wednesday. I hoped James would be there.

I spent the afternoon putting my office back into some semblance of order. I had a creepy feeling that whoever had ransacked my trailer had been motivated by more than a search for Binky's video. The logical place for a flash drive was my desk, but the whole office looked like a hurricane had hit it. Whoever had done it had been vindictive, even enraged. By late afternoon, I'd done all I could for the time being. My garbage can overflowed with broken glass and crockery, a couple of shredded pillows, the smashed remains of my old monitor, and other destroyed stuff. None of it was worth much, but some of it had meant something to me and it would all have to be replaced. I wondered if the kid from the Geek Squad who had helped me a couple of times with computer problems would be able to salvage my hard drive. Most of it was backed up, but I'd been lazy lately.

There was still no sign of El Gato. He's like me. He hates violence.

I took a quick shower, dressed in a worn but clean shirt and my best pair of Levi's, and headed downtown.

Sandwiched between Rasta's pub and a school for prospective glass blowers, The Church of Redemption turned out to be a dilapidated house that had been reincarnated as a makeshift place of worship. A carved wooden sign in the small, neatly trimmed front yard displayed the church's name and its motto:

JESUS SAVES
ANYONE
ANYTIME

Jimmy's Ford pickup was parked in the gravel parking lot next to a collection of shopping carts overloaded with stuffed garbage sacks and worn out bicycles attached to ramshackle trailers. I parked a few yards away and glanced in the bed, not knowing what I was looking for but finding it empty anyway. On a hunch, I jotted down Jimmy's license plate number, something I should have done the first time I went out to Winetrout's.

A wooden wheelchair ramp, paved with asphalt roof shingles, switchbacked up to the front door. I chose the steps instead and stepped quietly inside.

Two large windows flanked the single door. One cracked window had been repaired with strips of duct tape. Hanging over the other window was a stained glass cross in vivid red, yellow, and gold that filtered what remained of the late afternoon sunlight. This time of day the cross would've looked better outside with the inside light shining through it than vice versa. Three large bare-bulb fixtures with cobwebbed mesh grates, the kind you might find in a rural high school gym, lighted the single room. A couple of dozen scratched, mismatched folding metal chairs were arranged in semi-circles around a scuffed wooden podium in the center. About half of the seats were occupied by a variety of leathery, weathered-looking souls. Many of the men were unshaven and most of the people looked and smelled like they lived on the street. A few had bedrolls stuffed under their chairs or perched on the seats next to them. Everyone was clutching a Bible and Bibles waited on the unoccupied chairs. The study group was already underway and heads turned when I entered. A large, pony-tailed man wearing black pants, a black turtle neck shirt, and a shiny silver cross on a shiny silver chain around his neck looked up and smiled.

"Welcome to the House of the Lord, brother. I am Brother Edward. Please take a seat and join us. We are in Romans." I recognized the voice from the message machine.

I looked around until I found Jimmy sitting in the front row off to one side. I took the empty seat next to him. The Bible felt heavy and unfamiliar. It had been a while.

Jimmy stiffened when I sat down. "What are you doing here?" He hissed, looking straight ahead.

"*'For the wages of sin is death, but the free gift of God is eternal life in Jesus Christ our Lord.'*" Speaking from memory, Brother Edward looked out over his motley flock. "Six twenty-three. Think for a moment and reflect upon what that passage means."

"Same thing you are, James. Seeking salvation. And forgiveness." I kept my voice as low as I could.

Jimmy locked his lips and turned his attention back to his Bible.

"You *are* seeking forgiveness, aren't you?" I whispered.

"You got no business being here. I told you to leave me alone."

"Why James, that's most unchristian of you. I was under the impression that the House of the Lord was open to all."

Brother Edward's voice boomed over the congregation. "'All *have sinned and fall short of the glory of God.*'" He paused and lowered his voice to room volume. "What is the Bible saying here in three twenty-three?" He paused for a moment, but when no explanation was offered by the congregation, he continued. "As I read it, the Bible says nobody is completely free from sin, but all are within sight of the glory of God. It does not say you are *beyond* the glory of God, only that you *fall short* of the glory of God. God will meet you halfway, but you have to take the first steps toward Him. There is hope for each and every one of us, if we look deep into our hearts and renounce sin." His voice had the cadence and solemnity of a late night AM radio preacher.

As if on cue, a chorus of mumbled amens reverberated around the room.

"What about you, James? You got anything to confess?" I asked in a stage whisper.

"Leave me alone."

173

"How about you and Summer Rain? You made that right with the Lord yet?"

Jimmy sat expressionless, like a block of rock.

"For the Scripture says, '*Everyone who believes in Him will not be put to shame.*'" Brother Edward was preaching right up my alley.

"When was the last time you saw Summer Rain, James?"

"She was evil. She was Satan." James' teeth were clenched as tight as a kid at the dentist.

"How's that?" I whispered. Suddenly I was aware that the nearest worshippers were paying more attention to us than to their Bibles or Brother Edward. I could feel the tension rising.

"Satan sent Summer to take me to Hell." Now Jimmy's teeth were chattering or grinding, I couldn't tell which. The veins in his neck were rigid with fury.

"That's not quite right, James," I said quietly. "You took yourself to Hell. On Friday the tenth."

"No." The kid was scared shitless, tense, trembling, ghostly pale. His knuckles were white. His hands were shaking so badly I thought he might drop his holy book to the floor. The image of David and Goliath came to mind. It was hard to believe this was the same scrapper who'd taken down a titty bar bouncer twice his size.

"You got my card. You know how to get in touch with me." I stood up and leaned down to Jimmy's ear and stage whispered, "Think about it, James. What would Jesus do?" By then we had the full attention of everyone in the room. You could have heard a pin drop. Or the cock of a Glock.

I paused at the door and surveyed the still room behind me. Jimmy looked like a powder keg about to blow. Even Brother Edward Beauchamp was silent. Something was missing, though, some small detail that was conspicuous by its absence. At first, I couldn't put my finger on it, but as I closed the door behind me, I realized what it was; there was no collection plate. A mystery for another day.

Two tall, skinny girls with big hair and fishnetted legs up to here tottered by on platform heels down the uneven, cracked sidewalk in the direction of the clubs. A month ago, one of them might have been Summer Rain Wycowski. How fragile it all is.

My confrontation with James had left me tenser than I cared to admit and I figured an IPA would settle me down so I followed the girls. I knew where they were going. I hoped Susan wouldn't mind my patronage.

CHAPTER THIRTY

It was past ten and three Ninkasis later when I left the Hot Body Club, my ears ringing from the music. Funny how sometimes high decibel noise can calm me down and quiet solitude can boost my tension level. Of course, the IPAs could have had something to do with it. Susan had the night off, which was disappointing. There wasn't anything in particular I needed to ask her, but it would have been nice to chat with her anyway, even if it was under the auspices of table dances.

The picture was still fuzzy, but pieces of the puzzle were beginning to fall into place. I couldn't wait until the next morning, so I took a chance and called Lucas on his cell phone.

"What have you got on what passes for your mind that can't wait until tomorrow, gumshoe?" Lucas sounded grumpy, not unreasonable given the hour. He's a morning person, something I learned long ago on our occasional fishing trips: By the time I crawl out of my tent, Lucas will already be laying his double taper across the ripples.

"I think I may have something. About Summer Rain's murder. Can you meet me at your office?"

"Now?"

"Yeah, now."

"Thirty minutes. This better be good."

"Less than that. I'm in the Whiteaker."

On my way over to the police station, I picked up a double mocha and a tall Americano at Dutch Brothers. I wanted Lucas wide awake.

I told him about my encounter with James Sundquist at the Church of Redemption and how wound up he appeared. Lucas ran Jimmy's plate number through the Department of Motor Vehicles database and brought up his driving record, an inquiry we should have made long before. Jimmy's record featured two speeding violations and a DUI. Then he entered Jimmy's full name – James Robert Sundquist – into the criminal records department. Not surprisingly, Jimmy had quite a history of misbehavior that had attracted the attention of law enforcement in whatever jurisdiction he happened to be. Most of his offenses involved minor drug possession or disorderly conduct confrontations of one kind or another. The sole felony on his record – a year-old aggravated assault arrest – had not been prosecuted for lack of evidence. Lane County is in a perennial budget crisis and the DA, who wants to get reelected and is eager to bolster his conviction rate, pursues only slam-dunks. I could see where Jimmy's legal tether had about run out, though, and why Charles Winetrout's offer was one he would have been a fool to refuse.

"I wonder what he was doing Friday the tenth," Lucas said.

"Why don't you ask him?" I said. "And while you're at it, why don't you ask him where he was yesterday about the time my office was trashed?"

"I'll be sure and do that, gumshoe. Let's back up for a minute, first. Connect Sundquist and Summer for me."

"James, or Jimmy as he was known in the old days, ran with the same gang of mall rats as Summer Rain. They were casual lovers." I thought about that for a minute. "No, casual lovers isn't exactly right. Jimmy had a thing for Summer Rain that went beyond sex, or rather wasn't so much about sex. What got his ball rolling toward Christ was a fight with the bouncer at the Hot Body Club, which started when he tried to prevent her from stripping in an amateur night contest. From what I heard, it turned into quite a brawl."

Lucas narrowed his eyes. "When was this? It never crossed my desk."

"It wouldn't have, Luke. You're homicide and nobody got killed." It gave me a little inner bump to one up Lucas for a change. Doesn't happen often. "Besides, the fight never made it past the door. Winetrout hushed it up."

"How'd he manage that?"

"It probably wasn't that difficult. He gave Jimmy a choice. Straighten up and fly right or he'd press charges. Given his record,

Jimmy probably would have spent some time in jail. As for the bouncer, getting banged up once in a while is part of the job description."

"And now Jimmy works for Winetrout as well." Lucas made it a statement rather than a question.

"No doubt part of the deal. Jimmy owes Winetrout big time, if you ask me."

"I'll tell you something, gumshoe, the more I learn about Charles Winetrout, the less I like him."

I just nodded. I didn't like Winetrout much, either, but I was in the unenviable position of having the old bastard as both my landlord and a client. "You know, amigo, we need to get out and get our lines wet. It's been a while."

Lucas swiveled his chair and looked wistfully at the dusty Orvis in the corner. "Yeah. Too long."

CHAPTER THIRTY-ONE

I stood on a narrow peninsula of soggy soil that jutted into a bend of the McKenzie River, laying my double-taper line upstream across the water, waiting patiently for a hungry steelhead to rise as my hand-tied leech fly floated past me in the brisk current. A light rain, more of a heavy mist, beaded on my hat and dripped down the back of my neck. It was a perfect time to be fishing; winter had not yet dumped enough snow to survive the still-warm afternoons and the river was beginning to swell with cool runoff, cold enough to entice the fish upriver to spawn. This secluded spot – not unlike the bend in the Willamette where Summer Rain's body had been dumped – was a favorite of mine. The only other person I'd ever brought here besides Lucas was my ex-wife and my now infrequent visits always provoked bittersweet memories of our early love and then our collapsed marriage. I hadn't wanted to be with anyone since. I thought of Susan and wondered idly if she would find it as beautiful as I did. I wondered if she even liked to fish.

A scattering of beer cans, cigarette butts and tangles of discarded monofilament line indicated that I shared my not-so-secret getaway with other anglers. It was one of the few places I knew where I had a reasonable chance of hooking a steelie from the bank without having to suit up in my waders and get in the water. Close to town, it was a good spur-of-the-moment fishing hole, although this time I'd come here as much to sort through what I knew about Summer Rain Wycowski's murder as to fish. Thankfully, I was alone.

Summer Rain's death was the most baffling, not to mention gruesome, case I had ever investigated. That's not saying much since my niche market consists primarily of cheaters; wayward men and women who stray over the matrimonial fence in the timeless quest for greener pastures and lusher valleys. Catching people cheating on their spouses may not be the best of professions, but it would take a sizeable stack of Franklins for me to change places with Detective Lucas Leonard of the Eugene Police Department Homicide Division.

There is a world of difference between looking for a rebellious runaway kid somewhere on the streets, a situation reasonably close to my narrow field of expertise, and discovering a mutilated corpse floating in a river. Murder is a police matter, the bailiwick of very competent cops like Lucas. I had reluctantly succumbed to Charles Winetrout's demand that I locate his step-daughter because at the time he hired me she was only missing, plus I hadn't yet realized that he wasn't her real father. Beyond that, I had my own admittedly selfish interests to consider as well. With nothing happening under the big tent of the illicit flesh circus, tracking down Summer had promised to not only provide me with some much needed cash but also to get me off the hook on my delinquent rent. At least temporarily. I knew I'd have to wrestle with the ethical ambiguities sometime in the future, but for now, how could I turn the old man down?

Suddenly the leech disappeared in a quick flash of silver, jerking me back to reality. The line tightened and zipped upstream. My Orvis bent double and my reel screeched as the angry fish charged away from the bank into the current. Patiently, I played the steelie, keeping just enough tension on the line to let him know I was there. He gained a few feet; I won back a few inches. We tugged back and forth for several minutes, my attention riveted on the opaque water, waiting for the shiny fish to surface. Gradually, as he wore himself out, the ratio changed and I began retrieving more line than I was yielding. Soon I'd coaxed the exhausted steelhead near enough to glimpse him. He was big, beautiful, at least ten pounds. I worked him closer and closer to the shallow, pebbly edge of the river and reached for my landing net.

"Cut him a little slack. You're going to snap your line."

I jumped at the sound of Lucas' voice. I had been so deeply engrossed in landing the writhing steelhead I hadn't heard him creep up behind me and I involuntarily jerked my pole. The line snapped back and went limp across my shoulder.

"Damnit. Now look what you did."

"Sorry about that. I didn't mean to startle you."

"Well, you did." I was pissed. This was my private Idaho and I didn't appreciate having it invaded, even by my fishing buddy Lucas Leonard. He couldn't have timed his arrival any worse. How long had he been standing there?

"Besides ruining my day, what are you doing out here?" I busied myself choosing another fly, waiting for Lucas to go on or go away, preferably the latter. It was sprinkling a little harder now, but he didn't seem to notice. Raindrops dimpled the river. Somewhere in the cold water my steelhead was swimming around, trailing a few feet of monofilament leader. How could all his buddies not fail to notice this and lose their appetites?

"James Sundquist is our guy. His DNA came back a positive match for the baby Summer Rain Wycowski was carrying."

"That fits. Now you have evidence tied to a suspect. I guess that lets Winetrout off the hook."

"Not quite yet. We got some other new evidence you're gonna love. The forensics guys found something interesting in Winetrout's garbage."

"And that would be…?" At the moment, I couldn't imagine anything in Charles Winetrout's garbage that would be worthy of my love. I wanted my solitude back.

"Two used condoms. Buried in the trash."

"I'm shocked, shocked, I tell you. Used rubbers in Charles Winetrout's garbage. What is this world coming to?" I wanted Lucas to go away and leave me alone and I told him so.

"These particular condoms had been used but they contained less than half a cc of, um, contents each. Not only that, they'd been carefully rolled up and stuffed back into their packets."

Now he was getting my attention. I stopped tying on the fly. "Gross." How did they know this? Who measured it? Why?

"That's not all. There were letters written with a black sharpie on the packets. 'AT' on one and 'EM' on the other."

It didn't take me long to decipher the initials. "Alex Trippitt and Elton Miller."

"My conclusion exactly."

"I'll bet you that trip on the Rogue the forensics geeks went nuts."

"Oh, yeah," Lucas said. "They had a field day. There was trace vaginal fluid on the EM condom and flecks of fecal matter on the AT one."

That was enough to snap me, however reluctantly, the rest of the way back from an idyllic afternoon of fishing to the matter at hand. The disgust factor was ratcheting up fast. I digested Lucas' information, trying to mesh it in with everything else I would have preferred not to know. I didn't feel like fishing any more, so I started packing my gear. "OK, you got my interest. Let's go grab a cup of coffee."

"Dutch Brothers on Seventh? Still your favorite place?" Lucas asked.

"Let's do VERO on Pearl. The back room there's a little more private." The steelies would have to wait for another day.

"I'll meet you there shortly." Lucas hesitated for a moment. "I'm sorry I…" he mumbled something to himself, perhaps reconsidering whatever he was about to say and then he retreated up the trail to his car without finishing.

It didn't matter; there was plenty to be sorry about.

*

Forty-five minutes later, the two of us were hunched over a couple of excellent coffees. I'd ordered a five-dollar Borgia, knowing that the Eugene Police Department would be picking up the tab to atone for the lost steelhead. Lucas drank the house blend, black. As long as I've known him, I've never been able to get him to explore anything beyond the basic cuppa Joe. I've given up trying. We were lucky to get a table; the place was full of students nursing lattes and enjoying the free Internet on their laptops. How the coffee shop stays in business with a clientele of slackers is a mystery to me.

"Let's brainstorm this from the beginning," Lucas said. "We're off the record here, understood?"

I nodded, "Aren't we always?" The one that got away was already fading from my memory.

"Sleazebag Charles Winetrout marries *HUSTLER* centerfold Krista Wycowski, who brings to their volatile union not only her own special charms, but a precocious teenage daughter, Summer Rain. Said daughter's what, fourteen, fifteen, going on twenty-four? Before long, Winetrout, being the letch that he is, is having sex with both mother and daughter."

"So far so good." The barista had painted an evergreen tree in the frothy milk and for the moment I preferred to look at it rather than spoil the artwork. One of the conundrums you're faced with in better coffee houses.

Lucas frowned. "Not exactly how I'd phrase it."

"Sorry, amigo," I said. "Lousy choice of words."

"How does the guy keep Summer from blowing the whistle? In the time-honored tradition of pedopapas everywhere, Winetrout showers the child with bling and cash. Remember the upscale cell phone? Tattoos aren't cheap, either, and the money for them had to come from somewhere. Not only that, but he allows her hang out and even perform at the Hot Body Club, a strip joint he conveniently owns."

"I'm with you so far." I gave in and sipped my Borgia and sucked the sweet creamy foam mustache along with a piece of orange zest off my lip. Lucas didn't know what he was missing. "Do you suppose that poor girl ever had a childhood?" I asked.

Lucas ignored my question. "You have to wonder, besides the toys and the cash, why does Summer put up with it?"

I took another sip of my coffee to avoid answering. I wanted to hear Lucas' take first. He wasn't having it.

"Well?" He asked.

"Here's what I think, based on what little I know," I said. "Up to that point in her young life, Summer Rain Wycowski has not had it easy. Her mom is on the game, struggling to make ends meet working the sex trade. We don't even know who her father is or was, right?"

Lucas shook his head.

"Could have been a relationship or even a marriage. Then, too, Summer Rain's biological father could have been one of Krista's johns. She may not even know herself who he was."

"Not relevant," Lucas said. "Go on."

"No, not at this point, anyway. But it does help paint a sad portrait of a throwaway kid. At any rate, one day her mom somehow gets discovered by none other than Larry Flynt and parlays centerfold status into a marriage with a rich big shot. Life in Oregon is good. No more hustling. Everything is peachy-keen, until something upsets the delicate balance. Maybe Krista finds out her sugar daddy is screwing her daughter and raises holy hell. Maybe Winetrout goes too far over the top. Maybe Summer Rain just gets disgusted with the whole arrangement. For whatever reason, the chemistry changes."

"Plausible," Lucas said, adding, "So far."

"Don't forget, for Summer Rain sex wasn't something she did for fun or enjoyment. It was a game. A tool to manipulate men. She'd learned what she knew from her mother." My conversations with Susan were swirling around in my head, along with vivid memories of my encounters with James and Krista.

Lucas Leonard sat quietly, taking in everything I said, nodding in agreement.

"So," I continued, "Summer Rain is no dumb bunny. She knows if she blows the whistle on Winetrout, there'll be one hell of an explosion. Even if she keeps her own mouth shut, sooner or later someone's going to figure out what's going on in the big house on the hill. I can tell you from experience, sexual shenanigans always have a way of coming to light, no matter how much the people involved try to hide them. However it's going to happen, it will happen, and when it does, it'll be bad news for our material girl."

I paused, waiting for Lucas to contribute his opinion. It was a long wait.

"So, what's your take? You make her out to be a manipulative vixen or an immature victim?" I asked.

"What's the difference? As far as the law is concerned, Summer Rain Wycowski is a minor. No amount of tattoos or makeup or hairspray makes her legal," Lucas said.

"Of course not. I was only curious about your personal impression." I'd already gone down this path myself and it was reassuring that Lucas was connecting the same dots with the same line. "So Summer ups the ante, decides to tip the scales in her favor."

Lucas nodded, still not smiling, still not saying much.

"Little Summer Rain Wycowski comes up with the brilliant scheme of blackmailing big, bad, rich Charles Winetrout. Never mind fancy cell phones and baubles and ink and whatnot. She perceives a way to get her hands on some serious cash. All she's gotta do is—"

"Enter the late Marcus Binkelman." Lucas interrupted.

"Exactly. Binkelman is handy with his camcorder. If Summer Rain can get video proof that the old man is forcing her to have sex with him, then she has all the marbles. So she sets up a particularly brutish encounter and hides Binky in the shrubbery outside to record it."

"You have to wonder how he got all the way out there, through the gate, and buried in the bushes without being seen."

"Hold that thought. I gotta use the restroom," I said, standing up.

I didn't really have to take a leak. What I wanted was a minute or two to think this through so I wouldn't be that far behind Lucas. Somehow, I could not get my head around Charles Winetrout committing murder, even to cover up a rape. And then there was the glaring inconsistency that he had hired me to find her. Had Winetrout really believed he could somehow plant evidence that would convict someone else without the truth being discovered? Did he really think that by hiring a private detective he would somehow be automatically exempt from suspicion? There were still too many loose ends for me to fathom. When I got back to the table, Lucas was working on a fresh cup of coffee.

"You really ought to try one of their lattes or cappuccinos," I said.

Lucas took up where he'd left off as if I hadn't moved.

"The story gets simple for a while. Summer confronts Winetrout with the video and demands cash. He pays her off. Once, maybe twice. It doesn't take long for him to realize there'll be no end to her demands. She's a ticking time bomb, just waiting to blow his life apart. One way or the other, she has to be shut up. Permanently."

Lucas paused and stirred his black coffee. It's an odd habit of his. I don't know why he bothers.

"All he has to do is devise a scheme that accomplishes the purpose without getting his own hands dirty and, hopefully, points somewhere else."

"Like to Elton Miller and Alex Trippitt?" I said.

"I don't think he planned that part to begin with. A lucky coincidence. Things just conveniently fell into place."

CHAPTER THIRTY-TWO

It was late afternoon by the time I got back to my trashed trailer. The light rain had matured into a full-blown storm and my driveway was a slick, muddy mess. Being a vintage single wide, the trailer didn't have the luxury of a mud room at either the front door, now hanging by a single hinge, or the back door. I took my boots off on the cinderblock porch before I went inside; no sense making the disaster any worse.

El Gato was still nowhere to be found and that had me worried. Whoever had broken in and ransacked the place had frightened the daylights out of the poor guy. It wasn't like him to stay outside in the rain and the storm was getting worse. I was tired and lay down for a nap but I couldn't sleep. In my mind, I kept coming back to Jimmy and Winetrout, struggling to make it all add up. Had Jimmy wanted Summer Rain dead because he perceived her as too great a temptation from his chosen path or had Charles Winetrout persuaded him to kill her? It made a kind of strange, twisted sense that depended on several premises: Summer Rain wanted to blackmail her stepfather and had conspired with Marcus Binkelman to video him raping her. The old man was smart enough to realize once he started down the blackmail trail there would be no turning back; it would only get worse and more costly. Technically, Oregon still has the death penalty on the books, but it's been over ten years since anyone has been executed and the governor has declared that there will be no executions on his watch. Winetrout likely rationalized the law couldn't do an awful lot more to him for killing Summer Rain than for raping and sodomizing her. And then there was the question of who had impregnated her.

The catch was that Winetrout would have to engineer Summer Rain's death while hiding his own involvement. If he could manage that, he could conceivably survive. The odds were against him, of course. Prisons are packed with killers who believed they had

187

committed the perfect crime, only to get tripped up by some small detail later. But he did have a useful tool in Jimmy.

James Sundquist had acquired a reformed sinner's heightened level of religious fervor; only a compass needle that has been stuck for a long time at due south can swing with such ferocity one-hundred-eighty degrees to the north. Furthermore, Jimmy owed Winetrout, his new-found benefactor, a huge debt of gratitude for keeping him out of jail and giving him a job.

Finally, I heard the cat door snap shut and a moment later my water-logged, orange tabby hopped on the bed and began licking himself dry. It was going to take a while. With El Gato home at last, his motor running at a fast idle, I was able to doze off.

CHAPTER THIRTY-THREE

El Gato woke me up just after eight the next morning kneading dough on my chest and meowing. Like Lucas, he was an early riser. If I'd remembered to leave food out for him, he might have let me sleep in. As it was, I'd been out cold for almost fourteen hours.

"Hey, fella, you hungry?" I grumbled, stretching as I got out of bed.

El Gato jumped down and bee-lined into the kitchen, his tail extended straight up like a dune buggy whip and his slack belly swinging side to side as if to illustrate his hunger pangs. Just in case I hadn't gotten the message, he batted at his empty food dish with his paw.

I scooped some kibble into his bowl, topped off his water, and flopped back under the covers to contemplate my next move. "So, Gato, where do we go from here?"

El Gato was too busy chowing down to pay any attention to me. Other than passing judgment on everyone who comes into my trailer, he isn't much help, anyway.

My mind churned with possibilities. I thought I had all the clues, but like a thousand-piece jigsaw puzzle, I couldn't get inside past the edge. The outline was in place but I couldn't position the interior pieces. Maybe some were missing. Maybe some were from another puzzle. Perhaps it was time for another chat with Jimmy. As much as I don't trust gut feelings, mine told me James Sundquist held the key to the mystery.

I forced myself out of bed again and got dressed. I debated – briefly – whether or not to take my Glock. Other than the time I emptied a couple of clips at a bull's eye target out in the woods shortly after I'd bought the weapon, just to see what firing it felt like, I've never pulled the trigger. None of my shots had been within the concentric circles and some had missed the target entirely. My lack of marksmanship had reaffirmed my conviction that shooting a

189

gun was the least desirable way of resolving any issue whatsoever. I finally gave in. If Jimmy was capable of murder, it would be better to have my Glock and not need it than the other way around.

For the umpteenth time, I wished I'd left Summer Rain's murder in the capable hands of Lucas Leonard and Eugene's finest. The minute her body had turned up floating like a spawned-out salmon in the Willamette River, I should have ended my involvement. Ironically, though, Winetrout had been right: There were places I could go and questions I could ask that would be off limits to the police. I couldn't imagine Lucas having a beer with Susan in the Hot Body Club, for example. It wasn't a position I wanted to be in, but there I was, anyway.

I stopped for a triple mocha on my way out Willamette Street, which was covered with maple leaves, fir needles, and small branches. The wind storm had stripped the deciduous trees bare and uprooted a sizeable fir that now partially blocked the road. A city road crew, decked in hard hats and fluorescent raingear, was flagging traffic into a single lane. Another worker, covered with wet sawdust, was attacking the fallen tree with a chainsaw. It was still early and I was counting on Jimmy being asleep. Finally the flagger turned his stand-up sign around from 'STOP' to 'SLOW' and the southbound lane started moving. I was on my way, but to what, I had no idea.

A post-storm fog had settled into the forest around the south side of Eugene and I nearly missed Winetrout's driveway. I punched in the code and the massive gates guarding the estate swung open in the gloom. As I drove slowly up the winding driveway, I could barely make out the outlines of the mansion. The garage with Jimmy's apartment came into focus as I got closer. I killed the engine and sat for a minute or two sizing up the scene.

There were drawn curtains over the apartment's windows, but the lights were on and I thought I saw a shadow cross the room. I could have been mistaken. Jimmy's truck was parked in its usual space, but I didn't see the born-again Christian anywhere. Time to move.

"James?" I called out as I rapped on his door. "James, you in there?" I felt hyper-vigilant, adrenaline rushing through my veins, my senses sharpened to the slightest provocation.

There was no response. I couldn't imagine where he would have gone on foot, but if he was home, he wasn't answering the door. Maybe he was outside, lying in wait. If Jimmy had killed Summer Rain he was obviously capable of anything.

I thought I heard a twig snap. I spun around, ready for an attack, but there was nobody there. I was way too jumpy. I closed my eyes and slowed my breathing and then I crept around the side of the hedge toward Jimmy's truck as far as I dared. My feet sounded like a backhoe in a gravel pit. Still, there was nothing. I must have been mistaken about seeing a shadow. I crunched back to my car.

I felt relieved and guilty. Or maybe the truth was I felt guilty about feeling relieved. As I slid into the driver's seat, I took a deep breath and realized I'd been practically holding my breath for the past ten minutes. I turned my tired Cherokee downhill.

In my last glance in the rear view mirror, I saw James silhouetted in the doorway of his apartment, bare to the waist, hands outstretched against the door jambs. I shifted into reverse and backed up the driveway and cranked the wheel so my passenger side window faced him. Cold air gushed in when I rolled the window down.

Jimmy glared at me, or through me, without moving or making a sound.

"James! You OK?" I felt around on the seat for my Glock.

Finally he spoke. "What are you doing here, Hunter?"

"I came to talk to you about Summer Rain."

"We already talked about Summer. I got nothing more to say to you about her. Or nothing else, either."

"Fine. Don't talk to me, James, save it for the cops. They'll be here soon."

"Leave me alone!" Jimmy spun around and ran into his apartment, slamming the door behind him. He emerged a moment later with a keychain on a lanyard and sprinted around to his pickup truck. With a cloud of blue smoke and a gnashing of gears, James Sundquist was on the move.

"Get thee behind me, Satan!" He shouted as he roared past, loud enough that I could hear him through his rolled up window.

I chased after him down the driveway. Jimmy didn't wait for the gate to fully open. He raked the side of his truck as he rammed his way through, braking only when he hit Willamette Street. He hung a left, sliding sideways, nearly clipping a southbound FedEx delivery van. The driver blared his horn and flipped a one-finger salute, but Jimmy was already gunning it down Willamette, taking his half of the road right down the middle. It wasn't difficult to keep up with him, but I needed both hands on the wheel and my full attention on the slick road. I wanted to call Lucas but I couldn't handle the distraction of even speed-dialing a cell phone without pulling over. It became a moot point when I hit a water-filled pot hole and my phone bounced onto the floor and slid back under the seat.

I knew this section of Willamette and apparently so did Jimmy, because he sped up. I glanced at my dashboard and saw the needle pushing seventy MPH. He had to know that the straight section we were on ended in a sharp, unbanked curve that fell steeply away on the outside. More than one careless driver had miscalculated the turn and ended up mangled or dead in the trees in the gulch or the river beyond it. A trio of white, wooden crosses sprouted from bouquets of faded plastic flowers at the apex of the turn, flanked by two yellow warning signs.

Jimmy showed no sign of slowing down. I didn't want to run him off the road, so I eased up on the gas hoping that he'd do the same. Instead, he gradually pulled away from me, side-slipping out of sight around the bend, still going full throttle.

A few seconds later, I slowed and rounded the turn. The Ford had slid off the street and was mired in the muck, jammed sideways against a thick Douglas fir. The front bumper was tangled in the remnants of a barbed wire fence. The rear wheels were still spinning, seeking traction that wasn't there. Broken pieces of the memorial crosses and one of the warning signs lay flattened in the mud. One of the crosses was skewered into the top of the grill like a grotesque hood ornament.

Jimmy had an agonized look on his face. He pounded the steering wheel. The engine roared like it would explode at any moment. Mud spewed from the rear end. The truck stained against the barbed wire and shuddered lower and lower into the muck. I could almost feel *his* adrenaline coursing through *my* body as I watched from the shoulder.

Jimmy sprang out and attacked the fence with a tire iron. He turn-buckled the barbed wire until it snapped, raking his palms and arms. The rusty wire snapped and whipped back against him, tearing a nasty gash across his bare abdomen. He threw the tire iron onto the seat. Jimmy stood for a moment, looking at the white cross. Blood flowed from the open wounds on his hands and his stomach. Then he yanked the cross out of the grill and climbed back into the truck.

"Jimmy! James! Stop! Wait!" I shouted. I got out of my car and slipped my Glock into my pants at the small of my back. "It doesn't have to be this way."

As I came around the back of my Cherokee, the Ford's tires found traction and the truck lurched up onto the road. The spinning wheels covered my windshield with sludge. Back on the pavement, Jimmy slid to a stop and jumped out holding the tire iron in one hand and the bloody cross in the other. I reached for my Glock, hoping I wouldn't need it. Jimmy waved the cross at me, yelling unintelligibly. Then he stood still for a moment with his eyes closed, his head tilted back, his arms raised in the air, his mouth open in a silent scream. Suddenly he seemed to reenter the present world. He tossed the iron bar into the pick-up's bed, jumped in still holding the cross, and fishtailed down the wet street.

I made a few quick swipes across the windshield with my forearm before I got back in, wedging my gun into the crack of the seat. Washer fluid helped the wipers smear a streaky blur. I reached under the seat for my cell phone but it was out of reach and Jimmy was disappearing. I floored the gas pedal and chased after him, guiding myself mostly by peripheral vision. Furiously, I squirted more fluid onto the windshield. Soon I'd cleared a spot I could squint through if I slouched down.

In the distance I could see flashing red warning lights and the fluorescent orange coat of the flagger holding the STOP sign. The fallen tree was still holding up traffic. A couple of cars were headed toward us along the thin edge of the one-way road. No brake lights; Jimmy wasn't slowing down. The flagger waved his sign frantically before leaping out of the way. Jimmy crashed into the tree head on. The truck somersaulted through the air, rolled twice down the bank, and came to a stop upside down.

I pulled over as far off the road as I dared and rolled down my window. Steam billowed up from the Ford's engine bay. The rear wheels were still spinning. I sat, paralyzed by the scene unfolding before me. Jimmy struggled through the broken windshield. His hands, already bloodied by the barbed wire, pushed at the shards of glass. He rolled through onto ground and crawled out from under the wreck. As he stood up, dazed, he steadied himself with his arms extended on the upside down grill. Fingers of fire escaped past the crumpled hood.

"Jimmy!" I shouted. "Get out of there. Get away from the truck!"

Jimmy leaned motionless, his head drooped forward, his bloody palms grasping the bumper for support. I don't know if he heard me, but he didn't respond. An instant later, it was too late.

A ball of fire exploded from the middle of the pickup. The flames reached upward and ignited a few low fir branches, cascading sparks onto the wreckage. The road workers, who had been petrified witnesses, either dove for cover or were knocked off their feet by the force of the blast. Maybe both; I couldn't tell which.

My last image of James Sundquist will be with me for the rest of my life. He sank to his knees as his body was engulfed by the flames. Slowly he brought his palms together and tilted his face skyward. I saw his lips moving but I couldn't make out his words. If I had to guess, they would have been something along the lines of 'nearer my God to thee'. A flaming branch fell and ignited his hair and settled onto his lap. Finally he pitched forward, a soundless ball of fire. I don't know if he was still alive at the end. I only know he made no effort to escape the fiery hell that consumed him.

In the distance, I heard the sounds of sirens. Operating as much on instinct and auto pilot as anything else, I reached into my Cherokee and grabbed my camera and snapped several photos. There would be plenty of time later to answer questions, give statements, and perhaps testify. For the moment, I was on sensory overload.

I didn't hesitate any longer than I needed to. I retrieved my cell phone from under the seat and called Lucas.

"Luke, it's me, Hunter. I'm out Willamette Street. There's been an accident. Jimmy's dead. I'm on my way down to the station." I hung up before the detective had a chance to say a word.

The sirens, faint at first, got louder and louder. The flagger, now covered in mud, stood in the middle of the street. I gave her my card and told her I was going directly to the police station and she waved me through. Half a minute later, a fire truck and an EMS mobile unit passed me racing south. I steered onto the narrow shoulder to give them as much room as possible, which wasn't much.

Lucas was waiting in the lobby of the police station with a grim expression on his face. I'd briefly contemplated stopping for coffee but figured the detective wouldn't appreciate any delay. I certainly didn't need any stimulation.

"What happened out there, anyway? I heard the fire department dispatcher on the radio but she didn't give any details." Lucas waited about two seconds before he repeated. "What the hell happened out there, anyway?"

"I drove out to see Jimmy." My teeth were chattering and I was having trouble getting the words out. "I wanted to question him some more. I thought maybe he'd crack. He did, but not like I expected. He wouldn't answer the door but I was sure he was home. His lights were on, his truck was there, and I might have seen a shadow. You know, signs of life." I stopped and took a deep breath, trying to settle my vibrating nerves. I could sense Lucas' impatience. "I'd given up, but as I was leaving, he came out with a crazed look on his face. Disoriented. I asked him if he was OK and he bolted. He screamed at me, jumped in his truck, and roared off."

"And?"

"And?" I was trying to explain what happened at the same time I was processing it in my own mind. Everything had happened too quickly and too recently for any retrospection. "I followed him. He tried to break the sound barrier on Willamette. You know that long straightaway right before the tight curve as you're coming into town?"

"I know where you're talking about," Lucas said.

"Jimmy lost control going into the curve. Not surprising, it's a nasty spot and the road was slick. Remember those three little white wooden crosses?"

"Three kids died there last year. Been drinking. Were in a Jeep, as I recall."

"They're not there anymore. He slid off the road and got his truck stuck in the mud and tangled up in some old barbed wire. I caught up with him and begged him to hold up. He wasn't having any of it, though, and as soon as he got untangled and unstuck, he took off again." I stopped to take another deep breath.

"We better get out there now," Lucas said. "Fill me in on the details in the car."

Lucas grabbed his windbreaker. "Only if it's urgent," he barked at Cheryl without waiting for a reply. We sprinted out the door to his Crown Vic. He lit up the flashing lights and the siren and in short order we were barreling south on Willamette Street.

"Go on," Lucas said as if there had been no interruption.

"A few hundred yards this side of that turn the storm has blown a big tree down across the road. They'd just started sawing it up on my way out. The road was still wet and slippery with fir needles. They were flagging traffic one way at a time."

"What time was that?"

"An hour ago. Not even." I'd been too excited to note the time.

Lucas glanced at his watch. "Go on."

"When I got to Winetrout's, Jimmy wouldn't come to the door, but his rig was there so I was sure he was hiding. As I was leaving, I saw him in my mirror. I stopped and he screamed at me and bolted for his truck."

"You already told me that part, gumshoe."

Traffic was slowing down and when we got to the point where it was stopped dead, Lucas steered into the oncoming lane, still at nearly full speed. I double checked my seatbelt.

"Yeah, I guess I did."

"So you chased after him?" Again, Lucas with the half question/half statement tone of voice.

"Yes. He nearly totaled a FedEx truck he was in such a hurry."

"Get to the part where he crashed."

I fast-forwarded in my mind past the part where Jimmy had slid off the road.

"Jimmy didn't stop or even slow down. At least, I didn't see any brake lights. He crashed head on into the tree and catapulted over it and landed top side down. His truck caught on fire just as he was climbing out."

"Jimmy didn't make it out of the truck?" Lucas asked.

"He dragged himself out through the broken windshield. I know this is going to sound weird, Luke, but from what I saw, Jimmy didn't want to escape from the fire."

"Come again?"

"I think he wanted it to be over, once and for all, permanently. That's my take on it, anyway."

CHAPTER THIRTY-FOUR

Traffic was backed up for at least a quarter mile on Willamette. Even with the siren screaming and the lights flashing, we were forced to slow down. It took us several minutes to inch our way up to the scene of the accident. When we got to a point where walking would be faster than driving, Lucas silenced the siren but left the lights flashing and we jumped out.

The fire crew was hosing down the charred remains of Jimmy's pickup. It looked to me like the fire was out but they weren't taking any chances. The storm had soaked the underbrush, which was fortunate. A blazing vehicle a few months earlier, during the dry season, would have been a disaster.

We arrived at the scene just in time to see a cluster of masked EMTs load a mummy on a gurney into the back of the EMT cube. An IV bottle swung from a chrome hook and a clear plastic tube disappeared into the bundle. It didn't seem possible that Jimmy could still be alive, but they wouldn't have been pumping saline into a cadaver.

"I doubt he'll make it." A young EMT with her mask pulled under her chin was talking into her cell phone but stopped when Lucas and I joined her. "Hang on."

"He's with me." Lucas pulled open his windbreaker to show his badge.

"He's very banged up. Cuts on his hands and stomach and face and he's pretty much burned all over. Any idea who he is?" The EMT produced a clipboard from under her slicker.

"His name is James Sundquist," I said. "He's the gardener at the Winetrout Estate."

The EMT furrowed her brow. "Winetrout, Winetrout, Winetrout. Why is that name familiar?"

"Fat cat mover and shaker," I said. "Mostly real estate stuff. He tries to stay out of sight and work his deals as a silent partner."

198

The EMT still looked confused.

"His place is that huge estate on the right going south." I pointed. "Stone wall, iron gates. I'm sure you've driven by it."

"Oh, yeah, I know where you're talking about. I always wondered about that place."

"Owns a strip joint in the Whit." I said.

"You're taking him to RiverBend Hospital?" Lucas said. Again it was half question/half statement.

"Initially," said the EMT. "My guess is if he's still alive when we get there, they'll stabilize him and airlift him to the Legacy Emanuel Burn Center in Portland."

"Thanks." Lucas started up the bank to his car. "You coming, Hunter?" He asked without turning around.

"Right behind you," I said.

We fell in behind the ambulance and I tried to calm down for the fifteen minute ride to the hospital. I could feel the adrenaline ebbing from my body. For the time being, Lucas was out of questions and for that I was grateful. I was out of answers.

CHAPTER THIRTY-FIVE

Even with his City of Eugene Police Department credentials, Detective Lucas Leonard and I were not allowed into the Intensive Care Unit. A uniformed cop stood guard at the door, clearly uncomfortable blocking a superior officer. Finally, after almost an hour, we were at Jimmy's bedside. I felt drained and in a serious state of caffeine depravation.

"I'll give you about five minutes. Maybe less. We're flying the patient to Portland." The nurse looked young and sweet, like she'd graduated from nursing school yesterday, but her attitude was all vintage Nurse Ratched.

James Sundquist was swaddled like a dead pharaoh from head to foot, connected to various pieces of medical machinery with tubes and wires. A heart monitor beeped weakly at irregular intervals. The only exposed parts of his body were his dirty toes. I couldn't see how we were going to be able to question him, how he would be able to give us any answers.

Lucas pointed to me and then at Jimmy. He made the talking gesture by opening and closing his fingers against his thumb. He pointed to himself and shook his head. "He doesn't know my voice," he whispered.

"James," I said. I leaned down to his head. "Can you hear me?"

There was no response. Not that I'd expected any. Lucas tapped me on the shoulder and pointed at Jimmy's toes and fluttered his fingers.

"James, if you can hear me, wiggle your toes."

We watched the motionless body, our eyes glued to his toes. The only sign of life was the thin green line of the heart monitor, mostly flat but occasionally broken with a weak, half-hearted spike. The kid was more dead than alive. I was amazed that the medical staff had allowed us into ICU. We'd be lucky to get a response of any kind at all out of Sundquist, let alone details about the last hours or minutes of Summer Rain Wycowski's life.

"James," I said, as loudly as I dared, "can you wiggle your toes?" I didn't want to shout. Nurse Ratched lurked like a shadow in the hallway.

Almost imperceptively, the big toe of Jimmy's right foot began to curl. If we hadn't been watching like El Gato at a mouse hole, we would have missed the movement. Then the toes on his left foot moved.

Lucas pointed to himself and to Jimmy and gestured conversation with both hands.

"James, this is Hunter. Jack Hunter. I'm here with Detective Lucas Leonard from the Eugene Police Department. Can you understand me?"

Slowly he curled his toes.

"We want to ask you just a few questions. If you want to answer yes, move your right toes. For no, your left toes. OK?"

Jimmy's right toes moved up and down.

"James, do you know anything about Summer Rain's death?" I asked.

For a moment, I thought we had lost him. His toes were still and the spikes in the green line became weaker and further apart, like leftover trees after a clear cut. I was glad the nurse wasn't in the room. Eventually, Jimmy curled the toes on his right foot.

"Ask him if he killed her," Lucas whispered.

"James, do you know who killed Summer Rain Wycowski?" I asked.

There was no motion.

"James, did you kill Summer?" Lucas asked. It was the first time he had spoken directly to Jimmy.

Still no signal from Jimmy's toes.

"James, listen to me. Do you remember the accident? The fire?" I asked.

Nothing. I had an inspiration.

"You are not in very good shape, James. I know you're in a lot of pain. There's a good chance you're not going to make it." I paused. In the silence, the beep of the heart monitor underscored my words. "Do you want to face the hereafter with something terrible on your conscience?"

Jimmy's toes were still.

"Do you hear those beeps, Jimmy?" Lucas asked. "Those are your heart beats. Can you hear how far apart they are?"

"Think about it, James." I leaned down and stage whispered to the side of his head where I guessed his ear would be, if he still had ears. "You will go to heaven or you will go to hell. Why don't you help us and help yourself?"

There was no movement in his toes.

The door to the room opened quietly and Nurse Ratched looked in. "You've got about another minute before we have to move him. Maybe less. The helicopter is on its way in."

"James, this is your last chance. Think about, about... Think about eternity. Think about your soul. Do you want to face God with this secret?" I asked.

The toes on Jimmy's left foot curled once.

"Did you kill Summer Rain Wycowski?" Lucas asked.

Jimmy curled the toes on his right foot. The spikes on the heart monitor were a little closer and reached a little higher and Lucas and I looked at each other. I nodded. A long two plus weeks had elapsed from the day Charles Thurgood Winetrout had blustered into my office to this almost imperceptible wiggling of James Sundquist's toes.

If the moment hadn't been so momentous, it would have been anticlimactic. It took a minute or so for it to sink in that this was what we had been waiting for. This was the final piece of the puzzle. We knew who Summer Rain's murderer was.

I closed my eyes and took a deep breath and let it out slowly. In my mind's eye, I saw a flash of silver on the far side of a swift, white-capped rapid. Droplets of water slid down my line as it rose from the Rogue. I could feel my Orvis bend against the draw...For an all too brief imaginary moment in time, my world could not have been more perfect.

Detective Lucas Leonard grabbed my arm and jerked me back from the bank of the Rogue River into the ICU room at RiverBend Hospital. He pointed to James' feet.

Astonishingly, before my open, unbelieving eyes, Jimmy scrunched his left toes. Dumbfounded, Lucas and I watched as the toe movement alternated between his feet.

"I don't understand, James. Did you kill Summer Rain Wycowski?" Lucas asked.

All ten toes curled and uncurled. I turned to Lucas and shrugged my shoulders.

"James, you killed Summer and somebody else helped you. Is that right?" Lucas shouldered me aside.

Jimmy clenched the toes on his right foot. His left foot lay still.

The door opened and Nurse Ratched, along with two orderlies, marched into the room. "That's it, Detective. You'll have to leave now."

"Who was it, James? Who helped you kill Summer?" Lucas asked. The intervals between Jimmy's heart beeps were lengthening, the spikes weakening. I could well imagine the half-dead swaddled soul feeling the flames of hell licking at his loins. Lucas was getting anxious.

"Luke," I said. "He can't answer like that. You can only ask him yes and no questions." I turned my attention back to Jimmy. "Was it Charles Winetrout? Did he help you kill Summer?"

"I'm ordering you to leave the room!" The nurse's voice was brittle and staccato.

"James!" Lucas shouted. One of the orderlies grabbed Lucas' arm but he shook him off.

There was a long, silent pause. Even nurse Ratched and her orderlies had become transfixed by the drama unfolding before us. Everyone stared at Jimmy's feet. Finally, the right toes curled once, twice and then quivered still. The dead spaces between the spikes in the green line grew wider and then the line flattened and the beeping stopped and became a steady tone.

James Robert Sundquist was dead.

CHAPTER THIRTY-SIX

Two days later, mid-afternoon, I got a call from Lucas Leonard. I was expecting it.

"Can you meet me for a cup of coffee?" As usual, it was more of a direct order than an invitation or request.

"Sure," I said. "Will the City of Eugene be picking up the tab?"

"I believe I can justify that."

"Well, in that case, VERO in an hour. I've got a couple of things to finish up here."

In fact, I still had a lot to do. Susan had gotten the previous day off and had come over in the afternoon. The plan had been to spend the afternoon and evening reassembling my trailer; setting up a new computer, repairing my door, finishing up where we'd left off before. A homemade dinner was also part of that plan and she had arrived with a bag of salad goodies and a couple of thick New York Steaks from the Market of Choice. We hadn't gotten very far with the chores, though. Budding relationships can be like that, I guess. At least we'd managed to hang a new door and if I lifted the knob slightly when I closed it, I could get it to latch and lock. My carpentry skills being what they are, I figured I was ahead of the game. I'm a private investigator, after all, not a house builder.

I had no qualms about spending Winetrout's money on repairs insomuch as it was his trailer and most likely his boy Friday who'd done the damage to it. I wasn't sure how long I would want to be there, though. The place was a dump and maybe it was time I admitted it and looked for another place to live.

Lucas sat across from me, thoughtfully stirring his black coffee, flipping through his spiral notebook. I, of course, had ordered a Borgia.

"Do you remember the exact day Charles Winetrout hired you to look for Summer?" Lucas asked, without looking up.

I thought for a moment. "I think it was on the tenth or eleventh. He gave me a cash retainer so I can check my bank record to be sure."

"How much did he give you?" Lucas asked. Now he did look up.

I paused with my big coffee cup half way to my mouth and peered across the froth at him.

"Sorry, none of my business. I don't need to know that."

"Two thousand dollars."

"Moving on," Lucas continued. "Marcus Binkelman's body was found on Tuesday the fourteenth, which puts his time of death sometime on Sunday or Monday before."

"That sounds about right," I said.

"When was it you got the flash drive from him?"

"What are you getting at?"

"Nothing, don't worry. I'm just going over the details to make sure I haven't forgotten anything. The first pre-trial hearing is tomorrow, you know."

"Must have been a day or two before that. Again, I can check my bank statement. I took a cash advance in the middle of the night."

Lucas flipped his notebook shut and rested his elbows on the table. "I want to make sure every 't' is crossed and every 'i' is dotted. Getting a conviction won't be a slam dunk."

"Why is that? You don't think there's enough evidence?"

"We don't have anything actually tying Charles Thurgood Winetrout to the murder of Summer Rain Wycowski."

"You have evidence tying him to her rape."

"Almost. Only almost."

Charles Winetrout was awaiting trial in the Lane County Jail on multiple charges, including first degree murder, rape, sodomy, and conspiracy. The district attorney was busy preparing for the court battle, which, despite the grisly nature of the crime and the depravity of the defendant, looked to be a long and difficult uphill struggle. At least, that was the impression I was getting from Lucas.

"It is clear Charles Winetrout intends to claim that James Sundquist killed Summer Rain Wycowski and disposed of her body," Lucas said. "He can also contend that since the face of the rapist never appears in the Binkelman video, it isn't him."

"I see what you mean," I said. "That's the difference between our jobs. Your investigations end up in criminal court, mine only in divorce court."

"We need twelve people to send him to death row. All he needs is one person with a doubt."

"We don't have a smoking gun or a first person witness. Winetrout's done a good job of keeping his hands clean and the breaks have all gone his way. Whether it was on purpose or not, the video never shows his face." Lucas took a sip of his coffee and went back to stirring it. "Catching Krista in the act with Miller and Trippitt must have seemed like manna from heaven. He suddenly had incontrovertible DNA evidence that could send two innocent men to death row in his place. When that fell apart, there was always Jimmy to take the fall."

"So who do you think actually killed Summer Rain?" I asked.

Lucas frowned and shook his head. "You can make a case for either Sundquist or Winetrout."

"Come on, Luke, what do you think? What would you take to the judge?"

"Truthfully?" Lucas said. "I think they acted in concert. Getting rid of Summer satisfied both their agendas."

"I believe a stronger case can be made against Winetrout. He had the motivation."

Lucas set his spoon down. "Sundquist had a messianic complex. Look at it through his eyes. Summer, especially Summer being pregnant with his child, was living, walking proof of his fallibility in God's eyes."

"She did represent the devil to him." I agreed. I remembered the morning of Jimmy's death, the confrontation we'd had, his last words. 'Get thee behind me, Satan!' "Probably a lot more difficult to establish that as motive in court, though, especially with him dead."

Both the DA and the defense attorneys were anticipating the judge's ruling on the defense's motion to suppress Binky's video. Since Winetrout's face never appeared on screen, Winetrout's lawyers would argue that the video was prejudicial. The DA was prepared to counter that the man in the video was indeed Charles Winetrout, defined by his gold Rolex, his shape, his huge, stretch-marked belly. With the only three people who could testify definitively dead, it would be interesting to see how the judge ruled.

The best argument the DA had going was James Sundquist's death bed confession; the central issue being whether or not flexing one's toes could be considered communication, let alone constitute a confession. That would be the second major legal question for the judge to decide. Counting the nurse and her two aides, there had been five of us in the hospital room when James Sundquist died. We would all be called to testify but with a half-dead Sundquist on life support, the drugs flowing through the IV into his body could have rendered him incapable of coherent thought. The defense attorney would certainly argue as much.

"So, what evidence do you have that you can use against Winetrout?" I asked.

"We have the condom wrappers with Miller's and Trippitt's initials. We found a turkey baster in the kitchen, but it was clean. You can find basters in half the kitchens in America."

"At least the kitchens that celebrate Thanksgiving."

Lucas ignored my comment. "We found a roll of duct tape in the garage, but none in the house."

Again, I thought, half the households in America probably had a roll of duct tape somewhere. I knew I kept a roll around and I'd have bet a Franklin Lucas did, too.

"You have the DNA match for Sundquist and Summer Rain's fetus," I said.

"That doesn't help put Winetrout in prison, gumshoe. In fact, it hurts the case. A smart lawyer – and Winetrout's hired the best – can argue that Sundquist murdered Summer and disposed of her body by himself."

"I guess we'll find out," I said.

"Jury selection starts in a week."

"Keep your fingers crossed."

Lucas shook his head. "I don't like trusting felony convictions to crossed fingers."

We sat for a few beats, me scooping the last of the orange zest/whipped cream quilt from the bottom of my cup and Lucas stirring his now-cold coffee.

"Is there anything more you can do?" I asked. "Before the trial?" I added.

"That's why we're here," Lucas said. "I don't think there is."

"Then let's get the hell out of Dodge for a couple of days. We owe ourselves that."

"What do you have in mind?"

"Same thing you do, amigo. Fall run. Rogue River.

Lucas nodded and smiled a rare smile. "Sounds good, gumshoe."

EPILOGUE

I am perched on a partially submerged rock a few feet out from the south bank of the Rogue River. On the other side, thirty feet away, Lucas Leonard is standing thigh-deep in the water. His Orvis fly rod is clenched in his right hand, his landing net hangs from a carabineer at his left side. The crystal-clear, cold Rogue splashes against my ankles and his hip waders. Neither of us utters a word; this is what we do best as friends and we do it without much need to chit chat. The only sound comes from the river splashing over the rocks and the gusts of cluttered, fresh wind rustling the remaining leaves from the madrone, chinquapin, and tanoak trees that line the banks. There hasn't been a flicker of interest in the fly at the end of my line and I am beginning to wonder if we've already missed the fall steelhead run.

A few feet behind me, on dry ground, Susan St. Marie, also known as Charity, relaxes in a folding camp chair, alternately watching us and thumbing through a People magazine. She is bundled against the chilly late November afternoon in a fleece-lined Patagonia duster I lent her and she has a sleeping bag wrapped around her legs. Half her face is hidden behind a faux-fur earmuff hat and oversized dark glasses. Susan confided she'd never been an outdoorsy type, but that she'd be willing to give sleeping with me in a tent a try. I liked the 'with me' part.

When I floated the idea to Lucas of bringing Susan along for our long weekend in the wilderness, I'd expected some resistance, or at least one of his patented scowls. Fishing trips have always been private bonding time for the two of us, but my gruff buddy had surprised me. He'd interviewed Susan in the course of compiling evidence for the aggravated murder case against Charles Winetrout and he must have sensed, as I had, something tender and vulnerable hidden in the heart of the slender dancer.

209

Over the course of the past few weeks, Susan and I have become closer and closer, to the point where in the same breath she'd both invited me to move into her apartment and asked me to please not visit her at work any more. As she'd whispered to me in an intimate pillow-talk conversation, 'Charity is a stripper, but inside the suit of armor she's gotta keep up around her, Susan St. Marie is a shy, modest girl.' She'd paused and giggled to herself and then explained, 'How can someone have a suit of armor on when she's running around bare-ass naked?' I found her ironic, cockeyed view of the world and her third-person place in it endearing.

El Gato, who had taken to Susan from the first time she'd visited, early on graced her with a feline stamp of approval; he brought her a half-eaten mouse, sharing his dinner. She was never in my trailer for more than a few minutes before he was weaving his figure eights through her ankles or purring extravagantly in her lap. Perceptive and astute, he hadn't even gotten pissed off when Susan and I loaded my Cherokee with camping and fishing equipment, dumped weekend rations into his bowl, and left. 'Guard the place, kitty cat. Keep the bad guys out.' Susan scratched his back and he arched in appreciation. El Gato blinked his golden eyes at her, switched his tail once or twice, and curled up on her side of the bed.

So here we are, the three of us, decompressing from the events of the past couple of weeks. Being a homicide detective, Lucas likes to say he prefers having nothing to do. I have an interesting new client lined up, a mid-fifties something gay man who suspects his younger lover of infidelity. The potential betrayal is indicative of the changing times, but standing in the serenity of the bubbling Rogue, I'm in no big hurry to get back to Eugene. This will be my first same-sex case and I'm not even sure what to call it: Marital (queer-conjugal? same-spousal? New terminology is needed to describe our changing world.) infidelity tends to create a kind of dramatic arc of perception in the jilted party. It begins with mild suspicion and progresses through predictable stages of disbelief bolstered by scraps of evidence. The man's voice had been troubled but not desperate. Yet.

Susan demanded a week off and the acting manager at the Hot Body Club hadn't been happy. 'What are they gonna do, fire their best dancer?' Susan said. 'They're already short staffed. Dumping Charity would just make matters worse.'

Charles Thurgood Winetrout is awaiting formal sentencing in the Lane County Jail. Half way through the jury selection process, the DA agreed to a plea bargain deal: Winetrout would plead guilty to rape, sodomy, and aggregated assault and spend twenty years to life in prison. In return, the murder and conspiracy charges would be dropped and he would avoid life without possibility of parole and possibly the death sentence. The death sentence is still technically on the books in Oregon, but the current governor has declared a moratorium and there hasn't been an execution in the state in years. I suspect that not knowing how future governors might view lethal injection factored heavily into Winetrout's assessment of his situation. It certainly would mine.

"Fish on!" Lucas shouts, jerking me back into the present. I watch his line zip back and forth through the bubbling current. I begin reeling in my own line to give my buddy a clear shot of landing his catch. I don't want the frenzied, erratic movements of the steelhead to get our lines tangled.

Susan stands up and tiptoes across the damp pebbles until she is as close to me as she can get without wading in. I hold out my hand and she takes it and jumps onto the rock behind me. There is barely enough room for the two of us and she wraps her arms around my waist for balance. Susan's first trip to the Rogue River feels good to me and I hope it does for her, too.

"Is it a big fish?" She asks, avidly watching the tense, quiet struggle.

"Looks like it is. Check out his rod." Lucas' Orvis looks like a U-turn on a traffic sign. He reaches down and unclasps the net's handle from his wader suspenders and slips the safety lanyard over his wrist. Most anglers would play the fish out until it was exhausted and then carefully beach it. That's what I would do. But that isn't Lucas' style. When he's fishing, Lucas abandons the careful, methodical caution and control that he uses when he's a cop. It's the one activity in his life that he leaves open to fate.

The steelhead breaks the corrugated surface of the water with a stunning display of aerial aerobics, splashes back in, and rises again, writhing at the end of Lucas' taper.

"Cut him a little slack, amigo," I yell. "You're going to snap your line."

"I taught you how to do this, gumshoe. Remember?" Lucas shouts back.

"Yeah, right. I guess I forgot."

This is a traditional exchange between us, nearly word for word. Whoever hooks the first fish claims bragging rights. Later, whoever has landed the biggest fish assumes those rights.

"Are you guys always like this with each other?" Susan asks.

"Like what?" I answer. I reach my free hand behind us and cup a bundled cheek and give it an affectionate squeeze. Susan hugs me a little tighter. "We have our rituals."

Lucas' face is shadowed by his hat, but I can imagine him grinning. If he manages to land that baby, we are going to have one fine dinner.

*

That evening, the three of us huddle on logs around the campfire, wrapped up in fleece against the early winter Rogue Valley chill. Dinner was excellent. There is nothing tastier than a fresh-caught wild steelhead, barbecued over an open fire by the side of the river where it lived, and there is no better river than the Rogue. Congress, for once, got it right when it chose the Rogue as one of the original Wild and Scenic Rivers back in '68.

Lucas has done justice to his nine-pounder, grilling it to perfection under a tin foil tent and basting it with butter, lemon and cilantro. I've cooked up a pasta primavera side dish on my Coleman stove with fresh fettuccini, Chanterelle mushrooms, Chinese sugar peas, sun dried tomatoes, and homemade pesto sauce. Lucas and I wash the feast down with several bottles of hoppy IPA from the

Standing Stone Brewery in Ashland, just a few miles south. Susan sticks to a crisp Chardonnay from one of the new vineyards in the Applegate Valley. I'm not a wine drinker, so I didn't pay attention.

'I like beer fine, but if a girl gains too much weight and gets fat, she can't earn a living.' It was one of the few references to her profession as an exotic dancer she'd made on the three-hour drive south from Eugene.

For me, Summer Rain Wycowski had been a search for a missing person and for Lucas, a homicide investigation. But Summer Rain had been Susan's friend and out of deference to her, Lucas and I agreed ahead of time not to talk about her murder. So, when I look up at the full moon with its misty winter halo and feel a chilly breeze nipping at the back of my neck and say, 'Summer's almost gone', I'm not thinking clearly.

No one says anything for several beats. Susan, who is down to about a half a pack a day and is making a concerted effort to quit altogether, reaches a Marlboro toward a glowing ember. "That's not right, mister," she says, "Rainy's not almost gone. She's totally gone." Her cheeks are wet and shiny in the firelight. "I miss her."

The 'mister' part stings. I try to put my arm around her, but she scoots away.

"She was lucky to have you as a friend," Lucas says.

"Fat lot of good it did her," Susan answers.

I feel like my foot is still stuck in my throat. "And without your help, we'd still be trying to figure out exactly what happened."

"What exactly did happen?" Susan takes a deep drag on her cigarette and then studies it for a moment before she flicks it into the flames.

Lucas and I look at each other over the fire and I nod to him.

"You sure you want to hear all this again?" He asks.

"I asked, didn't I?"

Lucas drains the last of his IPA, spikes it neck down into the sandy ground between his legs, and reaches into the ice chest behind him for another. He peels his koozie off the empty bottle and slides it onto the fresh one. Using the back edge of his knife, he pops the bottle cap into his lap. He's drawing this out, taking as much time as he can.

"Winetrout had been sexually abusing Summer almost since she and her mom moved in," Lucas says.

"How can you be so sure about that? You weren't there, right?" Susan asks.

"We interviewed the housekeeper, Consuelo. With Winetrout in jail, she was scared to death ICE would find her and deport her. It took a while for her to trust me enough to open up. Consuelo actually speaks more English than she lets on, but of course we had an interpreter. The court planned to keep her in Eugene at least long enough to testify at Winetrout's trial and after that the Police Department promised do what it could to help her with the immigration people. Now, of course, that won't be necessary.

"Consuelo was in a perfect position to know everything that went on in the household. Because she was undocumented, she was afraid to go anywhere or say anything to anyone, but that didn't mean she didn't see everything. Consuelo knew about the parties, heard the fights, the whole shebang." Lucas pauses and tosses another chunk of wood on the fire, sending a geyser of orange sparks into the moonlit sky.

"I've only met Consuelo once, you know, for just a sec. We didn't really talk. You're sure she knew that bastard was raping Rainy?" Susan is persistent, maybe hoping for some wiggle room between what her friend had whispered to her that night in Shari's and what Consuelo might have testified to in court if there had been a trial.

"OK," Lucas says, "here it is." He scrapes at the neck label with his thumbnail. "Consuelo walked in on them in his office one morning, bringing his coffee. Winetrout had his back to the door and was arguing with someone on the phone, so she naturally assumed he was alone. Consuelo didn't see Summer on her knees under the desk fellating him until she set the tray down. Summer looked up and made eye contact with her without missing a stroke. Winetrout kept yelling and didn't pay any attention. He probably didn't even know Consuelo had been in the room until he saw the coffee tray on his desk."

"You would think Consuelo would have, I dunno, done something. Said something," Susan says.

"Done what? Said something to whom?" Lucas asks.

Susan shakes her head. I keep my mouth shut, too.

"How long did you know what was going on?" Lucas is persistent.

"Long enough." Susan answers. "Too long, actually."

"And you never came forward, either." Lucas' voice is steady; the reprimand is in his words. He's pushing the issue a little too hard, I think, but I don't know what to say or how to fit into their tension, so I keep my mouth shut. Susan St. Marie, I've learned, is quite capable of taking care of herself.

"Rainy told me what she told me in utter confidence," Susan says. "She made me promise never to breathe a word to anyone. She said she had her own plan to deal with him."

"And that plan was to blackmail him," Lucas says.

"That's not how she put it, but yeah, I guess you could say that."

"Would you have been willing to testify to that under oath?"

"I could have testified to what I think she meant, but Rainy never used the word blackmail."

The conversation is morphing from a friendly fireside chat to a police interrogation, but it wasn't my job to interfere. I can't quite see what he's after, since there won't be a trial. The plea bargain agreement made it all moot.

"You told me before you have no idea when the blackmail part started." Lucas says.

"Rainy always had plenty of cash on her. How was I supposed to know exactly how she got it?" Susan's voice has taken on a defiant tone.

Lucas shrugs his shoulders.

"He nearly got away with it." I say.

"What about Binky?" Susan asks. "Do you think Winetrout killed him, too?"

"It's tempting to believe Charles Winetrout had a hand in Marcus Binkelman's death." Lucas says, "I'd love to be able to give the DA evidence to prosecute him for another murder. The truth is, though, I can't find anything courtroom-proof that links the two of them. The autopsy established that Binkelman died of a methamphetamine overdose. The coroner confirmed that he'd been addicted to crystal meth for some time. Among other things, Binky had facial lesions, his teeth were falling out, and he had early onset tuberculosis, probably from living on the street."

"Binky was a mess," Susan says. "We all saw it. We all knew it."

Lucas goes on. "It's a high bar. To support a murder charge, you have to prove that someone knowingly sold or provided him with drugs that had an unusual imbalance of ingredients, or simply gave him enough typical street grade meth to be fatal if he used it all at once. In the unlikely event you got that far, you'd next have to prove premeditation, that the provider intended the drugs to cause his death. And that is all before you even have a suspect."

"Which," I say, looking directly across the fire at Lucas, "we don't have one of."

"Which," Lucas answers, "we don't have one of."

Lucas, Susan and I sit in awkward silence. Susan fidgets with an unlit Marlboro and Lucas fidgets with his bottle of beer. It doesn't feel like the right moment to ask Lucas to reach me another beer, so I just stare into the fire. We all know where Binky got the money for the fatal overdose. None of us want to talk about it.

Lucas breaks the silence. "The night Winetrout walked in on Krista having sex with Miller and Trippitt, he was furious, or he pretended to be furious, but he recognized an opportunity when he saw one. After he'd kicked them out of the house, he saved their used condoms. It must have seemed like a gift from heaven." Lucas pauses and starts to take a drink of his beer, but stops and studies the remains of the neck label instead.

After a few moments, he continues. "It tied up all the loose ends for him nicely. Krista was in Portland, out of the picture. If she came forward now, after Summer was dead, somebody would be sure to

216

ask why she didn't do something at the time to protect her. Where were her protective maternal instincts when her daughter was at risk? Binkelman, who had shot the video, was dead. Sundquist had stolen the incriminating flash drive and it didn't occur to Winetrout that there might be a copy floating around somewhere. The only thing left to do was to get rid of Summer's body."

"Something's missing here, amigo" I say. "How could Winetrout be sure you – the police – would make the connection? What if I hadn't saved the cigarette butts and the toothpick?"

"Winetrout assumed that Miller and Trippitt would have records somewhere and wouldn't be able to come up with good alibis. It was fine with him if they went to prison," Lucas says.

"That's a big assumption to make, that both of them couldn't beat DNA proof."

"I don't know, gumshoe," Lucas says. "That's something that might have come out at a trial. You might want to think about what your answer would have been under oath." Now Lucas tilts his IPA back, drains half the bottle, and wipes his mouth with the back of his hand. "Whatever Winetrout's plan was, you saved him the time and trouble."

"Yeah," I say.

Susan isn't saying anything. She is mesmerized by the fire and I can't tell how closely she is following the discussion.

"He figured when Summer's corpse was discovered with their semen in her, the DNA matching would put them away forever. It must have felt like sweet revenge. Those guys were the reason he dumped his trophy wife in the first place."

"Payback can be a bitch," Susan mutters, shaking her head. She has been following the conversation after all.

Lucas ignores her. "He needed help, though. Disposing of Summer's body was more of a job than he could manage on his own."

"That's where Jimmy came in," I say. "Getting Jimmy to help was easy. For starters, Jimmy was no stranger to violence. The guy was a scrapper with a criminal record who'd lived more years as a bad-ass than he had as a born-again Christian. Second, he became an accomplice when he broke into my trailer and stole the flash drive. And, don't forget: He had a huge debt of gratitude to Charles Winetrout for keeping him out of jail after the brawl with the bouncer at the Hot Body Club and then giving him a job and even a place to live."

"Modern day indentured servitude," Lucas says.

"No," I say, "that more accurately describes Consuelo. I'll get to her later."

"Speaking of Consuelo, where is she now?" Susan asks. "She seemed like a nice lady."

"She's still at Winetrout's residence," I say. "Where else is she going to go? Back to Guatemala? I don't think so."

"OK. Dumb question," Susan says.

"Sorry, I didn't mean to sound harsh."

Susan smiles. "Don't worry about me, Jack Hunter, I can take it when I deserve it."

"Anyway, Jimmy's biggest motivation was his convoluted relationship with Summer." I feel like I'm on a roll. "In my opinion, James Sundquist developed a messianic complex. Someplace deep in his tortured soul, he became convinced he was the reincarnation of Jesus Christ. A lot of tangible evidence supports that; his attendance at the Church of Redemption, the tattoo of Jesus on the Cross on his arm, his insistence on being called James instead of Jimmy, even his Saints baseball cap."

"Lots of people get tattoos and go to church and don't kill people," Susan says. I'm trying to figure out if she has a soft spot for Sundquist or just wants to make Winetrout shoulder the whole load by himself. Not that it matters.

"Lots of guys don't have girls like Summer Rain Wycowski jerking their chain," I said. "Jimmy believed Summer had been sent by the devil to corrupt him and drag him back to his old, evil life and he felt powerless to resist her. Whenever she came around, flaunting her sexuality, the darker, worldly side of his old self came out. Saint James faded away and Jimmy the player took over."

"You never told me exactly how she died." Susan says.

"How she died?" Lucas asks.

"Exactly," she repeats. "What exactly it was that killed her." She drags the word 'exactly' out, emphasizing every syllable.

"Asphyxiation," Lucas says. "What we theorize is this: Winetrout couldn't admit to himself that he was a slave to his own demented debauchery, but he did recognize that he was enslaved by both Summer's wantonness and her demands for money. Ironically, he was just as much her captive as Sundquist was. Like Sundquist, he desired Summer and at the same time he felt trapped by her. He concluded that killing Summer was his only option, but he was compelled to have sex with her one last time." Lucas falls silent and pokes at the embers with a stick, sending a fountain of sparks crackling upward.

"Don't stop on this girl's account," Susan says. She still hasn't lit her cigarette.

"Psychopathology never retreats, it only advances."

"Psycho what?" Susan asks. "What do you mean?"

"Somebody who is criminally insane doesn't get better, they only get worse. Charles Winetrout is one sick puppy. He was getting desperate, losing his grip, waiting for the perfect opportunity. Something pushed him over the edge, maybe another demand for money, maybe a bout of impotence. We may never know, but whatever it was, something inside the man snapped. He tied Summer up, gagged her, whipped her, and raped her. My guess is that they'd been there before. Winetrout was into bondage – remember the video? – so she probably went along with it, at least for a while. By the time Summer realized he intended to kill her, it was too late. He suffocated her, possibly with a pillow, but more likely he just pinched her nostrils shut. We believe Winetrout had sexual intercourse with her while she was dying and maybe even after she was dead."

"That is fucking disgusting. I don't know what you call it, but it's truly...yuck." Susan finishes her sentence with a full body shudder.

"Necrophilia," Lucas says. There is an edge in his voice that wasn't there before. "The word for having sexual intercourse with a corpse is necrophilia."

219

"Thanks, I needed to know that," Susan spits back.

"You did ask," I say.

"We'll never know the events that happened that night for sure unless he tells us. He's made his deal with the DA, so that isn't likely, at least unless and until the DA decides to bring some additional charges." Lucas tips his IPA back and drains the last half of the bottle.

"Plea bargain. What a crock. What'd he get? Twenty to life?" Susan's voice has the hard grittiness I haven't heard since my first meeting with her.

"There was no trace of Winetrout's DNA on Summer's body. He undoubtedly used a condom. Plus, she'd been in the river for a while."

"What about the video?" Susan asks.

"What about the video?" Lucas answers. "We can make an educated guess that the man is Charles Winetrout, but we can't prove it. There could be dozens of fat men in Oregon who wear fancy watches and sodomize young girls, and since we never see his face, it could be anybody."

"I don't think there's any doubt it's him," Susan says. "Rainy didn't know anyone else like that."

"Educated guesses don't hold up well in court."

"You know," Susan says, "all the time I worked for him at the Club, I knew he was a sleaze ball nut case. Brittany has been up—"

"Brittany?" Lucas asks.

"Brittany's another dancer I work with. She's been up to his place a couple of times for parties and she's told me things I'd just as soon not hear about. I like Brittany and all, and I am a dancer, a stripper I guess if you get right down to it, but that doesn't mean I go beyond that."

"Did I miss something?" Lucas asks. "Should I know this Brittany?"

"No," I say. "You shouldn't. Investigating consensual sex among adults at a private residence which happens to be the home of a murderer would be like issuing a jay walking ticket to the driver walking away from a fatal hit and run accident." The metaphor may be fuzzy, but I'm sure he gets the point.

"Right." Lucas picks around the dying embers of our campfire with a stick but doesn't add any more fuel. We sit quietly for several minutes, listening to the peaceful sounds of the river and the cicadas.

This time, when I try to put my arm around her, Susan doesn't edge away.

"This girl's getting sleepy." Susan yawns for emphasis and leans her head on my shoulder. "She's ready for her big adventure sleeping outdoors in a tent."

Later, after we've brushed our teeth at the river's edge and had one last pee in the bushes and are clenched together in my North Face, zip-together sleeping bags, I say, "I'm glad this is over. When we get home, I want to get back to doing something I know how to do."

The full moon is beginning to shine through the mosquito netting roof of my tent, illuminating part of Susan's face.

"And where is home going to be, Jack S. Hunter?"

"My full name, huh?"

"Which reminds me," Susan says. "You've never told me what the 'S' stands for."

"Strange."

"What?"

"My middle name is Strange. Jack Strange Hunter."

Susan pulls away, extends her arms, and leans over me. "Wait a minute, mister. You're telling me that you track down cheating husbands and wives for a living and your name is Strange Hunter?"

"Jack. Don't forget my first name."

"Jack Strange Hunter?"

Neither of us says anything for a few beats and then something funny occurs to me.

"And I'm zipped up in a tent on the Rogue River with an exotic dancer named Saint Mary?" I can't quite bring myself to call her a stripper.

Susan has no such problem. She slaps me lightly, playfully, on the cheek. "No, Jack Strange Hunter. The stripper's name is Charity and she's nowhere near here." She lies back down and molds her body into mine. "So, what about it?"

"What about what?" I ask, always the dummy.

"Where is home going to be when we get back?"

The moon has migrated across the night sky and hangs overhead like a lantern. I want to shift around so I can look into Susan's face, but I'm chicken. I wonder if Lucas, in his tent on the other side of the fire, can overhear our conversation.

"I don't know. Were you serious about your offer?"

"Serious as a heart attack," Susan whispers as she rolls on top of me. Her long, blonde hair falls down around our faces, filtering the moonlight and forming a tent within a tent.

"You sure you want an old guy who makes his living hiding in bushes peeking through motel windows to move in with you?"

"Depends on how you would feel about living with a girl who swings around a brass pole naked in a bar every night."

I consider that for several beats. Ms. St. Marie is quick on the uptake, no doubt about that.

"What about El Gato? I love that old cat. I couldn't leave him behind."

"El Gato," she says, "is the best part of the deal." And with that she gathers her hair behind her, opens her mouth, and kisses me.